MW01134573

HAWKE

Taylor James

HAWKE

Taylor James

A TSJ Publication

ISBN: 1478131039
ISBN-13: 9781478131038

DEDICATION

To the readers of the world. What would authors do without them.

CONTENTS

Chapter	1	1
Chapter	2	9
Chapter	3	16
Chapter	4	27
Chapter	5	41
Chapter	6	50
Chapter	7	60
Chapter	8	76
Chapter	9	94
Chapter	10	101
Chapter	11	115
Chapter	12	125
Chapter	13	135
Chapter	14	157
Chapter	15	175
Chapter	16	186
Chapter	17	209
Chapter	18	216
Chapter	19	224
Chapter	20	227
Chapter	21	237
Chapter	22	259
Chapter	23	261
Chapter	24	263

Chapter 1

Jaden Hawke leaned weakly against the toilet bowl and tried to think about anything except her roiling stomach. Since she had been bent over the bowl for quite a while, she thought there was a good chance she was empty. She flushed once again, closed her eyes, and sat back against the wall, limp and shaky. The phone rang distantly in her bedroom and she knew it was probably her agent wanting to know where the hell she was. She didn't have the strength to try and get it before it stopped and it went to voice mail. She was supposed to be reporting for her first practice with the Dallas Metros professional softball team this morning. Even her impressive list of accomplishments wouldn't erase the effects of a no show today.

She finally rolled to her knees and got slowly to her feet. She was still shaky, but the cold sweats were abating. She went to the sink, brushed her teeth, and used mouthwash liberally. In her bedroom, she pulled on shorts and a long sleeved tee shirt then added warm up pants before finally looking at her phone. One missed call.

Stan Marsh. She ignored it and slipped it into her pants pocket. She stopped in the kitchen, blew out a deep breath, and ran a hand through her short dark hair. She needed something in her stomach, but knew that she couldn't make herself eat anything yet. She took an energy bar from the pantry for later before grabbing her keys and heading out the door. Her gear was already in the truck so all she had to do now was concentrate on getting to the practice field as soon as possible.

She pulled into a parking spot at the field and was surprised by the number of vehicles already there. How many players did the Metros have?

"Jaden!" The shout reached her before she could fully exit the truck and she knew Stan was frantic by the timbre of his voice. "Where the hell have you been?" he exclaimed as he neared the vehicle. "Jesus! You look like you've been on a three day bender!"

Jaden winced visibly and made a calming motion with both hands. "I've been spewing into the toilet all night, Stan. I'm sick." She noticed movement then around a car in the row in front of them and lowered her voice. "I think it's food poisoning." She reached into the back seat of the truck and got her bag. It was then that she noticed the soft click and whirring of a camera and looked up with a scowl. Standing one row over was a lithe brown haired woman with a camera hanging around her neck taking her photo. Before she could explode, Stan stepped in front of her and blocked her from view.

"Jaden, it's media day," he said quietly. "They've been waiting for you. They've already taken pictures of the rest of the team but you know the sports writers will want their pound of flesh from you."

Jaden's shoulders slumped and she dropped her head. Crap. She should have known it wasn't over. She heaved a sigh and straightened up. "Okay, let's go." She resolutely kept her head down and Stan walked between her and the camera as they made their way to the field. To her surprise, the woman made no attempt to engage her in conversation or get a comment from her. She just kept pace with them from a row over and watched. Photographer only, Jaden thought. She's probably not allowed to speak to me in case she pisses me off so much that I won't speak to the reporter. She kept her head down anyway.

The rest of the team were scattered around the field still warming up when they got there. Some were throwing to partners, some jogged around the outfield, and others were on the ground contorting themselves into impossible positions to stretch out. There were a cluster of people in front of the backstop fence, and by the look of the cameras and notepads, Jaden assumed they were the press. The photographers fanned out and went into action when they realized who she was. She did her best to ignore them and dropped her bag near the dugout. The reporters held their ground and she figured they had orders to wait until they were given the word. They all watched her as she and Stan made their way to home plate where a small group of people awaited them.

Jaden recognized Georgia Tate. She had been the head coach of the Metros for the last two years. She was stocky with short bushy blond hair. She had on warm up pants and a windbreaker. Her face held the faint telltale lines at the corners of her eyes from too much time spent squinting into the sun. Jaden couldn't see her eyes behind her sunglasses.

Next to her was a man Jaden guessed to be the assistant coach, Robert Winslow. He was taller and heavier and sported brown hair that touched his collar not unlike that of the infamous first baseman of the Cincinnati Reds. He wore a blue baseball cap with *Metros* on the front and baseball pants with a blue stripe down each leg. He also wore stirrup knee socks in blue. A little over dressed for the first practice of the season Jaden thought. He frowned and lowered his clipboard to look pointedly at his watch.

The third person was a young woman, shorter than the other two and she watched them approach with a smile. Not a coach, Jaden thought. There were two men in suits and Jaden pegged them for front office guys.

"You know Coach Tate," Stan whispered as they walked. "The big dufus is Bob Winslow, her assistant coach, and the girl is the trainer. The two suits are Greg Brown and Steve Cutter."

"Okay," Jaden nodded slightly. She kept her eyes on Coach Tate while trying to keep her face a blank as zoom lenses captured her image in rapid-fire style. Her stomach rolled a little and she swallowed quickly trying to squelch it. *Please don't let me be sick right now.*

"It wouldn't hurt if you looked like you were glad to be here." Stan urged in a whisper.

Jaden plastered a quick smile on her face and took the offensive as they met the group. She held out her hand. "Coach Tate. I'm sorry for being late. I've been up half the night with a touch of food poisoning."

Georgia Tate shook her hand and gave her a curt nod. "Welcome aboard, Jaden."

"Bob Winslow," the man next to her said with a frown and shook her hand only because she held it out.

"Hi, I'm Danny Hightower and I'm the trainer," the young woman stepped forward and shook her hand with a smile still on her face.

"I'm Steve Cutter, president of the Donald Sutter Group. Glad to have you aboard." The man wore a blue suit with a striped tie and a lighter shade of blue shirt. He was just less than six feet tall and had soft hands. He shook her hand vigorously, smiling like a politician at a campaign rally and turned to the last man. "This is Greg Brown, also from DSG."

Greg Brown was of medium height and weight and had a little gray in the dark hair on his head. Jaden shook his hand and murmured hello.

"I promised the press they could have a few minutes," Steve Cutter said and turned toward the crowd against the fence, pulling Jaden beside him. "People," he called out and they surged forward. "Coach Tate tells me we have a lot of work to do today so please keep it brief." He smiled at them to show he was the good guy here.

The questions started to fly immediately from everyone and they all inched closer. Jaden tensed, feeling trapped.

"Please, one at a time," Mr. Cutter said loudly.

"Ms Hawke," the guy with the loudest voice won out. "Is it true you were involved with the daughter of Senator Paxton during the Olympic Games last year?"

"I'm sorry," Jaden responded quietly with her standard answer. "I do not comment on my private life." She was stiff with tension and fought to keep her hands clasped loosely behind her back.

"Come on, Jaden, we've all heard the reports of the wild parties Kendall Paxton throws. You were reported to be seen with her both in Japan during the Olympics and here in the states as well."

Jaden stood silently and kept her gaze over their heads. She presented the image of an immovable force. Meanwhile her entire body shook with the effort and her stomach threatened to turn itself inside out again.

"Jaden," another voice came out of the crowd. "Are you still seeing Kendall Paxton?"

"Ms Hawke, has Ms Paxton been in contact with you since her arrest?"

"Jaden, were you part of the drug ring the police discovered during the raid on the senators summer home?"

"Jaden, are you currently using drugs?"

"Jaden, tell us about you and Kendall Paxton. What's it like to be in a relationship with her?"

The questions and thinly veiled accusations kept coming at her, pounding her, flooding her already dizzy head with painful memories. She swayed briefly under the onslaught but kept her face still and closed least they see how the whole ordeal still affected her. She was very near the breaking point when Steve Cutter stepped forward with a raised hand and put a stop to it.

"Please. We're here as the Metros softball team not as a tabloid photo op. We would appreciate it if you would all give the past a rest and try and concentrate on the team. Jaden is here as our newest pitcher and that's all we're concerned about. Anything you'd like to know about that can be had by contacting our media department or our website. Thank you all for being here today." With that, he turned and they all walked back toward the dugout. Jaden relaxed a measure until she heard Steve mutter to Greg Brown, "Shit! Fucking dykes. This is exactly what I wanted to avoid! We don't need this kind of publicity, Greg." His back was stiff with anger. "Fucking media nightmare!"

Jaden and Stan slowed their pace simultaneously. Jaden saw her career go down the drain before it even got started. At least now, she knew how her new employer viewed her.

"Don't worry, Jaden," Stan said. "He's got nothing to do with the team. His job is with the owners group, nothing more."

"Yeah," Jaden nodded but wondered how many others had the same viewpoint. "At least I have a contract they can't get out of." She gave him a thin smile. "Did I ever thank you for that?"

"Yes," he grinned. "You did."

"Don't let Cutter get to you." Danny, the trainer, fell back to walk beside them. "He's just pissed because they're more interested in you than in him." She gave Jaden a smile. "You'll never see him again anyway."

Jaden nodded her thanks and smiled back at her. "I haven't exactly had that kind of luck lately."

"You'll be fine," she went on. "Once they see how well you pitch they won't care about anything else."

"Thanks. I hope you're right about that."

They had reached the dugout and the suits disappeared into the parking lot while the two coaches stood and waited for them to catch up.

"Stretch out and warm up," Coach Tate said. "When you're ready start throwing with Gillian Banks down in the bullpen."

"Yes Ma'am." Jaden dug her shoes out of her bag and sat down on the bench to change.

"I'm going to take off now, Jaden. Call me if you need anything, okay?"

"Okay. Thanks Stan. I'll talk to you later."

When he'd gone Danny still hung around the dugout. "You need anything, Jaden?"

"I could use a new stomach," she answered with a snort. "Mine is rebelling against what I ate last night."

"Let me see what I've got in my kit," she answered seriously and walked to where a jumble of jackets, towels, hats and other assorted junk lay at the far end of the bench. She opened a battered black leather case and rummaged around inside it. She emerged with a bottle of pink fluid and brought it back to Jaden. "Here, try this."

"God, you're a life saver," Jaden sighed and tipped the bottle to her lips. "Thanks."

Chapter 2

Sloane Ellison slipped a new SD card into her camera and stored the full one in the bag on her hip. She was the official photographer and web site administrator for the Metros. She had gotten pictures of every member of the team including the coaches earlier for posting to the site and was just waiting for the opportunity of get one of Jaden. She had plenty of photos of her but she wanted the one that would stand the test of time. She could change the web site but the photo she submitted to the rest of the media department for the program would be used for the entire season. She had been changing cameras in her car when Jaden had arrived and witnessed the exchange between her and her agent. The quick photo she had snapped was good for a tabloid paper maybe but was not what she wanted. When she saw the scowl directed her way she resisted the urge to keep snapping and simply kept pace with them and watched. She had all day to get her shot. She thought it might come during the press interview but had quickly realized it was nothing short of torture for Jaden. Sloane had kept her camera trained on her face and watched Jaden completely shut down. She thought it might very well have been the saddest thing she had ever seen.

She now sat in the stands behind home plate and watched as practice began. Pitchers and catchers worked together in the bullpen, infielders ran through drills and the outfielders fielded grounders and fly balls. Her gaze kept returning to the bullpen. She had a good zoom lens but she would still need to get closer for the shot she was looking to get. She got up, worked her way down to field level in a roundabout path so she was unobtrusive, and set up far enough away to go unnoticed. She sat cross-legged on the ground and zoomed in on the bullpen.

After warming up and stretching out, Jaden went to the bullpen area and took her place at the one pitching rubber left open. A solidly built girl with strawberry blond hair and catchers gear pushed off from the fence and picked up her mask. Presumably, this was her catcher.

"Just throw me some warm up pitches," she called to Jaden. "Let's see how it goes."

Jaden nodded and hoped her stomach stayed quiet. She took a deep breath and let her shoulders sag for a moment. Pitching was so second nature to her, she didn't need to think to do it and she had been blessed with a machine for a right arm. She threw a few half speed pitches and then a few at about three quarters speed, feeling the groove come back to her. The next three pitches she put some heat on the ball and heard the resulting pop of the catcher's glove with satisfaction. On the last pitch, the catcher stood and walked toward her. Jaden met her half way, a question on her face. "Hey," she smiled up at Jaden and held out her hand. "I'm Gillian Banks. It looks like we're going to be working together this season."

"Hey, Gillian." Jaden gave her a sincere smile as she returned the handshake.

"What kind of junk can you throw?"

"Well, I have a good change up, a decent curve, and a nice rise ball, besides the speeder."

Gillian grinned. "This season might just turn out to be fun!" She slapped her glove against Jaden's shoulder. "Let me show you our signals." She demonstrated the finger count for each pitch she would call then looked her in the eye. "I know you've been playing college ball and in the Olympics and I know you know what you're doing, but I know this league and the people in it. Understand?"

Jaden grinned down at her. "Yes. Gillian's in charge on the field."

"Damn straight!" she laughed in delight. "I think this might work out. Now, let's see some of that junk." She jogged back to the practice plate and flipped her mask back on.

Sloane kept her lens focused in on Jaden's face. She couldn't hear them from her position but it looked like they were getting along. Her camera recorded the transformation from reserved and stoic to relaxed and happy as she talked to Gillian Banks. Jaden took up her position again and before long the other two pitchers, Erin Coe and Susan Strange, were standing and watching her work out. Sloane widened her view range and continued to snap more photos. She captured everyone else standing and watching as Jaden released the ball to the target Gillian had set. It was classic. She was thinking it might make a good shot for the front page of the web site.

"Are we all having fun?" Coach Tate's voice bellowed making everyone jump. Erin and Susan hurried back to their positions and resumed their own practice.

Gillian stood up and removed her mask as the coach drew near. "Hey Coach."

"Tell me," she demanded.

"She's the real thing, Coach. She's got speed, junk, and control."

Georgia Tate grunted. "But?"

"No buts," she shook her head. "She's everything good you've ever heard about her."

"Is she going to be hard to handle?"

"Nope. She's already admitted I'm in charge on the field." Gillian grinned at her coach. "Shit, Georgia, I think I'm in love!"

"Yeah, well don't let that get around, okay? We've got enough bad press already. It was a fucking circus out there today."

"I don't care if it's a circus all season as long as she keeps pitching like she has today!"

"Pitching to a catcher is one thing but hold off on putting her in the hall of fame until we get into a game, Gilly. You might have to change your mind." She looked off toward the mound where Jaden was patiently standing, flipping the ball and catching it, waiting to be called on. "She said she was up all night with food poisoning."

"Shit, if she's this good when she isn't feeling well then I can't wait until she's healthy." Gillian's enthusiasm couldn't be contained.

Georgia Tate sighed. She badly wanted it to be true but couldn't let hope overshadow proof. Proof was what she needed to see. She had pushed the others into going after Jaden despite the whole scandal with Kendall Paxton erupting in the tabloids. She had seen her play in college. She had been in the stands during both of Michigan's wins at the national finals. She knew this kid had the talent. The big question was her personal life. She had been linked with the infamous Kendall Paxton, Senator Paxton's daughter, during the Olympics in Japan. Kendall Paxton was a highflying lesbian party girl and there had been photos of them together as an obvious couple overseas. Then last year the police had raided a party at the summer home of Senator Paxton and found illegal drugs, alcohol, and several guns along with an undisclosed amount of cash. Everyone had been arrested and taken to jail. Kendall's picture made the front page of the papers on a regular basis but this time it was her mug shot. She had looked strung out and slovenly. Jaden was not there at the time and no mention of her was made. Still, people liked to talk about beautiful, successful, rich women. Jaden Hawke met the criteria on all counts except for the rich part and Georgia Tate and the Dallas Metros took care of that with a substantial contract. Georgia knew her job now rested on whether she had been right in her judgment of Jaden.

She called for batting practice and the players divided themselves into fielders and batters in their natural order. "Erin, you start," Georgia called to her. "Take five batters then Susan and Jaden can finish up. Let's get started."

They all dispersed and Gillian went to Jaden's side. "We all rotate into the positions we play," she told her. "Pitchers and catchers get to hang out and chill until it's our turn to either hit or you're the one pitching."

Jaden nodded. "Okay, good."

"How are you feeling? I heard you were kinda sick today."

13

"Better. Danny gave me some magic elixir that seems to have helped."

"She's the best!" Gillian grinned. They took seats in the dugout and Jaden realized she really did feel better. She didn't notice Sloane dogging her every step until Gillian called out to her.

"Sloane, quit sneaking around and come meet our new star pitcher."

Jaden looked up to see the woman from the parking lot that morning. Sloane smiled tentatively at her and let the camera dangle from its strap around her neck.

"Sloane, this is Jaden Hawke. Jaden, this is Sloane Ellison, the official photographer and web nerd. You'll get used to her always being in your face with that damn camera. Be nice to her or she'll put ugly pictures of you on the web."

"Hello," Jaden nodded at her.

"Hi," she returned. "Uh, I'm sorry if I pissed you off this morning."

"Don't worry about it," Jaden told her. "I'm just camera shy."

"You shouldn't be," Sloane said without thinking. "I mean, you have marvelous cheek bones," she added quickly. "And you're very photogenic."

"That's not exactly why I'm camera shy."

Sloane quirked an eyebrow at her. "Yes, I can imagine." She slowly nodded her head. "I hate to bother you again, but I need a player photo for the program. Do you mind?"

"I'm telling you, man, give her what she wants or suffer the consequences," Gillian told her with a laugh.

Jaden sighed but smiled. "Sure. Click away."

"Would you come out here? I need the light to get the best shot."

Jaden stood and stepped back onto the field. "Where do you want me?"

Sloane's breath caught for just a split second. Want her? Who wouldn't? Jaden Hawke was a beautiful woman. However, Sloane had heard all about her and Kendall Paxton just like everyone else. She moved on from that thought and motioned to the fence in front of the dugout. "Right there is fine."

Jaden stood and looked into the camera as Sloane clicked off a series of shots. "How long have you been the photographer for the team?"

Sloane went down on one knee in front of her. "This is my second year," she answered then stood again. "A smile wouldn't hurt."

Jaden smiled and Sloane lowered the camera. "Can you relax a little? You look like you're posing."

"I *am* posing," Jaden laughed at her.

Sloane quickly snapped off another couple of shots as she did so. "That's it," she murmured.

Jaden laughed harder when she realized how she had been tricked. "You're sneaky."

"Thank you."

"That wasn't a compliment."

Sloane chuckled. "I know." She dropped the camera and raised her hands. "No tricks." She turned to the dugout. "Gilly, come on out here and get in on this."

Gillian bounded out of the dugout and stood next to Jaden. "You should make this shot the home page, Sloane," she declared as Jaden leaned an arm on her shoulder. "The heart of the team."

Sloane smiled as she caught the two laughing. "You may be right," she nodded as she looked at the captured images in the camera. "Thank you both."

Chapter 3

Jaden parked her truck in the lot and lifted her bag from the passenger seat. Most of the team was gathered on the sidewalk in front of the clubhouse, their luggage in a pile beside them. Their first game of the season was against Houston, about a five-hour bus ride down state. She was feeling cautiously good about the team and her place on it since everyone seemed to have accepted her. Her worst fear was the trips where they would have to stay overnight. She still suffered from the nightmare. The one that filled her with terrifying images, making her heart squeeze into a tight ball of lead within her chest. The one where she couldn't breathe, her lungs compressed flat, the fear so palpable it was a living thing inside her. She would wake gasping for air, her heart rate soaring beyond the safety point, her body drenched in cold sweat. She would be trembling, panicky, and often disoriented. What would happen if she had one of those on a road trip where she was sure to have at least one roommate? How would her team react to something like that? She hadn't been able to discern a pattern for when the dream occurred but knew stress was probably one of them. The food poisoning the night before the first practice had actually been the result of her dream. How could she explain something like that to anyone else? She shook off the dark thoughts and got out of the truck beeping it locked behind her as she joined her new team.

Jaden sat next to Gillian on the bench with Erin Coe on her other side as Susan Strange took the mound for the Metros. Even though she wasn't playing Jaden's heart thumped in excitement. It happened every time she entered a ballpark. It had been like that since she was a kid and she played in after school softball games. She loved everything about playing ball. She loved the bleachers, the announcer, the crowd, and the anticipation. It was the excitement of competition and the camaraderie with the other players. There was nothing quite like it to get her juices flowing.

The game was scoreless as they reached the bottom of the sixth inning. Susan walked the first batter who then reached second safely on a pitch that went into the dirt and skipped past Lindsey Jones, her catcher. Georgia Tate exited the dugout and called time out as she walked out to the mound. Lindsey met her there and they all conferred for a minute before Coach Tate returned to the dugout with a scowl. She flicked a glance at Gillian before taking up her post at the far end of the bench.

"Let's warm up a little," Gillian said, bumping Jaden's shoulder with her own. She grabbed her glove and led the way down the outfield foul line to the area set aside for the bullpen. "Just throw easy," she told her. "Just get your arm warm."

Jaden nodded and threw soft strikes, letting the motion become automatic. Gillian kept an eye on the game and when Susan walked the next batter, she signaled Jaden. "Give me some heat." Jaden nodded and popped Gillian's glove on the next three pitches. Gillian nodded, pleased with the speed. She stood and motioned her back to the dugout. "If she puts another batter on Coach will put us in. Are you ready?"

"Yeah."

"Good." Gillian slapped her on the back as they reached the dugout. "Put your jacket on." Jaden smiled. Gillian was acting like a mother hen. She couldn't tell if she was nervous about Jaden or just in general. Jaden had been through the first game on a new team too many times to be nervous about it. She had confidence in her own abilities.

Susan managed to get the next batter out when she hit a fly ball into deep left field but both runners advanced after the catch. Coach Tate got up and Gillian reached under the bench for her shin guards and chest protector. After a short conversation on the mound, Coach Tate looked toward the dugout and nodded.

"Show time, Hawke."

"I'm right behind you," Jaden said. She touched gloves with Susan as they passed on the field. "Good job, Suze. Let me get my feet wet here in the big leagues."

She reached the mound and picked up the rosin bag, bouncing it in her hand a few times before dropping it and stepping to the pitching rubber. She threw four soft pitches to Gillian then popped it on the last one before turning her back as Gillian fired a throw to Bebe Lennox at second base. The infield threw the ball around and Jaden got it from Sarah Nichols, the first baseman. She took her pitching position and waited for the batter to settle in the box. She kept her eyes on Gillian behind the plate until she got the signal. She wanted her to lead out with the heat. Her wind up was smooth and her delivery was nearly perfect. The batter watched it zip past her for a strike. Gillian called for the rise ball and the batter relaxed when she saw the pitch coming in low. It was a mistake. The pitch rose to cut through the strike zone for strike two. Gillian grinned behind her mask as she returned the ball to Jaden. The batter stepped out of the batter's box and looked down to her coach. When she stepped back in, Gillian called for the curve ball. Jaden laid it over the outside corner for a swing and a miss. Strike three. Now it was two outs with runners on second and third. The next batter settled into the box and Gillian signaled for another rise ball. The batter fouled it off behind the backstop. Gillian received a new ball from the umpire and walked out to the mound.

"What's up?" Jaden asked.

Gillian held her glove up to cover her face partially. "I would really love it if you'd either strike this bitch out or hit her with a pitch."

Jaden nodded, trying to keep a smile off her face. "I see. Which would you prefer?"

"I'd prefer you knock her head off but I guess I can't really ask you to do that."

"Well, just for future reference, I'm not totally opposed to hitting a particular batter given a good enough reason. On the other hand, it's not exactly the way I planned on making my professional debut."

"Then strike her out! Please?"

"I'll do it just for you," Jaden couldn't keep the giggle from her voice.

"I'm serious, Jaden."

"Tell you what—I'll pay you $20 if she gets a hit off me."

"You're on!"

Jaden had to stare at the ground to keep the grin off her face until Gillian was back in her catcher's position. She didn't bother looking for a signal. She was in charge of this batter. She threw a sloppy fastball low for a ball and didn't look at Gillian's reaction. She had her own way of doing this. The next pitch was again low, almost in the dirt. Jaden caught the ball, dipped her head, and turned her back to pick up the rosin bag. When she stepped back to the rubber, she put a frown on her face. She threw her fastball straight down the middle of the strike zone while the batter watched it. Now the count was two balls, two strikes. Jaden took the ball and stood facing the plate. The batter was hers to take and she knew it. She had set her up perfectly. She was definitely going with the fastball, but not the one she usually threw. She could throw a lot harder, just not repeatedly. The batter dug in, drew the bat back, and swung just as the ball landed in Gillian's glove. Strike three, inning over.

Jaden walked off the field nonchalantly while Gillian ran to intercept her, throwing both arms around her and laughing. "Damn, Jade, that fucking hurt my hand!" Everyone else slapped her on the back or shoulder as they ran off the field and into the dugout.

Jaden laughed down at Gillian. "You owe me big, Gilly."

"I do! That was fantastic!" She hugged Jaden again, making the breath whoosh out of her.

"What did she do to piss you off so much?" Jaden asked once they'd took seats on the bench again.

"Old history. She's an asshole," Gillian stated as if it were evident. "How hard can you actually throw, Jade?"

Jaden winced. Kendall had called her Jade. "Please, it's Jaden."

"Okay. How hard can you throw, *Jaden*?"

"You need to understand something," Jaden lowered her voice. "I can't throw that hard very often." She slipped her jacket on. "If I do I won't be able to pitch for a week or more."

"Got it," Gillian nodded. "It'll be our secret then." She grinned again. "Thanks. I owe you big time."

The team was juiced up by the escape from that inning and their bats came alive in the top of the seventh inning. They managed to score two runs on a double by Holly Winslett, the center fielder before ending the inning on a fly ball to right field. Jaden took her time returning to the mound and threw only two warm up pitches before waving off the rest. She faced only four batters to get three outs and the game was over. She was smiling as she came off the mound to shake Gillian's hand before going through the sportsmanship routine of shaking hands with each member of the opposing team. She was surprised when flashbulbs greeted her as they returned to their bench. She automatically ducked her head and swung down into the dugout. The smile vanished and a scowl took its place as she heard her name being called. She threw her cleats into her bag and jammed her glove in on top before lacing up her sneakers. Sloane suddenly appeared at her side.

"They're just local press, Jaden. They want a quote about the game, that's all."

Jaden heaved a sigh and dropped her shoulders. "Do I have to say something?"

"Not if you really hate it but it would be good for our team and the league."

Jaden sighed again but nodded when she saw the look on Sloane's face. She wanted to make Sloane happy. "Okay." She shrugged into her jacket, picked up her bag, and went outside.

Sloane held back to see how she would handle it but she needn't have worried. Jaden smiled and gave praise to Houston's team and said they'd gotten very lucky to win tonight's game. She was at ease, personable, and very charming.

When they were finished, Jaden turned for the exit with Sloane next to her. "Thank you, Jaden. You handled that very well."

"I know how to talk to sports writers," she said. "It's the other kind I can't stand."

"I can imagine," Sloane said quietly. When Jaden shot her a dark look, she added, "I just meant it can't have been fun having the paparazzi following your every move."

Jaden kept going, her eyes straight ahead, and said nothing. They were the last to board the bus and everyone else was celebrating. Jaden put a smile on her face and accepted all their congratulations on her debut game. She worked her way to the back of the bus and finally claimed the last seat as her own. She eased into the corner and relaxed, stretching her legs out to the aisle. Only a minute later, Sloane sat down in the seat in front of her. She turned and put her arm on the back of the seat and looked at Jaden.

"I'm sorry if I upset you back there. I didn't mean anything by it."

"Sloane, listen, I..." Jaden blew out a breath and ran a hand through her thick short hair. "I don't talk about that, okay? So, if you're looking for the whole sordid story, you're out of luck."

"I'm not interested in your story," Sloane snapped. "I'm sorry for bothering you." She rose and went up the aisle toward the front of the bus.

Jaden sighed. *Shit!* She put a hand over her face and tried to calm her breathing. She had just wanted to enjoy her first professional game. Was that too much to ask? She clenched her teeth against the tightening in her throat, hating that it could still cause her such pain. She fought hard to regain control of her emotions. She knew she should be able to put this behind her and not let it affect her so badly. She knew it intellectually, but she just couldn't get her head to stop sending the signals to the rest of her body, the parts that made her feel. She didn't want to feel.

When she was in control again, she stood and walked toward the front of the bus. Most of the players were sleeping, heads propped on jackets or against the window, a few on each other. She stopped in the aisle and cleared her throat. "Sloane?" When she looked up Jaden continued. "I want to apologize. I'm sorry about the way I spoke to you earlier. I was out of line." Jaden kept her voice low and dipped her head. It was dark in the bus so she was unable to see her face. She held her breath until Sloane turned to her.

"Apology accepted. Thank you."

"Uh, may I sit here?" She wasn't sure she was welcome until Sloane nodded and moved her jacket into her lap. Jaden slid into the seat with a small sigh. "I know I'm crazy," she offered. "I just...have a hard time with...that."

"It must have really been rough on you," she said softly, "for it to still be this upsetting."

"It was," Jaden nodded. "But still, I need to keep it to myself and not let it out like that."

Sloane turned her head toward her. "Maybe that's the problem—you keep it all inside."

Jaden swallowed. There was probably some truth to that, but there was no way she could share the things that had happened to her. She looked away and put a hand to her brow to rub it quickly. "I guess," was all she said.

Sloane hesitated but finally put a hand on Jaden's arm. "I know it sounds trite, but shared worry really is cut in half. Maybe you'll find someone to share it with some day and won't have to carry it all by yourself."

Jaden looked at the hand on her arm and felt a jolt along her spine. "Maybe I will."

Sloane removed her hand. "I hope so, for your sake." She leaned back against the headrest and returned to gazing out the window.

"How did you come to be the team photographer?" Jaden asked to keep her engaged in conversation.

"I was working for a company in Dallas that did the photo shoots for several of the ad agencies. I thought it would be fun. You know, models and everything."

"It wasn't?"

"Oh Lord, no! It was mostly boring as hell. I photographed table settings, dolls, towels, jewelry, food, and anything else you can think of, but no sexy models in their underwear."

Jaden laughed out loud. "You're kidding me!"

"Yeah, a little," Sloane admitted with a chuckle. "But it *was* boring. That part was true."

"So?" Jaden prompted her.

"So I saw a clip in the Morning News about the team needing another person in their media department and went down to ask about it. When I told them I was not only a photographer but also a web designer they practically hired me on the spot."

"And you like it."

"Well, there are still no sexy underwear models but at least it's not boring. It's not nine to five and I get to travel a little bit. And the players are all pretty nice."

"Most of them anyway." Jaden poked fun at herself.

"Yeah, most of them," Sloane smiled in the dark.

"How does your job work?" Jaden asked. "I mean, what photos go where and what does the web site do and all that?"

"I take all the photos and when you guys aren't playing, I'm in my office going through them. I pick the ones I want to put on the web, do a little editing, and then post them on the site."

"Wow, you're a one woman advertising agency."

"There are two others in the department," she allowed. "They do layout work for the program, get the opposing teams stats, arrange for printing, and buy TV and radio ads."

"I guess, I never thought about all the stuff that goes into it."

"There's a lot of work being done behind the scene," Sloane nodded.

"Maybe one of these days I'll take a trip up to the media department and check it out."

"That would be fun," she laughed. "The others rarely get to see any of the players unless they go to a game."

Silence settled over them then and they both relaxed in their seats. The bus was dark and quiet, and Jaden soon heard deep and even breathing, indicating Sloane had fallen asleep. She smiled. Sloane was nice, she thought. Maybe she had been too hard on her, too suspicious. She was concentrating on staying awake when she felt Sloane lean against her shoulder. She looked over and found her still fast asleep but using her shoulder for a pillow. She didn't know what she should do but it felt nice. She took the jacket from her lap and draped it over Sloane's shoulder.

Chapter 4

Jaden never got drunk, but she was drunk now, and pissed off. She was immeasurably pissed off. That morning she had opened the newspaper to see her picture plastered on the front page of the sports section, and directly next to it was a picture of Kendall Paxton. The headline declared Kendall was coming to Dallas to be with Jaden for the summer. The following column did little except rehash false 'facts' about Kendall's life and where Jaden fit into it. Jaden recognized the picture as one Sloane had taken on the first day of practice. She recognized the background. How could Sloane have done that to her?

It was late night and she was in a rough bar with even rougher women in it. The windows hadn't been washed since they were installed thirty years ago and the bar stools were in much the same shape. The seats barely held any padding and were cracked and full of cigarette burns.

She had been drinking steadily all day and had no idea where she was or how she had gotten there. She didn't care. The ceiling fan moved sluggishly, managing just to push the haze of smoke around. Jaden's eyes were rimmed in red and bloodshot as she slumped against the grimy bar in front of her. She downed the last of her drink and thumped the glass down on the bar. It made a small splash as it landed in a puddle of spilled booze. This was a bar where they weren't afraid to let their customers over indulge and her glass was quickly refilled.

"Hey, baby, how ya doin'?" A big woman in a jean jacket with the sleeves ripped out slid onto the stool next to her. She had on dirty blue jeans and boots and she smelled as if she lived in the bar, all smoke and booze. There was a tattoo on her upper arm, a heart cracked in two pieces.

Jaden turned away. "Not interested."

The woman sneered. "Not interested, huh? Well, maybe I don't care if you're interested." She put her arm across Jaden's shoulders and pulled her toward her.

Jaden exploded off the bar stool in a rage. She held onto the flabby arm and twisted it behind the big dyke's back then pushed her off the barstool. Several adjoining stools tipped over and cascaded around her. She got to her feet and blindly charged Jaden only get kicked in the stomach as Jaden turned away from her and lifted her leg in a sloppy but effective side kick. The bar erupted into a full-blown brawl as everyone got in on the act and soon all manner of things were flying through the air. An airborne beer bottle hit Jaden in the side of the head and she went down.

When she opened her eyes all she saw was a pair of legs and gravel. She heard sirens in the distance. She rose up quickly and hit the pair of legs behind the knees and the woman went down. Unfortunately, she went down on top of Jaden, causing the breath to whoosh out of her.

"What the hell are you doing?"

"She knocked me down!"

"Well, get the fuck off her and let's get out of here!"

The weight lifted from Jaden's chest and she sucked in some air. Before she could move, her arms were grasped and she was hauled to her feet. She struggled to free herself.

"Stop it, Jaden!"

Her left arm was yanked forward and she lost her balance. She would have fallen again but two sets of hands kept her upright as she was pulled along. She stumbled blindly, still struggling to free herself. The trip ended as she was pushed face down over the trunk of a car, and before she could recover, she was pulled upright and shoved into the back seat. They were in motion before she could move. The seat was softer than the ground had been so she thought maybe she would rest a minute and then when the car stopped she would be stronger.

"Damn! She's heavier than she looks! Can you get the door?" Gillian and Sloane pushed, shoved, and carried Jaden out of the car and up to the door of Sloane's apartment.

"At least I live on the ground floor," Sloane panted. "Lean her against the wall while I get the door open."

They put her on the couch and both of them sighed in relief. "Jesus! I can't believe we got her out of there!" Gillian slumped into a chair.

"Yeah, and just in time too," Sloane nodded. "Can I get you a beer?" She was still breathing heavily, more from tension than exertion.

"Yeah, thanks." Gillian watched Jaden sleep on the couch. "What the hell was she doing in that God awful bar?"

Sloane handed her a beer and settled into the other chair. "Looking for a fight maybe," she said.

"Well, she sure as hell found one." Gillian snorted and drank some beer.

"Or started one," Sloane corrected.

"Yeah, maybe."

"I think she's bleeding on my couch," Sloane said without any real concern for her furniture. "Should we roll her over?"

Gillian sighed. "Yeah, I just don't want her waking up and taking a swing at me."

They both got up and together they turned Jaden face up. Indeed, she was bleeding slightly from a small cut at her temple.

"Keep an eye on her while I go find something to put on that." Sloane returned a minute later with an alcohol wipe and a bandage. Jaden whimpered a little as Sloane cleaned the wound but did not wake up.

"I think we should put her on her side in case she wakes up spewing," Gillian advised. "She's going to have a hell of a hangover tomorrow."

"Oh yeah," Sloane agreed. "It's not going to be pretty." They put her on her side and Sloane got a plastic lined trashcan to put on the floor next to her head.

"Are you sure you'll be okay?" Gillian asked. "I can stay if you want."

"I'll be fine," she assured her. "You'd have to sleep in the chair and I'm not answering to Coach Tate for a crippled catcher. Go on home and I'll call you tomorrow."

When she had gone, Sloane locked the door behind her and stood looking at Jaden still passed out on her couch. She debated it for a minute but eventually undressed her down to her underwear. God, she was gorgeous! She had long muscular legs that led up to six-pack abs and wide shoulders. She looked hard, smooth, and soft all at the same time. She hesitated once again but then went ahead and unhooked her bra and pulled it from under her. She had slept in her bra on a camp out once and it had been horrible. The breasts that spilled from the bra were on the small side but full with pink nipples riding high. Sloane couldn't pull her eyes away from them. She wanted to touch her. She wanted to feel the weight of them in her palms as she cupped them. She wanted to see the nipples stiffen under her fingers. She unconsciously licked her lips and wondered how they would taste. She finally shook herself out of those thoughts and went into her bedroom to get a blanket to cover her.

The morning brought Sloane shuffling into the kitchen in a haze. She needed more sleep. She remembered her guest then and looked into the living room. Jaden was still passed out on the couch. She put the coffee on and went to take a shower.

She was on her second cup when she heard Jaden stir. She stayed in the kitchen not knowing how she might react to waking up naked in a strange place. It was a long time before she heard unsteady footsteps and then Jaden stood in the doorway wrapped in the blanket.

"Would you like some coffee?" Sloan asked quietly.

"Mmm." Jaden's mouth didn't open. She looked exactly like what she was, a woman hung over and recovering from a bar fight. Her hair stuck out at odd angles, the cut at her temple was bruising, and she was pasty white and shaking. Sloane waved a hand at a chair and got up to pour her a cup of coffee. Jaden had just managed to sit down when Sloane placed the cup in front of her. She huddled in the blanket and stared at the coffee as if she didn't know quite what to do with it. Sloane sat across from her and resumed reading the morning paper. She looked up only when she heard the cup clatter against the table. Jaden had a bad case of the shakes.

"I can make something to eat, if you..." Sloan started to say but stopped at the bilious look on her face. "Just coffee is good," she amended. She covertly watched as Jaden finally finished the coffee. She got up to refill the cup for her. "You're welcome to take a shower if you want. Your clothes are folded on the chair next to the couch." She watched Jaden's eyes and continued, "I was the one who undressed you last night." She seemed to be confused so Sloane added, "We can talk about last night when you're ready."

The phone rang and Sloane went to answer it in the living room. "Gillian is on her way over," she announced when she returned. Jaden looked surprised and confused. "She was with me last night when we found you." She could tell this information didn't help Jaden at all. "When you're ready," she repeated and returned her attention to the paper.

Jaden stared at the paper and something stirred inside her, something bad. She couldn't remember what. Her head pounded and her stomach felt seasick. She couldn't think. She took another sip of coffee but slopped some onto the table while trying to set the cup down.

Sloane got up, got a paper towel without comment, and cleaned it up. It was a bad case, Sloan thought. She went into the bathroom and returned with the same pink liquid that the trainer had given Jaden and some aspirins. She got a glass of water and brought it to the table. "Pink stuff first," she said before sitting once again.

Jaden pulled the blanket closer around her and took a shaky breath. She was dimly aware of her nakedness. Being in someone else's apartment was confusing and since she couldn't remember why she was here, she didn't know how to act. She was still at the table when Gillian arrived. She refused to be quiet even though Sloane shushed her.

"Jesus, Jaden!" she bellowed from the doorway. "You look like hell!"

Jaden winced and pulled her head into the blanket.

"Gilly, have a heart," Sloane pleaded. "Can't you see she's sick?"

"Sick my ass!" Gillian snorted. "It's her own fault." However, she did lower her voice. She noticed the blanket then and the fact Jaden was naked under it. "Did you two have a little fun after I left last night?" she laughed. "The last I remember she had on all her clothes."

"Stop it, Gilly," Sloane demanded gruffly.

"Aw hell, I'm just messing with her." Gillian sat next to Jaden and put an arm around her. "I'm sorry, Jaden. Get some more coffee down and we'll talk about it."

Sloan sighed. "Jaden, why don't you go take a shower? You'll feel better." Jaden gave her an appreciative look and nodded once. "I put fresh towels in the bathroom and help yourself to anything else you need." Jaden rose slowly and shuffled out of the kitchen. Sloane set a cup of coffee in front of Gillian and started a fresh pot. She had a feeling they were going to need it.

"Has she said anything?"

"Not a word," Sloan shook her head. "What should we tell her when she gets back? I'm sure she has no idea why she's here."

"We'll tell her the truth," Gillian shrugged.

Sloane sighed. "She blames me, Gilly. You know she does."

"It wasn't your fault, Sloane. We'll make sure she understands that."

They waited a long time before Jaden returned. She looked better but was still pale.

"You look almost human," Gillian grinned. "Have a seat."

Jaden remained standing. "Uh, I think I'd better just leave," she said very quietly.

"Don't you want to know why you woke up naked in Sloane's apartment with a nasty head wound, and a monster hang over?" Jaden hesitated, unsure. If she left, she would probably never get the whole story. Gillian patted the chair next to her. "Come on, Jaden, let us tell you what you want to know."

Jaden hesitated but finally took a seat at the table. "What happened?"

"Well, it's kind of a weird story," Gillian began. "Yesterday's Morning News had a picture of you on the sports page. There was also a picture of Kendall Paxton right next to it."

Jaden closed her eyes in pain as the memory came flooding back. She swallowed hard then bolted for the bathroom.

"My God, this is really upsetting to her," Sloane sighed. They sat in silence for a minute.

"What do you think it's about? I mean, I've broken up with women before." Gillian lifted her shoulders in confusion.

"This is way more than just a bad break up," Sloane said with conviction.

"You gave them my photo." Jaden's voice cut through her like a whip.

Sloane turned to find her scowling at her from the doorway. "It's not what you think."

"Then what is it?" she demanded.

"Jaden, the paper called and asked for a photo for the sports page," Gillian cut in quickly. "How was Sloane supposed to know what they were going to do?"

Jaden kept her eyes on Sloane. As angry as she was, had been yesterday, the look on Sloane's face made her hesitate. She looked stricken.

"I'm sorry, Jaden. I didn't know. I swear!"

"She's telling the truth," Gillian nodded. "Give her a break. Why would she do something like that to you? Nobody around here even knows why this is such a big deal to you anyway."

Sloane got up and reached out to touch Jaden's arm. "Please, Jaden, I didn't know. You have to believe me."

Jaden looked into her eyes and finally nodded. "Okay. I guess that makes sense."

"Okay," Gillian grinned. "Now sit down and tell us what you remember about last night."

Jaden sat down. "I don't remember much," she confessed. "I remember being so angry when I read that stupid piece in the paper. I just lost it. I wanted to break something."

"Did you?" Gillian asked anxiously.

"I don't know." Jaden put her head in her hands. She couldn't think through the pounding in her head. "I can't remember."

"Do you remember calling me?" Sloane asked.

Jaden started to shake her head but stopped quickly and whispered, "No."

"Well, we don't know where you were all day but last night you called Sloane around midnight." Gillian waited to see if it jogged any memory.

"Why?" Jaden raised her head to look at Sloane. "Why would I call you?"

"To cuss me out," Sloane said. "You blamed me for giving them your photo."

"Oh, God," Jaden mumbled. "What did I say?"

"You said, 'Fuck you'. I couldn't understand anything after that except the word photo."

"Jesus! I'm so sorry, Sloane."

"Well, no harm done." Sloane gave her a small smile.

"Do you remember where you were?" Gillian asked.

"No. A bar obviously."

"You were in Maxine's in south Dallas."

"Oh, God!" Jaden covered her face with her hands again.

"Yeah," Gillian nodded. "That pretty much says it all."

"What did I do and how did you find me?"

"We think you started a bar fight." Jaden groaned at that. "And we got lucky in finding you. After you called Sloane, she called me. We pieced things together and figured you were pissed off and drunk. So we started searching the bars around here and I ran into someone I know who mentioned she saw you at Maxine's."

"Oh God," Jaden said again.

"When we got there you were on the floor, bleeding. We managed to duck the flying beer bottles and drag you out of there. We brought you back here and that's it." Gillian leaned back in her chair with a sigh then came forward again. "Oh yeah, you knocked Sloane down in the parking lot."

Jaden was shocked. Her jaw dropped open and she turned wide eyes to Sloane. "No."

"Yes," Sloane nodded. "I don't think you knew who I was though. You just weren't done fighting."

"Are you hurt? Did I hurt you?"

"I'm fine," Sloane assured her. "Don't worry."

"Oh my God, I don't believe this." Jaden hung her head in shame. This was not like her. She didn't fight and she definitely didn't fight her friends. "I'm so sorry, Sloane," she said again.

"You were just reacting," she assured her. "And I fell on top of you so you got the worst of it."

"I don't know what to say."

"Shall we assume Kendall Paxton is not on her way here?" Gillian got them back on track.

"No." Jaden shook her head. "She better not be coming here."

"Where did that story come from then?"

"I have no idea," Jaden sighed. "Reporters just make shit up." She stood and paced across the kitchen. She ran her hands through her hair and sighed deeply. "When will people let this go?" She returned to the table and sank back down in her chair.

"Other than the two of you dating and her being the Senator's daughter, what's the big deal?" Gillian wanted to know.

"The big deal is that I don't want to ever be connected to her again." She sighed deeply. "Listen, we had a little fling and that was it."

"Come on, Jaden. If that was it, you wouldn't still be so nuts about it," Sloane pointed out.

"She has a point," added Gillian.

Jaden put her head in her hands again to cover her eyes. She couldn't let them know how deeply this affected her still. "You don't want to hear the story, trust me. It's just the same old thing. Women fall for each other, they separate, the end."

"Really?" Gillian's voice dripped with disbelief.

"Really. Well, except for one of them is the rich daughter of a senator and everything she does is reported on and she knows it."

"And that's all there is." Gillian made it plain she doubted it.

"Pretty much."

"And that's why you got drunk and started a bar fight last night."

Jaden sighed and leaned back in her chair before looking from one to the other. "Okay, I'll tell you the story but you have to swear it doesn't get out of this room." She paused. "I met Kendall in Japan at the Olympics. We went out, had a good time, you know?" They were nodding at her, waiting. "We would ditch the paparazzi, have dinner and then hit a bar and do some dancing." She closed her eyes briefly. "It was fun. We laughed a lot; I remember that. We'd go back to her hotel and we'd sneak in the back door." She had a small smile on her face but now it disappeared. "Everything changed when we got back home. It seemed like she was one person there and a completely different one here. We ditched the press in Japan, but she couldn't seem to get away from them here. She thought it was funny when she'd grab me and they would take a photo of it. It was like she was doing it on purpose."

"Why?" Sloane asked quietly.

"I...uh, finally figured that out, but it was a little too late."

"What do you mean?" Gillian prompted.

"She was the wild little rich daughter of Senator Paxton here in the states. She had a certain reputation to maintain. Her friends were right there encouraging her to be wilder and more outrageous. It was way too crazy for me. She was drinking constantly and I finally realized she was doing drugs. It seems she and her friends kept me hanging around because I was good for a laugh." Jaden drew a shaky breath. "She managed to ditch the press for a couple of weeks so they followed me constantly thinking I'd lead them to her." She paused and her eyes were unfocused and filled with pain as she remembered. "Anyway, I left and that's the end of that."

Sloane watched her and thought that wasn't nearly all of it, even as bad as it had been for her. "I'm sorry, Jaden. That sounds horrible."

"What about that big party where she got arrested along with half of the notable lesbians in California?" Gillian wanted to know.

"I was gone by then. You know as much about that as I do. Maybe getting arrested was good for her. Maybe she got some help." Jaden kept her eyes on the table.

"I'm still confused about the article in the paper. Why would someone make that up?"

"I don't know. If the tabloids can't find anything for real, they just make stuff up, and then it makes its way into the real news and nobody knows the difference. She must be hiding out and they can't find her right now."

"Maybe she's still in jail."

"No," Jaden shook her head. "Daddy wouldn't have allowed that. I'll bet she was out before the ink dried on her mug shot."

They sat for a while in silence until Gillian got up. "Shit, Jaden, I'm sorry all this happened. Just promise me that you won't go looking for a fight if anything else happens, okay? Next time you might not be so lucky to have us rescue you."

"Yeah, okay. I just thought all that was behind me and I got blindsided by it. Thanks for being there last night. I appreciate it."

"I've got some things I need to get done so I'm going to take off." Gillian flicked a look at Sloane. "Call one of us the next time you feel like that, okay?"

"Yeah. Thanks, Gilly."

Sloane walked Gillian to the door. "Thanks for everything, Gilly."

"I'll see you later." Gillian smiled at her with a knowing look. "Take good care of her."

Chapter 5

It was their day off, but Jaden's voice mail held a request for an appearance in Coach Tate's office at ten o'clock. She parked her truck in the lot and got out. She was nervous. She figured this was about the article in the paper and she didn't have any defense.

The offices were on the second floor of the clubhouse and she took the elevator at the rear of the building. The door to the office was open so she rapped her knuckles on the frame.

"Come in, Jaden." Coach Tate was at her desk. Coach Winslow was standing at the filing cabinet, a drawer open in front of him. He moved to his desk as Jaden entered the room. Georgia Tate waved to a chair and Jaden sat down. "I asked you to come in because of this." She turned the sports page so Jaden could see it. "Have you seen it?"

Jaden made a face of distaste. "Yes, I've seen it."

"And?"

"And nothing. I don't know anything about it."

"You expect us to believe that?" Coach Winslow's voice dripped with sarcasm. "It's all about you!"

Jaden clenched her jaw and forced herself to remain calm when she felt anything but calm. "I didn't talk to anyone from the paper."

"Then how do you explain it?" Coach Tate asked calmly.

"I can't explain it," Jaden said and shook her head. "I was as surprised as you."

"Oh, come on, Jaden! It just didn't appear by magic! The paper had to have talked to someone. Maybe Senator Paxton's daughter called the paper and let them know you'd invited her down to Dallas," Coach Winslow suggested with a sneer.

"I didn't invite her here!" Jaden's voice rose. "I haven't talked to her!"

"Maybe she invited herself then," he suggested with a shrug.

"Is she on her way here?" Georgia asked.

"No!" Jaden turned back to her. "You have to believe me! I haven't talked to her." She took a deep breath to calm down. "I don't know anything about that article in the paper. I didn't talk to anyone at the paper. I didn't talk to Kendall. I don't *want* to talk to her." Jaden was stiff with anger and frustration.

Coach Tate sighed and leaned back in her chair. "I have to be honest with you, Jaden. We don't want this season to be turned into a media circus." She folded her hands across her stomach. "The team owners will not allow what happened in L.A. to happen here." She gave her a hard look. "They will let you go if anything like that happens." What she didn't say was that she would be gone right behind her in that case. "I will not tolerate having this season turned into a spectacle. Do I make myself clear?"

Jaden nodded. "Yes. But I'm telling you, I don't know how that article got into the paper and it's not true." She stood. "You do whatever you have to do." She turned and left the office. She was angry and upset and turned the wrong way. The door at the end of the hall opened and Sloane came out. She smiled at Jaden.

"Good morning."

"Hi."

"Can I buy you a cup of coffee?" Sloan asked. "Or are you busy?"

"Coffee sounds good," Jaden nodded.

Sloane led her down another hall and into their break room. There were several tables with chairs, a sink, refrigerator, and two microwave ovens. A large coffee maker sat on the end of the counter. She handed a paper cup to Jaden and took a ceramic mug with her name on it from a cabinet for herself. She poured for Jaden then filled her own. "Do you take anything in it?"

"No," Jaden shook her head. "Black is fine."

"So, what brings you here on your day off?"

"I was sent to the principal's office for writing dirty words on the blackboard."

Sloane choked on her coffee, nearly spilling the entire cup before she could set it down. She finally took in a wheezing breath and wiped her eyes, laughing. "Damn, I almost shot coffee out of my nose!"

Jaden laughed. "I'm sorry." Her anger melted instantly when she heard Sloane's laugh.

"Okay," Sloane coughed once more. "I'm okay." She wiped her eyes again. "What words did you write and on whose board?"

"It seems like it was the front office blackboard."

"And the dirty words?"

"I can't say." Jaden grinned. "I'm afraid I'll get into trouble again."

"Would one of them happen to be Kendall?"

Jaden made a face and took a sip of coffee. "You're very perceptive."

"Are they pissed?"

"Yeah, they're pissed all right," Jaden sighed. "Coach Tate said if I turned this season into a circus they'd cut me loose." She shifted her gaze to the middle distance across the room. "Like I have any control over it."

"I'm sorry." Sloane knew it was inadequate, but couldn't think of anything that wasn't.

"Coach Winslow acted like I was lying to them and practically accused me of setting the whole thing up."

"Maybe he just wants to get a look at Kendall up close," Sloan said with a grin. "He's like every other guy. It seems they're all interested in seeing two women together," Sloane said, trying to lighten things up.

Jaden laughed. "What's up with that anyway? It's not like they'd be invited to join in."

"I don't know." Sloane laughed with her. "I never could understand it either."

"It must be a guy thing."

"Must." She agreed.

"So, what are you working on today?" Jaden wanted to change the subject.

"I'm doing some sorting and filing right now. It's boring. I've put up the picture of the Ohio team and their stats on the web site for the next game. And I've chosen Sharon Peck for our spotlight player." Every three or four games Sloane picked a player and did an interview type article that she then put on the web site. It was a way for the fans to get to know a little more about the players they came to watch.

"So Sharon is your target, huh? Does our left fielder know it yet?"

"Yes," Sloane nodded with a smile, knowing Jaden wasn't looking forward to being the one in the spotlight. "I have a simple questionnaire I give out and all you have to do is answer the questions honestly. It's painless."

Jaden snorted at that. "I'm sure."

"It is," Sloane said. "It's just routine stuff like where you grew up, what school you went to, things like that."

"And who's the most famous person you've ever f..."

"No," Sloan cut in. "I would never do that to you." She looked Jaden straight in the eye. "You don't have to be afraid of me."

Jaden sighed, but knew she had been fooled into believing in someone before with disastrous results. "Yeah, okay."

Sloane knew she wasn't convinced and while it hurt, she realized it would take time before Jaden trusted anyone. "Nothing goes on the site that hasn't been cleared by the player."

Jaden nodded absently and took another sip of coffee. "I may not be here long enough to find out if that's true."

Sloane jerked in surprise. "Don't say that." She put a hand over Jaden's on top of the table. "Don't even think it."

Jaden looked at their hands and her heart skipped a beat. "Thanks."

"Jaden, it was just one thing in the paper. When she doesn't show up everyone will forget about it."

Jaden gave a small sigh. "Thanks again for rescuing me from the bar the other night. I have a feeling I'd already be gone if the police had gotten there before you."

Sloane surprised her by laughing. "It was a first. I'd never even seen a bar fight before and I'd never been in Maxine's before either."

"And did you like it?" Jaden teased.

"There were some interesting people there," Sloane nodded with a grin. "Lots of leather and tattoos."

"So you like that kind of thing?" Jaden asked with a lift of a brow.

Sloane raised her own brow in response. "Maybe." Then she laughed. "Who can wear leather in this Texas heat?"

"Personal hygiene does not seem to be at the top of any of their lists."

"Do you remember anything more about that night yet?"

"A little. I remember a big ugly dyke coming on to me. I think that's what started the fight."

"Wow. I'll have to remember not to say anything suggestive to you then."

Jaden gave her a swift once over and felt her heartbeat ratchet up another notch. "Don't let that stop you," she murmured.

Sloane's mouth went dry. Had she heard her right? She cleared her throat and chanced a look at Jaden but she was draining her coffee cup and stood up.

"Are you going to show me what you do up here with all your photos?"

"Sure." Sloane recovered and got up. She rinsed out her cup and turned it upside down on the drain board before leading Jaden back to her office.

It was a large room divided into three areas by shoulder high partitions. She waved to the area on her right. "Stan, this is Jaden Hawke, our new pitcher. Jaden, this is Stan. He designs the layout for the programs and advertising copy." Jaden and Stan exchanged waves. Sloan then waved to her left. "And this is John. He's in charge of buying the printing plus the TV and radio advertising and helps Stan on layouts and anything else that needs to get done." Jaden smiled and returned John's wave. "And the back wall is mine." Sloane waved her into the space she commanded. "I take team and individual photos, edit them, and publish and maintain the web site." She sat at the counter that stretched the length of the room and waved Jaden into a chair.

"Is that your creation?" Jaden pointed to the large plasma monitor in front of Sloane.

"Yes. This is the Dallas Metros home page." Sloane smiled. "What do you think?"

Jaden moved closer. The team photo dominated the page with a stylized banner logo on top and Sloane had made a watermark of the inside of the stadium for the background. Each player was listed along with positions played, as well as both coaches. Moving the mouse over a name resulted in a small pop up window showing the current stats. There was a link to the schedule, one for a diagram of the stadium, and another one for the seating chart and ticket information. There were links to buy memorabilia from the fan shop, reserved seating for future games and links to the web site of their next opponent. Another link led to a page that held individual player photos with several candid shots of each. There were even shots of the coaches.

Jaden smiled at Sloane. "Wow, I didn't know Coach Tate knew how to smile."

Sloane laughed. "Yeah, she hasn't shown it much yet but she can be fun."

"This is great, Sloane. Really. Very impressive."

"Thanks." Sloane felt her cheeks redden. "Do you not have a computer?"

"A laptop," Jaden nodded. "So what do you do with all the photos you don't use on the web site?"

"I keep them," Sloane grinned. "I never delete a photo unless it's out of focus or unusable."

"That must take up a lot of space."

"That's why they make external storage devices."

Jaden grinned. "I should know better than to question you about your craft." She looked around the space and appreciated the tidy and organized workstation. "You've got quite a set up here."

"I love this work," she admitted. "It's everything I love all rolled together and then they pay me."

"I know what you mean," she nodded. "I love playing ball. I don't know what I'll do for a living if I get booted off the team."

"Don't worry about something that hasn't happened yet," Sloane said quickly. She looked up at the clock and put a hand on Jaden's arm. "Would you like to have lunch with me?" She held her breath.

"Yes," Jaden said while still looking at the hand on her arm. It was warm where it touched her and Jaden felt a tingle all along the nerve path. She couldn't look away until Sloane stood up and broke the contact.

"Great!" Sloane finally exhaled. "Do you have a preference?"

Jaden could finally move again once Sloane had removed her hand from her arm. "Uh, no. Anywhere you'd like is fine with me."

"Okay. Mexican?"

"Sounds good."

"There's a little cocina down on Young Street that's pretty good."

"In Deep Ellum?"

"Yeah. Right across from The Bone Yard club. Have you been there?"

"Not to the Mexican place."

"How about The Bone Yard?"

Jaden grinned. "I might have peeked in the door a time or two," she admitted.

"That's a wild place some nights," Sloane commented as they left the office.

"Nothing compared to Maxine's," Jaden laughed.

"Well, there is that," she admitted.

Chapter 6

"Stan, I don't know if I can go back there." Jaden was on the phone with her agent and she was pacing her apartment as they talked.

"You have to go," he said again. "What possible reason can you give for not going?"

Jaden's hand trembled and she pressed the phone tighter to her ear. "I don't know!" She had to fight to keep from screaming at him. *He was her agent; wasn't he supposed to take care of things like this for her?*

"Jaden, it'll be fine. You're worried about nothing. If the press is there, you just don't talk to them. You can do that, can't you?"

"It's not...I just don't know if I..." She stopped. She couldn't tell him she was more afraid of things inside her than the press. "Okay, you're right. I can do this."

"That's my girl! You'll be fine. Just say 'no comment' to everything and keep your head up."

"Yeah, okay."

"Don't let 'em get to you, Jaden. Remember, you're the best. Go out there and show them that."

"Okay. Thanks, Stan." Jaden hung up and sank down on her couch. *Shit!* Their next game was against L.A. and they were leaving tomorrow. They would stay in L.A. overnight and then go on to Portland the day after. She couldn't miss this trip. She would just have to suck it up and hope for the best.

At the check in desk at the hotel Gillian found Coach Winslow on his cell phone sending a text message and simply took one of the key cards from his hand and motioned Jaden to follow her. By twos and threes, the rest of the team followed her lead, took keys and carried their bags to the elevators.

"We room together on the road," Gillian told her. "If that's okay with you."

"Sure, I'm good with that," Jaden nodded.

They stopped outside their room and Gillian swiped the card and opened the door. "Which bed do you want?"

"Closest to the bathroom," Jaden said. "In case I need to puke in the middle of the night." She laughed so Gillian would think she was kidding.

"Okay." Gillian put her suitcase on the other queen size bed and slung her player bag next to it on the floor. "Oh, by the way, we'll have another roommate tonight too."

"Who?"

"Sloane's bunking in with us." Gillian looked up just in time to see the flicker of apprehension cross Jaden's face before she hid it. "You, being the pitcher, get your own bed," she continued. "We wouldn't want one of our stars to be tired from having to share a bed." She grinned over at her. "Unless they want to, of course."

Jaden managed to laugh. "Whatever."

Jaden tried to calm her nerves as she stretched out on the grass in the outfield. She bent one leg to the side and leaned forward to place her forehead on the opposite thigh. She held it for thirty seconds before releasing and bringing the bent leg forward again. She wore her uniform pants and cleats but only the blue sleeved under shirt. She hoped she looked just like every other player on the field. She had resolutely kept her head down as they'd entered the stadium and refused to acknowledge the questions thrown at her. Her teammates had closed ranks around her and shielded her from the blinding flashes of the photographers.

Gillian finished her own warm up routine and searched out Jaden. "Hey, Rookie, are you ready to throw a few fast balls?"

"Sure." Jaden followed Gillian to the dugout and they retrieved their gloves.

"You're not nervous, are you?"

"Not about pitching," Jaden assured her.

"Relax," Gillian told her. "Nobody can get to you down here." She tossed her the ball.

"Okay." Jaden tossed the ball back easily, just using the motion. "Thanks, Gilly."

"Hey, it's my job to take care of my pitcher."

The game began and Jaden felt the familiar excitement seep into her psyche. She was pitching today and she was jazzed. When she took the mound for the first time, everything else faded away. She was in the zone and it wouldn't have mattered where they were playing.

Dallas was ahead 1-0 going into the last inning. Gillian trotted out to the mound. "Just close this sucker out, Jaden, and we can go get a steak and a beer. How about it?"

"I'm all for that."

L.A. had other ideas. They put the first batter on with a hit up the middle. Jaden struck out the second batter but the third batter moved the runner around on an error by Dallas's third baseman, Rachael Walker. Jaden struck out their fourth batter and now stood facing the fifth batter of the inning. Gillian squatted behind the plate and flashed the signal for a rise ball. She expected a fastball and fouled the pitch off behind the backstop. Gillian called for another rise ball and the batter once again fouled it off for strike two. Jaden put the next pitch on the outside corner but the umpire called it a ball. She turned on the mound and hefted the rosin bag a couple of times before taking her pitching position. Gillian called for the fastball but the umpire called it low for another ball. She blew out a breath and tried to relax. They needed this out. Gillian hesitated but finally gave her the sign for the pitch Jaden called the *smoke*. Without hesitation, Jaden nodded. The umpire called it low for a ball. The count was full. Jaden was getting frustrated with the umpire and it must have showed because Gillian trotted out to the mound.

"It's okay," she said quickly. "Don't let him get in your head." Jaden nodded and looked over Gillian's shoulder to where the batter stood. "Look at me, not her. She's nothing. She's just a bat. She isn't cute, she doesn't have a name, and she's not going to be a hero tonight. Got it?"

"Yeah, I got it."

"Okay. How's the arm?"

"I'm good."

"What do you want to do?"

"*Smoke*."

"You sure?"

"Yeah. Let me try it again. How blind can he be?"

"Okay. Down the middle then."

Jaden took in a deep breath, let it out slowly, and centered herself. She focused on Gillian's glove and fired the ball past the batter, who managed a valiant swing, but didn't have a prayer of connecting. The radar gun showed 78 mph. Strike three—end of game. Jaden grinned down at Gillian as they both walked off the field.

"Shit, Jaden!" Gillian exclaimed, pulling her glove off as they neared the dugout. "That hurt!"

"Yeah, me too," she said, touching her arm.

"No! Oh, man! Please tell me you're kidding."

"It'll be okay," she said. "I'll get to rest it for the next few days and I'll take care of it."

The visitor's locker room consisted of lockers on both sides of the main room with benches in front. Past that, was a large open area holding an array of food and drinks that were catered at every game. Off to the side of that were the showers and training room. Jaden sat in front of the locker she'd chosen and kicked off her cleats. All around her the rest of the team were doing the same. The press invaded their space within just a few minutes. Most of the players were still dressed, at least those that cared about strange men being among them. Jaden kept her head down, but it didn't take them long to find her.

"Jaden, did you invite Kendall Paxton to the game tonight?" A slender red haired reporter spotted her first. Before she could figure out how to escape the rest of the news herd crowded around her.

"We heard Kendall was at the game at your request. Is that true?"

"Will you be seeing Ms Paxton while you're here?"

"Is Kendall staying with you, Ms Hawke?"

"Jaden, is Kendall in Dallas?"

"Jaden, we've heard you and Kendall got married last month. Can you confirm that?"

Gillian stood up just as Sloane appeared in front of Jaden. "Gentlemen, if you have any questions about how great a game Jaden pitched tonight, please, be my guest. If not, then please exit the locker room so the team can shower and dress."

They all looked at her then back at Jaden, not moving. Gillian moved closer and began a movement that could only be interrupted as physically threatening. Jaden stood up and put a hand out to stay Gillian.

"Gentlemen, please write this down because I'm only going to say it once. I am not involved with Kendall Paxton. I have not seen or spoken to her in many months. She is not in Dallas nor do I know where she is. There is no story and that is the end of the story. Thank you." With that, she grabbed the bottom of her uniform shirt and pulled it over her head. The undershirt followed and then she calmly peeled her pants off and let them drop to the floor. Clad now in just her underwear she grabbed her kit and headed for the shower room. She ignored the reporters as Gillian and Sloane began herding them toward the exit.

They high fived each other as the door closed behind them. "Good job, Gilly."

"Yeah. That was fun!" Gillian laughed. "Let's hope this is the last time we have to do it though."

Jaden emerged from the showers and Sloane caught her breath as she watched her walk over to the food table wearing only clean underwear now. She was magnificent. Tall and muscular but sleek like a racehorse. Her dark hair was short and still wet from the shower and she absently brushed a strand back from her eyes. Sloane knew her eyes were a grayish green that changed depending on the color she wore. She also knew her lips were full and her cheekbones were high like a models. She felt her stomach tighten and the blood rush between her legs as she watched her. When her breathing became faster she realized she couldn't just keep staring at her. She tore her eyes away.

Jaden looked up and smiled. "Hey, Sloane."

"You handled those guys pretty well, considering," she said and was surprised when her voice sounded normal.

"Considering what?" Jaden continued to sample the food and fill her plate.

"Considering you were pissed as hell."

Jaden nodded slowly but smiled. "Yeah, I was."

Sloane walked over to the table too and picked up a plate, helping herself to an assortment. The team began coming out of the showers and either going to their lockers or the food table. Some were in their underwear like Jaden and some elected to get fully dressed before eating.

Jaden tilted her head toward her locker and Sloane followed. They sat on the bench and ate from paper plates, saying nothing. It was calm and comfortable and Jaden began to relax. She set her plate down and began dressing, pulling on jeans and a polo shirt.

Sloane thought once again how great she looked. She dipped her head just as Jaden swiveled to sit down again. She was sure Jaden didn't need or want another woman obsessing over her. Fortunately, Gillian joined them then and quickly dressed before sitting on Sloane's other side.

Sloane looked at the bottle of water in her hands. "What I'd really like is a cold beer," she said.

Gillian laughed and Jaden smiled at her. "Where are we going for this beer?" Gillian wanted to know.

"I know a bar not too far from here."

"Lucille's?" Jaden asked.

"Maybe," Sloane hedged. "Have you been there?"

"Duh, Sloane. I lived here for almost a year."

"Oh, yeah," she laughed.

"Have *you* been there before?" Jaden wanted to know.

"Yeah, once," she grinned. "I went last year when we played here."

"Did you have a good time?"

Sloane giggled before she could stop herself. "Yeah, it was fun."

Jaden looked past her to Gillian who was just finishing her meal. "Did you go, Gilly?"

"Yeah," she nodded. "And if I remember correctly, Sloane had a *very* good time."

"What!" Sloane screeched, turning on her. "What are you talking about?"

Gillian and Jaden both laughed so hard they nearly fell off the bench. Sloane punched Gillian in the arm. "You're lying, Gilly. Take it back!"

"Take what back?" she asked, flinching as Sloane raised a fist again. "All I said was you had a good time. Didn't you?"

"That's not what you meant, Gilly, and we both know it! Now take it back!" Sloane hit her again in the shoulder.

Jaden pushed Gillian away as she tried to take cover behind her, laughing the whole time. "Don't hide behind me!" She slid off the bench and into the center aisle, leaving the two to settle things between them.

"Come on, Gilly, you're letting a girl beat you up," Jaden taunted.

"Who are you calling a girl?" Sloane turned on her.

Jaden held her hands out in front of her. "I didn't mean it!" She laughed, but backed quickly out of range.

Sloane turned back, but Gillian had escaped and she was behind the food table where everyone else was laughing at her. She put her hands on her hips and glared at her, daring her to move.

Jaden thought she looked adorable standing there and glaring at Gillian. She just wanted to hug her. Instead, she motioned to Gillian. "Come on, no fighting. Truce." She looked at Sloane. "Truce." Gillian came slowly toward them. "That's it," Jaden nodded, as they got close once again. "Now, you two kiss and make up."

"What!" Sloane lashed out and hit Jaden in the upper arm.

Gillian immediately lunged at Sloane and wrapped her up, pinning her arms to her sides. "No hitting, Sloane." She easily moved her a few feet away while Jaden squeezed her eyes closed and gritted her teeth in pain.

"Let me go, Gilly!"

"She hurt her arm," Gillian whispered in her ear.

Sloane stopped struggling immediately and Gillian let her go. "Oh, God. I didn't know, Gilly." She turned a stricken face to her.

"I know." Gillian looked back at Jaden. She was sitting on the bench again, her right arm in her lap.

"Jaden, I'm so sorry!" Sloane rushed to her side.

"Shhh." Jaden cautioned but smiled. "It's okay. You didn't know." She reached out with her left hand and took Sloane's. "Don't worry."

Sloane sank down beside her. "Oh God, Jaden! I didn't mean to hurt you."

"I'll be fine," she assured her.

"Can I do anything?" she asked anxiously.

"No. I just need to rest it."

Gillian joined them on the bench. "See, Sloane, you're violent nature finally got you in a mess."

"I'm going to get violent on you, Gilly, if you don't shut up."

Chapter 7

Lucille's was a hopping place. Jaden went in the back door alone and took a seat at the end of the bar. She had told Gilly and Sloane to go ahead without her so she could ice her arm. She swept the room and saw several of her teammates among the crowd. She ordered a beer and watched Sloane dance with a woman she didn't recognize. Sloane moved with a sensual grace and rhythm that made Jaden's heart catch. She was beautiful. She stared. She couldn't help herself.

"You're drooling." Gillian slid onto the stool next to her. "Go ask her to dance with you."

Jaden shook her head and was finally able to look away. "Let me buy you a beer."

"Sure." Gillian caught the bartender's eye and held up her bottle. "How's the arm?"

"It's okay," she shrugged.

"No more throwing the *smoke*," Gillian told her sternly. She took a swallow of her new beer. "At least not twice in a row," she added with a grin.

Jaden grinned back. "I just wanted this win so bad, Gilly. It was worth it."

"Yeah, I know, but there's a lot more games to play."

"I'll be fine." Jaden's eyes strayed to the dance floor again. Sloane was leaving the floor with her dance partner's arm around her. She experienced an intense stab of jealousy that surprised her. It was totally unexpected and she was unprepared to deal with it. She resolutely turned back to her friend. "Gilly, how come you're still single?" She needed not to think about Sloane right then.

"Aw hell, Jaden." Gillian ducked her head with a grin. "There's just so many women, you know?"

Jaden laughed. "Yeah, I know."

"I mean, we're in so many different cities during the season and there's always women hanging around. How can you not look?"

Jaden nodded. "Looking is one thing but touching is another."

"Yeah," she acknowledged. "I like the touching part." She laughed and Jaden joined her. How could you argue with that? Jaden was no stranger to groupies and the easy availability of sex.

"Do you know anybody in here tonight?" Gillian asked.

Jaden shook her head. "No. You're on your own tonight."

"No problem." Gillian swallowed more beer and swiveled on her stool to survey the room. "I love California women."

Jaden laughed. "Go get 'em, Gilly." Gillian went in search of love for the night and she searched the crowd in the direction that she'd seen Sloane disappear. She found her in a booth with three other women. She was laughing and Jaden felt her heart melt. She was so beautiful. She sighed and thought about what asking her to dance would mean when she saw Sloane move to the dance floor with the same woman as before. It served as a cold slap in the face and brought Jaden up short. She remembered Gillian's words then. There were, indeed, many women in many cities. Perhaps Sloane was taking advantage of the situation too. She sighed again and stood up. Maybe she'd be better off somewhere else tonight. She went quietly out the back door while Sloane watched her go in disappointment.

The night was dark, hot, and muggy. The sweat rolled down her face and she wiped her brow. She cursed out loud. The house was dilapidated with peeling paint and a sagging porch supported by rotting pillars. Knee-high weeds and abandoned objects littered the yard. There were no streetlights and it was dark and desolate. She got out and made her way to a front door that was wedged open by warped and uneven floors. Her heart was doing double time in her chest and her stomach was in knots. It was blacker than midnight inside and she strained to see as she crossed the threshold. Her lungs were desperate for oxygen. It felt like she was breathing under water. Voices, shrill and sharp, came from the left. She thought she heard her name on a sob. There was a small light near the floor and she turned. Her arm was grasped in a tight fist and she screamed. The grip tightened, threatening to tear her arm off. She kept screaming and fighting the hands. She tried to run. She had to get away!

"Jaden, wake up!" Sloane leaned over the bed where Jaden was thrashing and screaming. "Jaden!"

Jaden lashed out, swinging wildly. Sloane captured her hands finally, but not until after she'd taken a shot to the head. "Jaden, wake up!" Sloane was close to panic. She held onto her wrists and finally pulled Jaden off the bed. When she hit the floor, Sloane released her instantly, fearing she had possibly hurt her. *Oh God, what have I done?* The thought was all she had time for before Jaden lunged up from the floor and took Sloane back in a wild rush. She literally lifted her off her feet and pushed her roughly against the wall. Her eyes were open but wild with fear.

Sloane looked into them and stilled her struggling. "It's okay," she said softly, her eyes never leaving Jaden's. "It was a dream." She put her hands on Jaden's hips and felt smooth skin beneath her fingers. "You're safe now." Sloane forced her body to relax within Jaden's grip. She could feel Jaden's heart thundering in her chest. Her jaw was clenched tightly and she pressed hard against Sloane, trapping her against the wall. "We're in the hotel room, Jaden. It was a dream. You're okay now." Sloane kept her voice soft and non-threatening and never took her eyes off Jaden's. It took a minute before she saw the fear begin to recede and felt her relax minutely. Her breathing slowed and Sloane knew she was finally becoming aware of her surroundings. She moved the hand on Jaden's hip in a small, soothing circle. "Hey," she said with a small smile. "You okay?"

Jaden blinked, focused on Sloane, and blinked again in confusion. She eased her grip a bit. Sloane stayed against the wall. "What..." Jaden took a step back and Sloane could see her swallow hard. She wiped a shaky hand over her face.

"You had a dream." Sloane still spoke softly. "You're okay now."

"Oh God," Jaden moaned and bolted past Sloane into the bathroom.

Sloane sighed when she heard her retching. She gave her a few minutes and when all was quiet, she went in. Jaden was slumped against the toilet. She took a washcloth from the rack and wet it in the sink. When she kneeled next to her Jaden shook her head and mumbled, "Go away."

It broke Sloane's heart when she realized Jaden was crying. She ran a hand up Jaden's back and patted her gently. "It's okay, Jaden. Just relax." She laid the towel over Jaden's hand and continued to rub her back softly. "You're not the only one to ever have a bad dream. It's okay." Jaden finally curled her fingers around the towel and raised it to her face as she sat back. Sloane rose to her feet beside her. "Come on," she urged. "Come rinse out your mouth."

Jaden sat with the washcloth to her face and she thought she wasn't going to move but then she sighed and put a hand down to leverage herself up off the floor. She brushed past Sloane and stopped at the sink. She dug into her bathroom kit and produced a small bottle of mouthwash. Sloane went on into the bedroom and waited.

When she reappeared, Jaden seemed ill at ease and embarrassed. "Uh, I'm sorry..."

"Don't be," Sloane quickly interrupted her. "Are you feeling better now?"

"Yes." Her eyes darted around the room as she strained to deal with her embarrassment.

Sloane reached out and took her hand. "Relax, Jaden. You had a bad dream and it made you sick. It's nothing to be embarrassed about." She pulled her toward the bed and made her sit. Jaden was wearing only boxers and a

64

cropped tank top and Sloane was having difficulty keeping her eyes off her.

"Did I...hurt you? When I pushed you against the wall?"

"No," she hastily assured her. "Not at all." Without thinking, she raised a hand to her jaw where one of Jaden's wild swings had connected.

"Oh God, you are hurt!" Jaden exclaimed. She reached out to touch Sloane's face. Her touch was soft and tender and she stroked her jaw with a gentle brush of fingertips. "I'm so sorry. God, Sloane, I'd give anything not to have hurt you."

"I should have ducked," she smiled, "or stayed out of reach." She hoped Jaden couldn't tell how her touch affected her.

Jaden sighed and dropped her hand. "It's a dream I've had before," she said without looking at her. "And...I get sick some times."

When she fell silent, Sloane took her hand again and squeezed it lightly. "Can you tell me about it?"

Jaden looked at their hands entwined and resting on Sloane's thigh. "I have to...go into a house." Her voice was hoarse and strained already. "It's dark and I can't see anything." She absently wiped a hand over a brow that wasn't sweating. "I'm scared but...I have to go inside. I hear my name and then...," Jaden's grip tightened almost painfully on Sloane's hand. "Someone grabs me." She was breathing heavily.

"It's okay, Jaden," Sloane hastily told her. She squeezed her hand quickly. "It's over now. Just tell me what happens."

Jaden tried to keep it together but she was having difficulty. "That's it. That's the end. I scream but nobody comes. Nobody comes to help." The last came out in a whisper.

Sloane raised her other hand to slide up Jaden's forearm in a soothing stroke. "Do you know why you have the dream? Is it the same dream every time?"

"Yes." Jaden was calming down now that she had said it and she just wanted to put it behind her. "It's really not too bad." It was sinking in that Sloane had witnessed her break down.

Sloane felt her start to pull away. "If you don't get to the bottom of it, it'll just keep coming back, Jaden. Do you want to go through this all season?"

Jaden withdrew her hand and stood up. "I need a drink."

It was clear that Jaden was done with confession. Sloane stood with a sigh. "If I go down the hall to the machine will you let me back in the room?"

"Of course." Jaden knew she was being an ass, but she'd just put all her emotions and feelings out there for Sloane to judge her. What the hell must she think of her now? She couldn't allow any more of her weaknesses to show. She just couldn't.

"Then I'll be back in a minute." Sloane pulled her jeans on and grabbed her wallet from the dresser. When she tapped on the door a few minutes later it opened immediately. She handed a Coke to Jaden.

"Thanks, Sloane." Jaden tried to convey her apologies by her tone but figured it was a futile effort.

"You're welcome." Sloane returned her wallet to the dresser knowing their heart-to-heart was over. She didn't have any right to hear any of it but still, it rankled. She sat down on the opposite bed. She looked at the clock on the nightstand. "I wonder if Gilly got lucky tonight."

Jaden sat on her bed and popped the top on her drink. She knew Sloane was ticked, because she'd clammed up and she felt bad about that. After all, Sloane had done a lot for her. "Sloane, I'm sorry." She wasn't any good at this sort of thing and didn't know what else she could do.

"Don't worry about it," she shrugged. "I hope Gilly gets back by the time we have to leave tomorrow morning. Coach gets ugly if anyone's late."

Jaden sighed and dropped her head. "I'm sorry, Sloane."

"I said don't worry about it," Sloane told her. "It's something you don't want to talk about. I get that, I do."

"Sloane...the dream is real. Something that really happened. To me."

Sloane looked at her in surprise. "You were actually in the dark house?"

"Yeah." Jaden kept her eyes on the floor. She was already shaking. "I promised a...friend I'd...pick her up there."

"Why? Did you think something bad would happen to her?"

"I didn't know for sure but I suspected." Jaden put both hands to her face. They were trembling.

"Was it a drug house?" Sloane asked quietly.

"Yeah," Jaden nodded, still not looking at her. "She called me. She was scared to death. She needed me to come get her out of there." Jaden's voice broke on the last sentence.

Sloane could hear the anguish. "You think you failed her?" she asked cautiously.

"No." Jaden wiped her eyes. "I got her out of there that night."

Sloane tried to connect the dots and figure out the story but failed. "So why do you think you're still having the dream about it?"

Jaden took several long swallows before standing to pace the room. Sloane was captivated by the flat expanse of belly showing beneath the cropped top and the wide shoulders that were now hunched in pain. Her long legs ate up the carpet and she spanned the room in just a few strides.

"There...was someone else." Her voice wavered at the end and she stopped at the windows to stare out into the parking lot through a gap in the heavy curtains. She was breathing heavily.

"Kendall!" Jaden screamed her name when she saw her lover. She was kneeling beside another woman. She scrambled to her feet and rushed, sobbing, into Jaden's arms. "I knew you'd come for me, Jade. I knew you would! We need to get out of here!"

But Jaden stared at the woman on the floor. She wasn't moving. "Kendall, we need to help her."

"No! Jade, we have to get out of here! Hurry!"

But Jaden crossed to the figure on the floor and knelt beside her. She wasn't breathing and her eyes were wide open. She was dead. Death came in the form of a needle sticking out of her arm.

A door opened on the other side of the room then and a man emerged, shouting at them. Jaden reeled back and fell on her ass in fright. She scrambled up in panic and screamed at Kendall to run but Kendall was already gone.

Jaden made it out of the room but he caught her at the front door. His hand was bruising when he tried to drag her back into the house. Then he let go as a rotting plank gave way under his weight and he fell through the porch flooring.

Jaden ran for the car and didn't look back.

She came back to the present with a start. The Coke can was crushed in her fist and the brown liquid dribble down her arm. Sloane was beside her.

"Give me that," she said quietly, taking the can from her nerveless fingers. She noticed blood mixing with the soda and took Jaden by the elbow. "Let's go into the bathroom and clean up."

When she'd washed Jaden's hand and arm, she found a small slice along the side of her left ring finger. "It's not too bad," she said. "Hold this tissue against it until it stops bleeding." Jaden silently did as requested and Sloane found a bandage in her kit and bound up the wound.

Jaden didn't speak again until she was once again sitting on her bed. "Thanks. Again."

Sloane shrugged it off. She was watching Jaden's breasts as they strained against the tank top. She could see the nipples through the thin fabric and unconsciously licked her lips. "Are you okay?"

"Yeah."

"Do you want to tell me the rest of it?"

"I don't know...if I can." Her breath was already coming faster. The prospect of actually putting it into words terrified her.

Sloane rose and kicked out of her jeans and sat on the edge of Jaden's bed. "Lie down." When she did, Sloane snapped off the light. She sat back against the headboard and reached for Jaden's hand in the dark. "Just tell me whatever you can."

Jaden's fingers tightened in her hand. "There was another woman there. With Kendall." She was unaware it was the first time she'd said that name. She stopped and Sloane could hear her struggling. "She was...I wanted to help her but Kendall was screaming at me to leave." Jaden moved restlessly on the bed, unable to be still.

"Did you leave with her?" Sloane's voice was soft and non-judgmental.

"No." Jaden tossed her head from side to side. "I went to check on her. She was on the floor. She...wasn't...I couldn't get her to..." Jaden jerked upright with panic in her voice. "She was dead!" Anguish did not adequately describe the way she sounded.

"Jesus!" Sloane whispered.

Jaden pulled her hand away and tore at her own hair. "A needle. She OD'd." She was talking fast now, unable to get the words out quickly enough. "A guy came at me and I ran. Kendall was gone. I almost made it out but he caught me at the door." She unconsciously gripped her arm in the same spot he had. "I got away and I ran for the car. We got out of there as fast as we could."

Sloane ran a hand soothingly along her spine. "He would have killed you."

Jaden sat hunched over her knees, her whole body trembling. "I thought so...at the time." It was almost a whisper.

"You would have brought the police," Sloane said. "He couldn't let that happen."

"No," Jaden shook her head in the dark, "he couldn't."

"What happened?"

Jaden wiped her face. "I called the police and reported it but I never heard back from them. Another dead druggie was all it was to them."

"But you got Kendall out of it."

"Yeah, I got her out of it." Jaden sniffed and wiped her eyes again. "I took her home and then I left. Forever. I never saw her again."

Sloane thought about what that had cost Jaden. She'd wanted to do the right thing, but couldn't. And her rich bitch girlfriend left her behind when she tried. She put a hand on her shoulder softly. "Maybe you should try and get some sleep."

Jaden let go of her knees and stretched out on the bed. "I don't think I can."

"Just give it a try." Sloane still sat with her back against the headboard and when Jaden moved restlessly against the sheets she eased a hand into her hair and let her fingers glide over her scalp. "I'll be right here. Just relax."

Jaden stilled at her touch, her breathing slowly turned into a deep and even pattern, and she finally slept.

When Gillian returned to their room early the next morning she found Jaden spooned against Sloane's back, her arm across her waist, holding her. She grinned. She wanted to laugh out loud and wake them but they looked so cute together she let them sleep.

Jaden stirred at the sound of the shower and nestled her head against the back of Sloane's neck. It felt good and she tightened her arm around her, pulling her closer, before sinking back into sleep.

Sloane woke to a very pleasant sensation between her legs. Jaden had rolled almost on top of her and her leg was tight between Sloane's. Her hand was against her breast and she could feel her nipple harden immediately. *Oh God*. Her pelvis rolled against Jaden's thigh as if it had a mind of its own. The sound of the hair dryer finally penetrated her brain and she jerked fully awake. *Gilly's back!* She tumbled out of bed and Jaden woke up.

"Gillly's back," Sloane told her breathlessly.

Jaden sat up and yawned. It took a minute for Sloane's agitation to register. "Oh. Were we sleeping together?" She examined a faint memory.

"Yes."

Jaden thought about that a second. "Thank you."

Gillian chose that moment to enter the room. She tried but failed to hide her smile. "Good morning, ladies. Sleep well?"

Sloane scowled at her. "Don't start, Gillian."

"Whoa, my full name. This must be serious." Gillian grinned and continued on to the dresser. She pulled on shorts and a shirt and proceeded to re-pack her traveling bag.

Sloane opened a drawer, took out bra and underwear, and headed for the bathroom without a word.

Gillian looked at Jaden. "She seems..."

"Yeah," Jaden nodded, "she does." She looked at Gillian. "It's not what you think and she needs you to know that."

"Hey, I don't care," Gillian told her. "You guys can do whatever you want."

"I mean it, Gilly. Nothing happened. Don't tease her about it. Okay?"

Gillian shrugged. "Sure." Then she grinned. "Can I tease you about it?"

Jaden laughed. "Sure, as long as I get to inquire as to your whereabouts last night."

"Ah, I see." Gillian laughed. "We might need to exchange stories one day."

"Yours will be infinitely more exciting than mine, I assure you."

It was still early when the three of them entered the dining room and they had their choice of seating. Sloane remained quiet even though Gillian refrained from teasing.

They were drinking coffee when Coach Winslow entered the restaurant alone. He looks like hell, Jaden thought. He hadn't shaved and there were dark circles under his eyes as if he hadn't slept at all. His face was grayish and slack. He moved slowly and she saw his hands shake when he picked up his menu. He hadn't noticed them yet.

"It looks like he really tied one on last night," Gillian quietly remarked. "He's in bad shape."

"I didn't know he was a drinker," Sloane remarked.

"Well, now you do," Jaden said. "I hope he had a good time last night."

"Maybe he got lucky too," Gillian laughed until she caught sight of Sloane's expression. "Well, whatever he did, he's paying for it now."

By the time they finished their breakfast, Coach Tate had joined Coach Winslow. She nodded to them as they filed past. "The bus will be here at ten o'clock. Have your bags outside by then so we can load up and get going."

"We're on it, Coach," Gillian grinned down at her.

She harrumphed and turned to Jaden. "What did you do to your hand?"

"Oh." Jaden held out her hand in surprise. She had forgotten the cut altogether. "It's just a cut, nothing serious."

"Well, make sure you take care of it."

"Will do, Coach."

They boarded the bus and by unspoken agreement made their way to the seat that stretched across the back of the bus. They could see everyone and everything from there as the others arrived. "How did you cut your finger?" Gillian asked as they sat.

"On a coke can," Jaden said nonchalantly.

Gillian looked at Sloane but she was busy checking her camera bag. When she turned back, Jaden was yawning and stretching. She grinned. "Want to tell me about last night?" she asked in an undertone.

"Sure."

"Really?" Gillian asked in shock.

"Really," she answered. "I was thirsty and Sloane bought me a coke from the machine down the hall."

"Yeah, yeah. Then what?"

"When I was done with it," Jaden grinned at her and leaned closer. "I crushed the can and cut my finger."

Gillian gave her a disgusted sound and turned to Sloane. "She's no fun," she complained.

"Oh, really?" Sloane looked past her to Jaden, who smiled back at her. "I think she's a lot of fun."

Jaden laughed at that. "Come on, Sloane," Gillian wheedled. "Talk to me."

"Sure, Gilly. What would you like to talk about?" Sloane had one of her cameras out and she was fiddling with the settings. She looked up and hit the flash right into Gillian's eyes.

"Ahhh! Damn it, Sloane!"

Sloane laughed and got up. "Sorry." She threaded her way back through the bus, stopping to talk to and greet the rest of the team as they settled into seats. She snapped photos as she went and hoped she would get something good enough to put on the web site. She'd updated the site last night with the results of the game with L.A. but she liked to change the photos often to keep the site fresh and current. She swung down the steps and snapped several photos of Coach Winslow loading their bags into the luggage compartment of the bus. She fleetingly wondered if he was feeling any better. She hoped so. She turned then and caught Coach Tate coming out of the hotel. She was wearing sunglasses and her perpetual frown. Sloane smiled. She knew behind the scowl lay a good heart and she liked her.

Chapter 8

Portland was winning by three runs and Jaden secretly hoped she didn't have to play. Her arm, while fine with ordinary tasks, would not hold up to another pitching session. And the *smoke* would definitely not be available. Beside her Gillian was hoping the same thing.

"Come on, Erin, get this batter!" she yelled. She nudged Jaden's knee with her own. "Can you go today?"

"If I have to."

"Let's hope you don't, then." Gillian raised her voice again to yell encouragement to her teammates on the field. "Do you have something going with Sloane?" She kept her voice low even though they were sitting at the opposite end of the bench from the others.

"Why do you ask?" Jaden kept her eyes on the field as Erin threw a strike to even the count.

"Maybe because last night you were both in the same bed," Gillian grinned, "and you were holding her."

"No, I didn't mean that." She turned to look at her. "I meant why do you care? Do you have an interest in her?"

"Only as a friend," Gillian said quickly. "I'd like to see her with someone again."

"Again?"

"Well, it's not like she's been a nun," she snorted. "She's had girlfriends before."

"Serious ones?"

"I think she'd better be the one to tell you that kind of stuff."

"Hmmm, something went wrong then," she murmured.

They both stood up and clapped then as Erin ended the inning with a strike out and the team came to the bench. They lost the game but Coach Tate opted to take their chances with Erin to the end. They filed across the field shaking hands with the Portland team and returned to the dugout to pick up their gear and head to the clubhouse and the visitor's locker room.

"So, you never answered my question," Gillian remarked as they relaxed in the locker room. They'd both filled plates from the spread and they were eating while waiting for everyone else.

"What question was that?"

"About Sloane," Gillian said in an exasperated tone.

Sloane chose that moment to snap their photo and Gillian was the one who scowled at her this time. "What about Sloane?" she asked with a dangerous glint in her eye.

Jaden bent her head over her plate to hide her grin and left Gillian to fend for herself.

"Hawke." Coach Tate and Coach Winslow were both approaching trailed by two unfamiliar men in bad suits.

"Yeah, Coach?"

"We need to speak to you, alone please." Coach Tate looked nervous and uncomfortable as the two strangers pushed forward. Sloane moved away but looked back at her with a bad feeling.

"Ms Hawke, I'm Detective Miller and this is Detective Voss from the Portland Police Department." When Jaden kept silent, he went on. "We'd like to search your equipment bag and your luggage."

Jaden kept her face blank but her mind worked furiously to put the pieces together. Something bad had happened. She didn't know what but it had to be very bad to have the police come for her. "What's this all about?" she finally asked.

"There's been a...murder." Detective Miller said it quietly but his eyes never left her face. "In Los Angeles."

"What's that got to do with...?" Her breath caught in her throat as it hit her. "Kendall?" she asked in a strangled whisper.

"Yes, Ma'am." While that conversation was taking place, Detective Voss had started a search of her locker.

She was stunned. "Kendall's dead?" Murdered, she silently amended. It must be a joke. It just couldn't be true. She put her head in her hands. She would have believed dead from booze or drugs but not murder! When she felt a hand on her shoulder, she looked up into Coach Tate's compassionate eyes.

Detective Voss turned to her. "Is this your cell phone, Ms Hawke?" He was holding up a black cell phone with a flip open cover.

Jaden looked up in surprise. "No. Did you find that in my bag?"

"If it's not yours, then whose is it?"

"I don't know but it's not mine," she insisted. "Mine is red and it's in my suitcase."

He put the phone into a plastic bag and sealed it. "Ms Hawke, we're going to need you to accompany us to the police station."

"What!" she exclaimed. "You're kidding!"

"Please, Ms Hawke." Detective Miller held out his hand. "We'll get this straightened out down at the station. We just need to ask you a few questions."

"I'll send someone down to get you," Georgia Tate said in a vote of confidence. "Don't worry. We'll see you later."

Jaden looked from her to Coach Winslow. He turned away without meeting her eyes. Detective Miller took her arm while Detective Voss gathered everything except her uniform. The room was silent as they led her out. At the last moment, Sloane stepped in front and leaned in to whisper in her ear. "Don't worry. We all know you didn't do it. Hang in there, Babe."

"Please. Miss." Detective Miller put a hand out to touch Sloane's shoulder.

Sloane let her lips brush across Jaden's cheek as she moved away. "It'll be okay."

Jaden wasn't in handcuffs, but she felt as if she were. They put her into the back of their sedan with Detective Voss sitting next to her. She thought about whom to call with her one phone call. She didn't exactly have many friends, and those she did have, just watched her being accused of murder.

"What happened?" Jaden asked the man sitting beside her. He stared straight ahead and didn't answer. "Why are you arresting me?"

"You're not under arrest at this time," he answered without looking at her.

"Well, you could have fooled me," she retorted. "How did Kendall die?" She squeezed out the last word but both men remained silent once again. Her world had been rocked and she tried to regain her equilibrium. It was proving impossible. She was confused, off balance and frightened like never before. She was going to jail! They must think she had something to do with killing Kendall. How could they think that? "I didn't do it," she said. It seemed important for her to say it out loud. "Do I need a lawyer?"

By the time she was led into the police station, Jaden was so nervous she was afraid she would throw up. Once inside the station they put her in a small room with a table and two chairs and left her alone. She slumped into one of the molded plastic chairs that were chipped and scarred. Her mind was locked on the fact that Kendall Paxton was dead. How could that be? Sure, she was wild and out of control, but dead? Her hands were shaking. Images rolled across her mind's eye. She had been smiling and beautiful, sweet and sincere, fun and laughing. She'd been all of those things plus incredibly sexy. Those were the things she remembered during the good times, the times they shared while in Japan. She had also been manipulative, self-involved, condescending, and a total bitch. Every time Jaden had tried to walk away, she would show the side of her she knew Jaden loved to bring her back. It seemed unbelievable that she'd just talked about that last night with Sloane. It was all too much and Jaden put her head down on her arms.

An hour later the door opened and Detective Miller entered. He carried a file folder which he laid on the table across from her. Jaden watched him silently, resisting the urge to demand information. He flipped the file open and lifted a few pages as if checking facts about her. It was exactly what he was doing. He finally cleared his throat and looked at her. "Can I get you anything, Ms Hawke? Coffee? A Coke?"

"No thanks," she answered. "You can tell me what's going on though."

"Last night, Los Angeles police found the body of Kendall Paxton. She'd been murdered."

"How? What happened?"

"They have reason to believe you were in contact with her yesterday," he said slowly.

"That's not true!" Jaden fought not to jump up from the table. "I didn't talk to her yesterday." She leaned across the table. "I was with the team all day and night. Ask any of them."

"You were with the team until after the game. Where did you go after that?"

"I was at a bar," she sighed. "Half the team saw me there."

"And after that?"

"I went back to the hotel."

"What time was that?"

"I don't know." Jaden shook her head.

"Can anyone verify your story?"

"I went back to the hotel alone."

"Then you could have left the bar and gone to meet Ms Paxton." He lowered his voice. "Is that what you did? I'm told you know L.A. pretty well."

"No!" she shouted. "I haven't talked to Kendall in over six months," she added. "I didn't talk to her yesterday."

"Would you object to giving us a set of finger prints, Ms Hawke?"

"Why?"

"So we can clear you if you're innocent. That's what you want, right?" As Jaden thought about that, he continued. "Or you can let us send you back to L.A. and they'll take your prints there."

The threat wasn't lost on her. She didn't know what to do. She was innocent, so why not give them whatever they wanted? The door opened and Detective Voss motioned to Detective Miller. They closed the door and Jaden was left alone again. How could this be happening? What was going on? *Oh God, Kendall, what did you do to get yourself killed?* She was pacing when Detective Miller finally returned.

"It seems your lawyer is here," he stated flatly. "He's downstairs."

Jaden stared at him in confusion. "My lawyer?"

"Yes. Come with me, please."

She followed him down the stairs but wondered if at any minute they would cuff her and put her in a cell. When they got to the bottom, a man in a charcoal suit stepped forward. He switched his battered briefcase to his left hand and held out his right to her.

"Ms Hawke, I'm David King, your attorney."

"You're free to go but keep yourself available," Detective Miller said with an edge to his voice.

"Ms Hawke will be returning to her home in Dallas. You can contact her there."

"It's Los Angeles that cares, not me."

"Then you'll be able to tell them when asked." He took her arm and turned her toward the door.

"What about my stuff?" Jaden asked. "Do I get it back?"

"They're keeping the phone they found in your bag and the one in your luggage. You can have everything else back. We'll stop on the way out and get it. You'll have to sign for it so you should check to make sure everything is there."

"How'd you get to be my lawyer?"

"I got a call from a friend of mine in Dallas."

"Must be a good friend."

"We went to law school together. Now he'll owe me a favor." He laughed. "That's the real commodity in this world."

Jaden's head was swirling with everything that had happened. She had so many questions, which needed answers and so much more that she needed to absorb and understand. She needed time to think. When she'd signed for her stuff, he took her suitcase and she followed with her equipment bag. "What do I do now?" she asked as they pushed through the door to the street.

"I think she has the answer to that," he said and motioned toward Sloane who was waiting at the bottom of the steps. He went down the stairs and set the suitcase next to Sloane, said a few words to her, and then walked off. Jaden still stood at the top of the steps.

Sloane looked up at her. "Are you planning on staying here tonight? Or would you rather stay with me?"

"You," Jaden said through the catch in her voice. "I choose you."

Sloane smiled and when Jaden reached the bottom of the steps, she hugged her. "It's good to see you out of there," she whispered.

"It's good to be out," she whispered back as they parted. "Who do I thank for this lawyer guy?"

"A friend of mine," she answered. "I know a guy in Dallas."

"Thank you."

"We couldn't let you hang out to dry here in Portland, could we?"

Jaden smiled back into twinkling blue eyes. "I can't thank you enough, Sloane. I don't know what would have happened to me if he hadn't gotten me out."

"They would probably have put you in a cell for the night and, depending on what L.A. has, put you on a plane back there tomorrow," David King said as he re-joined them. He handed Sloane an envelope and turned to Jaden. "They're trying to match your fingerprints on the phone they found."

"Why? I wasn't anywhere near her."

"The cell phone they found in your bag had the number of Kendall's phone in its memory as being called the night she died."

"But that's not my phone!"

"They found a duplicate phone near Ms Paxton's body and it had the number of your phone in its calls received log." He held up a hand as she started to protest once again. "On the surface it looks like you called her and arranged to meet."

"If that's the case then why am I standing out here?"

"Those are the only things they'd tell me but I think something is throwing their theory off. Something doesn't fit and they're waiting for the rest of the evidence to come in. That's my best guess." He patted her on the arm. "Be careful and it wouldn't hurt to try and work out a time line for when you had an alibi." He turned to go once again. "Tell Keith I said he owes me one." He touched Sloane on the arm as he left.

"Thank you," Jaden called after him. When he was out of sight, she turned back to Sloane. "Now what?"

She looked up the street. "I called a cab. It should be here soon."

"And then? Are we heading back to Dallas?"

"Not tonight," she said absently as she kept her eyes on the street. She glanced back at her. "We're stuck here for tonight. Ah, here it comes."

The cab took them to the Hilton Hotel and Sloane helped carry her bags in. They by passed the check in desk and went straight up to the eighth floor where Sloane swiped a key card and opened the door. "We were lucky to get a room tonight," she said as she closed and locked the door behind them.

That explains the single queen bed, Jaden thought. She set her bag down against the wall and stood uncertainly. "How can I ever thank you for this, Sloane?"

"No thanks necessary, Jaden. I'm just glad they let you go." She was folding the cover down the bed as she talked. "Why don't you take a shower? It's late and I know you're tired."

"I don't know if I can sleep," she answered. "My head is jumping with all kinds of shit."

"I can imagine." She sat on the side of the bed and kicked off her shoes. "Maybe you can at least rest."

"I'll try." Jaden took her kit and went into the bathroom. When the hot water hit her body, she realized how exhausted she really was. The past twenty-four hours had taken a toll on her. She let the water pound her for long minutes before reaching for the soap. When she emerged, Sloane was already in bed and only a dim light from the bedside lamp was on. Jaden slid in beside her and Sloane opened her eyes.

"Feel better?"

"Yeah."

"Good. Try and get some sleep." She reached out and snapped off the light.

Jaden tried to relax but she was still wired and restless. She finally rolled onto her side away from Sloane and hoped she wouldn't keep her awake. How could Kendall be dead? Who would kill her? How was it possible? And why make it look like Jaden had called her? Was someone trying to frame her for murder? It didn't make any sense. Who hated her that much? She jerked as a hand slid down her side under the covers and draped over her stomach.

"You need to get some rest," Sloane whispered in her ear.

Jaden held in a breath and tensed as her hand moved in small soothing circles against her skin. It left a hot trail in its wake. Her abs contracted as Sloane's fingers brushed the top of her boxer shorts. "I...uh...don't think that's going to help me sleep, Sloane." She clutched the pillow beneath her head.

"But you're not thinking about jail, are you?"

Jaden smiled and laid a hand over Sloane's, stopping its movement. "No, I'm definitely not thinking about that." She shifted onto her back. "Didn't anyone ever teach you it's not nice to tease?"

"Who says I'm teasing?" Sloane slid a hand back across her stomach.

Jaden stopped her hand again. "Sloane..."

Sloane sighed. She'd made a mistake. "I'm sorry. I...we both need to get some sleep." She quickly turned away but Jaden held onto her hand.

"I think if you get to touch me then I should get to touch you back."

"What?"

Jaden rolled onto her side and propped her head up on her hand. "Fair is fair." She slid her hand under Sloane's tee shirt and stroked over her belly. "You're so soft," she whispered and leaned down to kiss her.

Their lips met in a light brush, each hesitant at the first touch, but then pressing together more firmly. Jaden ran her tongue over her bottom lip before taking it into her mouth slowly, sucking gently. Sloane pushed her tongue between her lips and they both fell into the kiss, tongues dueling and dancing together. Jaden rolled on top of her and ran a hand up Sloane's chest to cup her breast. Her thigh pressed between Sloane's legs and she pushed against her, while her thumb and forefinger captured a nipple. It puckered instantly at her touch and she squeezed and tugged at it while she did the same to her tongue.

Sloane pulled her mouth free to gulp air. "Jesus!"

Jaden dropped her head to her throat and kissed her softly but the hand at her breast stilled and her thigh became less rigid. She kissed her way up Sloane's neck to her jaw and then back to her mouth. Sloane put a hand into the hair on the back of her head and held her tightly. The kiss deepened and Jaden was beginning to lose herself again. She hadn't known a kiss could be like this. It was soft, intense, and threatening to consume her. She never wanted it to stop.

Sloane had taken notice of the change of pace and released the hold she had on her hair.

"Baby, you okay?"

Jaden held herself over her and looked into eyes dark with passion. She took in a shaky breath. "I'm fine. I just got a little carried away. I'm not usually like this." She meant, she didn't normally attack a woman with the fervent disregard of an adolescent boy.

"Like what? A great kisser? Hands that know exactly what I want?" She reached up to stroke Jaden's cheek. "That's really too bad, because I thought this might actually be the start of something very...exciting."

"Oh, yeah?" Jaden tried to breathe around the tightness in her throat.

"Yeah," she answered. "But if you're not up to the job then let me know now so I can move on." She moved her pelvis against Jaden's leg, letting her feel the heat and moisture between her own.

Jaden groaned in response. "Damn, Sloane."

"Yeah," she breathed. "You like that?" She moved against her again and touched her cheek with soft fingers. Jaden turned her head and kissed her fingertips.

"Yes," she gulped. "I like it." She leaned in to kiss her once again. "I like it a lot."

"What are you going to do about it then?" It was all Sloane could do to keep from ripping Jaden's clothes off.

"Take your shirt off. I want to touch you." Her voice was rough with need. She shifted to settle between Sloane's legs and helped her pull the shirt over her head. She had full breasts as Jaden knew and she wanted nothing more than to have her mouth on them.

"Take yours off too," Sloane demanded. "I want to feel you against me."

She sat back to pull her own shirt off and tossed it on the floor. When she looked back, Sloane was sliding her underwear down her legs.

"Come on, baby," Sloane urged. "I need to feel you— all of you."

Jaden quickly got out of her boxers and tossed them next to her shirt. She lost her breath when she eased back on top of Sloane. If she died right then, she'd be happy. She lay a moment just feeling the skin under her, hearing the breath of her lover, inhaling the intoxicating scent that was Sloane. She was wet and aroused to the point of embarrassment, throbbing with need.

"That feels so good," Sloane murmured in her ear as she began a slow, sensuous grind under her. She rubbed her hands down Jaden's sides, caressing the sides of her breasts as they pushed against her own. Their bodies slid together. Sloane ran a hand over Jaden's back and down to her ass, gripping and squeezing, pulling her even closer. All the while, she was kissing and nuzzling where Jaden's shoulder joined her neck and making incoherent noises that were driving her mad with desire.

"Oh God," Jaden panted. "Sloane...wait. I'm...so close I'll go off if you even touch me. Give me a minute."

"I can't wait, baby." Sloane pushed a hand between them and cupped Jaden's sex, sliding through her wetness. "You feel so good, Jaden. So wet." She circled her clit and felt her jerk in response. "Oh yeah, that's it, baby. Feel me." Sloane was panting as hard as Jaden now and worked to keep control. She had an arm over Jaden's back and held her tight against her, wanting to fuse herself with her and become one. Jaden began to move against her hand as she gave up control completely. Sloane slid farther down and pushed into her. She was so wet she was able to enter her easily and it made her head spin. Sloane wasn't sure she could ever let her go. "Do you want to come now?"

"Yes." Jaden's eyes were squeezed shut as she concentrated on every feeling coursing through her body because of this woman. "Please," she panted.

Sloane went back to her clit, slid over it softly, before placing a finger on both sides and began to stroke and squeeze. Jaden's body moved with her and within seconds, she stiffened and caught her breath, straining into a shattering climax. Sloane kept her hand tight against her as she jerked and throbbed in the aftermath. Jaden finally slumped, boneless, against Sloane's chest, breathing hard, her heart pumping furiously. Sloane kissed her cheek and held her tightly. "Oh, baby, that was so great," she breathed into Jaden's ear. "So good." She stroked Jaden's back, and continued kissing her, while she recovered.

Jaden felt the lassitude of after sex steal over her as she lay in Sloane's arms. It would be so easy to fall asleep there, safe and secure. Nothing bad could ever happen to her while she was here like this. She felt Sloane's hand slip from between her legs and she took a deep breath and rolled off her. "Jesus, Sloane," she muttered. "That was unbelievable."

"You like?" Sloane asked softly in return as Jaden slid her hand up to cup her breast.

"Oh, yes." Jaden leaned over her and took a breast in her mouth, the nipple running stiffly over her tongue. Sloane arched her back, urging her to take even more. All thoughts of sleep were gone now as Jaden kissed Sloane deeply while settling herself between her legs. Supporting her weight on one hand, she ran the other over her breast again. "You are so gorgeous." She rolled the erect nipple between her fingers and tugged as her hips began a slow rhythm between Sloane's legs.

Sloane's breath became harsh and ragged immediately. She touched Jaden's hand. "Harder, baby," she gulped. "I like it hard. Make me yours."

Jaden felt a surge of desire all over again. She tugged on her nipple harder, squeezing and releasing, in time with the thrust of her hips.

"That's good, so good," Sloane moaned. Jaden released her breast and she whimpered. "Oh God, don't stop."

"Easy, honey, just a minute." Jaden adjusted her position and put a hand between her legs, stroking the inside of her thigh. She could smell her need and inhaled deeply. "Bend your knees, honey." Sloane did so immediately and let one leg flop to the side to open herself completely to her. "Oh yeah," Jaden moaned. "Like that. That's it. That's my girl." She opened her and rubbed against her entrance softly, just wanting to feel the velvety folds that were slick with need and waiting for her. She avoided touching her clit, wanting this to last.

Sloane had other ideas. "Fuck me, Jaden," she moaned. "Come on, baby, I need you to fuck me!"

Jaden entered her with two fingers and drove deep, twisting and turning as she withdrew almost completely, then driving in again deeper and harder. Sloane grunted with the force of it but pushed back, wanting more. With each drive, Jaden's thumb bumped her clit and in less than a minute, she could tell Sloane was rapidly climbing to a climax. She withdrew completely and added a third finger and Sloane's breath caught in her throat. Jaden knew she wanted it, knew it was good for her, and pushed slowly but steadily until she was buried deep inside. Sloane was panting. Jaden stayed still a moment, just enjoying the feeling of being so connected to her. She moved her wrist and let her fingers brush against her and with a hand low on her belly she could feel her own hand move inside her. Sloane cried out softly and moved against her. "You okay, honey?"

"God, yes!" Sloane gasped. "So full, Jaden...Your hands..." She panted another breath, but couldn't continue speaking. She couldn't think any more. All her thoughts were centered between her legs and on the woman who was in control of her.

Jaden leaned up to take a nipple between her lips, sucking hard, making Sloane whimper and throw her head back. She hadn't thought she had room for any other pleasure, but this drove her to the edge. Jaden felt Sloane's body adjust to the girth of her fingers and began to move her hand again. "You're doing great, honey," she crooned to her as she slowly pumped in and out. Sloane's hips matched her rhythm, climbing once again. "You're so close, honey. I can feel it," Jaden told her a short time later. "Do you want to come now?"

"Yes. God, yes! Please. Make me come for you," she begged.

Jaden drove deep, held her there, and put her mouth on her clit, sucking hard. Sloane exploded, crying out loudly as wave after wave rolled over her. Jaden released her clit, but her fingers were trapped inside, locked by the fierceness of her orgasm. She laid her head on Sloane's chest and could hear Sloane's heart pounding beneath her ear. Many minutes later Sloane's grip on her hair relaxed and her hand fell limply to the bed. Jaden turned her face to place a kiss against her stomach. She slowly pulled her fingers out causing Sloane to jerk upright. She quickly took her into her arms and laid her back down on the bed, pulling her against her. "You're wonderful," she whispered against her cheek. "So beautiful and so good."

"Jaden..." Sloane couldn't believe what had just happened to her. Jaden had affected her in ways no other woman ever had. While she was recovering from an absolutely life shattering orgasm, Jaden was holding her gently, rocking her, making her feel wanted, and whispering endearments in her ear. She had never felt so content. She put a limp arm over Jaden's stomach and put her cheek against her shoulder. "Baby."

"Yes, honey?" Jaden asked softly. "What can I do for you?"

There it was—the crowning touch. This gorgeous, strong, independent woman, who had already given her the moon and the stars, wanted to know what else she could do for her.

"Nothing," Sloane sighed and fell asleep.

Chapter 9

Jaden woke to the sound of the hair dryer in the bathroom and she was briefly disoriented. It all came blooding back an instant later. Sloane. The beautiful, sexy, mesmerizing woman who she made love with last night. Her heart jumped in her chest followed by a rush between her legs.

Sloane appeared in the doorway then, her eyes searching out Jaden. The sheet was down around her waist and it occurred to Sloane that she hadn't been able to pay proper attention to Jaden's breasts the night before. She looked up into her eyes finally and what she saw there made her knees weak. She cleared her throat and moved into the room.

"You'd better quit looking at me like that," she said while holding Jaden's eyes with her own. "Otherwise we might not make it out of the room."

Jaden threw off the sheet and swung her legs over the side of the bed. "And that would be a bad thing because..." She stood up and watched Sloane's eyes darken with instant desire. That answered the morning after question of whether there was anything left to pursue.

Sloane struggled to lift her eyes to Jaden's face. "We have a flight to catch."

As they settled into seats on the plane to Dallas, everything came rushing back. Jaden felt the heavy blanket of despondency settle around her before they even took off. She was the prime suspect in Kendall's murder. She was undoubtedly out of a job. She was sure they had already called to inform her of that but the police had confiscated her cell phone. Her life seemed to be out of control and right now, it felt as if she'd been heading for this for a long time. She looked out the window next to her seat, but in her mind's eye she saw Kendall as she'd been the day they'd first met. She was without make-up, wearing a USA tee shirt and shorts. She was sitting in the first row of the stadium above the US team's dugout and cheering them on. She smiled at Jaden and winked, just as she started down into the dugout. Jaden had missed a step and she almost fell on her ass. Every inning after that Jaden made it a point to look her way when they were coming off the field. After the USA team had won, Kendall was waiting for Jaden at the gate and she passed her card to her. Her cell phone number was on the back. Jaden didn't know who she was then, but hadn't wasted any time calling her. They spent as much time together as they could manage after that. If she had remained the same sweet, fun loving, woman she'd been during that time, Jaden thought they might very well still be together. She sighed. If. A big word. Too big to contemplate.

Sloane leaned close and touched her hand where she was gripping the armrest. "We'll figure this out. Don't worry."

"Yeah."

Sloane extracted a small notebook from her carry-on bag along with a pen. "Let's get started."

"On what?"

"On what happened the night Kendall was...killed."

"Well." Jaden thought back to that night. "We won the game, left the park, and took the bus back to the hotel."

"That was about nine o'clock." Sloane wrote in her book.

"Yeah," Jaden nodded. "Then you and Gilly went out to Lucille's. Right?"

"Yes. Gilly and I got there about ten o'clock since it's close to the hotel."

"I was back at the hotel putting ice on my arm," She continued, "so, no alibi for that time frame."

"Okay. When do you think you got to the bar?"

"Well, I usually ice my arm for about an hour when I'm on the road. Twenty minutes on, twenty minutes off and another twenty on again."

"Did you go anywhere else first? Before you got to Lucille's, I mean."

"No. I dumped the ice in the sink and changed my shirt and went straight to the bar."

"Okay. That puts you at Lucille's between eleven-thirty and midnight."

Jaden nodded. "Sounds about right." She looked at Sloane. "I saw you dancing when I went to the bar."

"I know. I saw you too," Sloane said absently as she studied what she'd written.

"You looked like you were having fun."

Sloane gave her a sideways look. "Gilly was sitting at the bar with you not long after you got there, right?"

"Yes. She was telling me how much she loved California women."

Sloane gave her another look. "How long after that did you leave?"

"I left when you started dancing with that bleached blonde again."

Sloane didn't bother looking at her this time. She wrote an approximate time in her book. She sighed and thought back. She'd seen Jaden leave. She'd been hoping she could have gotten her to dance with her and was disappointed when she'd left so soon. "When did you get back to the room?"

"I went straight there from the bar," Jaden vowed. "When did you get back?"

"I left the bar about two o'clock, I think." She wrote it down. "You were already there and asleep when I came in."

"Okay. So what time frame are we looking at for my lack of an alibi?"

"You were alone for just a little over an hour before showing up at the bar and then again for an hour and a half to two hours after leaving the bar."

Jaden blew out a breath. "So what does that tell us? We don't know when she was killed or even where she was killed."

"No, but we know when it had to have happened if they're trying to pin it on you. That's something and you may have to give this time line to the police." Sloane put a hand on her thigh. "It's something that might help you."

Jaden nodded but looked unconvinced. "Who is your lawyer friend? I'm going to need to meet him."

"Keith Braden. He's a nice guy. You'll like him."

"I'll have his children if he gets me out of this fucking mess," she swore.

"No, you won't," Sloane said with some heat. She laid a hand back on her thigh and squeezed. "We'll have a major disagreement if that happens."

Jaden was pleased but tried not to show it. "Don't worry. I don't think any self-respecting man would want me anyway."

Sloane looked her up and down, lingering on the vee between her legs. "Oh, I don't know," she murmured. She raked her eyes back up to her face and seemed to remember where they were. "You should try and get some sleep."

"Yeah," Jaden sighed. "I'm worn out." She smiled as she closed her eyes.

After they landed and collected their luggage, Sloane turned on her cell phone and called Gillian. Thirty minutes later, she pulled to the curb in front of them and popped the trunk open.

"Ladies, it's good to see you again!" She gave both of them a big hug. "Let's get your bags into the trunk and get out of here." She steered them through the maze of ramps and parking garages, through the tollbooth, and finally got on the freeway. "You okay?" she asked Jaden.

"I'm fine," she automatically said. "A lawyer got me out of jail yesterday."

"Did they actually arrest you?"

"No, but they were talking about sending me back to L.A. where they probably would have." She sighed. "I've been told to keep myself available."

"I tried calling you."

"The police took her phone," Sloane said from the back seat.

"Are both of your cars still at the stadium?" Gillian asked abruptly. "I was heading for your apartment, Sloane."

"Unless someone stole it mine is still at the field house," Sloane said.

"Mine too," Jaden added.

"Okay." Gillian mentally adjusted her route and they were soon pulling into the parking lot of the stadium. "Listen," she said as they unloaded their luggage, "how about if I buy pizza and beer?"

Jaden hesitated, not wanting to go through the whole story again but Sloane accepted. "That would be great, Gilly. Thanks. My place?"

"Sure. I'll be there as soon as I can." She got back in her car and drove off as the two of them were digging in their bags for their keys."

"Sloane..."

"Follow me, Jaden. Please. We'll have something to eat and tell her what's going on. Everyone will want to know and this way we'll only have to tell the story once. Gilly can tell the rest of them."

Jaden knew she was right and she didn't want to leave Sloane without talking about last night. "Okay," she gave in. "See you there."

She parked her truck in a visitors slot and Sloane was waiting at the door for her. "Do you want to...?" She didn't know if she should finish the invitation to stay the night with her or not.

Jaden looked at her expectantly as she entered Sloane's apartment. "What?" When she got no answer, she turned. Sloane was looking at her and Jaden knew what was on her mind. "Let's talk after Gilly leaves. Okay?"

"Yes." Sloane nodded in relief. She picked up her bags

and went into her bedroom to unpack. "Make yourself at home. I'll just be a minute."

Chapter 10

Jaden was exhausted. Between slices of pizza, they took turns recounting everything that happened after the police had taken her to the station.

"What's going to happen now?" Gillian asked when the story was finished.

"I don't know. What's being said upstairs?" Upstairs meant the coaching staff and the owners group, DSG.

"Coach hasn't said anything yet. She called off practice today so nobody knows a thing." She turned to Jaden on the couch. "Everybody's behind you though, Jaden."

"I think she's asleep." Sloane smiled with affection at Jaden, who was slumped against the arm of the couch with her head propped up on her hand.

Gillian looked back to Sloane. "Is there something going on between you two?"

Sloane debated her answer. She had been friends with Gillian since she first began working for DSG but this thing with Jaden was different from anything she had ever encountered. "I don't know if it's going anywhere," she finally said. She owed Gilly that much.

"So there is something?" Gillian probed gently.

"Yes, something," she admitted. Her eyes strayed back to the couch. "I just don't know what yet."

"But it might be something serious?"

"You're pushing, Gilly," she warned.

"I'm sorry." She sounded contrite. "But if you think it could be, you have to think about what will happen if she's arrested. What will that do to you?" Gillian gave her a hard look. "This is about murder."

"Yes, I know," she nodded, a distant look in her eyes.

Gillian spoke again before she could go down that path. "Think, Sloane. If there's something there it won't hurt to wait."

"She didn't kill Kendall!" Sloane said fiercely.

"I know," Gillian quickly agreed. "But that's not to say they won't arrest her anyway. Is that something you want to go through?"

"Damn it, Gilly!" Sloane was furious with her. "She's not Kerry!" She softened her voice with another glance at Jaden.

"It could be worse." Gillian would not give up. "I remember what a basket case you were back then. I don't want you to go through that again."

"It's not the same thing," she stubbornly maintained. "She isn't abusive."

Gillian thought murder was about as abusive as it could get, but didn't say so. She sighed. "All I'm saying is you should be careful. Even though we both know she didn't do it, this could still hurt you in other ways."

"I'm not the same person I was back then, Gilly."

"I know. You're beautiful and intelligent and you deserve the best woman in your life." Gillian looked at the sleeping figure on the couch. "Just promise me you won't let that happen again."

"I promise."

Gillian knew it was a promise that Sloane couldn't keep. She got up. "I'd better get going. Get some sleep."

Sloane walked her to the door. "I won't let her hurt me, Gilly. But thanks for worrying about me." She kissed her on the cheek. "Goodnight."

After she left, Sloane cleaned up the remains of their dinner while trying not to think about what Gillian had brought up, or rather, whom she had brought up. Kerry Saunders, her former lover. She absently put a hand over her left wrist. Kerry had charmed her way into Sloane's life and Sloane had actually thought she'd found 'the one' for a short time. She had a good job downtown, made great money, and treated Sloane like a princess. She was shorter than Sloane at 5'6", and where Sloane's hair was a light brown that was streaked with natural highlights, Kerry's was just mud brown. While she might not have been the most gorgeous woman Sloane had ever dated, she made Sloane feel like *she* was.

Both of them had brown eyes and Sloane had learned to read those eyes in terms of what would happen to her. She became adept at reading the signs and trying to forestall the inevitable. That was after she had moved in with her. Before they lived together, it was like a living honeymoon. Whatever Sloane wanted and the sex had been great. It all changed when Sloane moved into her apartment. As if that signaled total and irrevocable ownership, Kerry became the monster Sloane soon came to know.

It started out small, a temper lost to something trivial, an argument over nothing, but it continued to escalate until Kerry had slapped her for a perceived slight. She had been shocked, but Kerry had apologized profusely and promised it would never happen again. And it hadn't for at least a week. Then Kerry went for drinks with the boys after work and came home late and drunk. She had practically raped her that night. She still remembered it. It was the first of many sexual assaults under the guise of consensual sex. *"I know you like it rough. How about this? Is this rough enough, bitch?"* She would proceed to use her own violent actions and put the blame on Sloane. It only got worse from there and eventually she broke Sloane's wrist when she held it in a vice-like grip at an unnatural angle against her back as she violated her from behind using one of her collection of toys, venting anger against some unknown source. It was the last straw and it propelled Sloane to the emergency room. Gillian had made her file a complaint with the police even when she didn't want to go that far. And she made Sloane move in with her until she could find another apartment. A month later, they arrested Kerry in a domestic disturbance call at another woman's apartment. During that same period, she had been stalking Sloane and she had reported it to the police at Gillian's urging. It was her additional complaint about Kerry that led them to arrest her.

She sighed now as she stood over a sleeping Jaden. She couldn't imagine this woman becoming violent with her. She was smarter now. At least she thought she was. "Jaden." She shook her shoulder softly. "Time for bed, babe."

Jaden stirred and opened her eyes. "Is..." she cleared her throat. "Is Gilly gone?"

"Yeah. Come to bed."

Jaden got up and stretched, shaking out her hand. "I'm sorry I fell asleep."

"You're exhausted, Jaden," Sloane told her. "It's fine."

"I'll go on home," she said without looking at her. "Call me tomorrow?"

Sloane took her hand. "You can stay here with me tonight. I can't call you tomorrow—you don't have a phone."

"Oh. Yeah." She yawned until her jaw cracked.

"Come on, let's go to bed. We'll talk tomorrow."

Jaden allowed her to lead her into the bedroom. "You have a nice place here, Sloane. I forgot to tell you that the last time I was here." She kicked off her shoes.

"I think you had other things on your mind that day." She remembered suddenly how she and Gillian had rescued her from a bar fight; a fight Jaden had admittedly started over Kendall Paxton. She swallowed hard as Gillian's words came back to haunt her.

Jaden sensed a change in her attitude. "I'd be happy to go on home, Sloane. You don't have to do this."

"No, I want you to stay," Sloane said quickly while wondering how she'd picked up on her hesitancy.

"How about this? I'll promise not to touch you tonight. We'll both just get some sleep. Okay?"

Sloane was both relieved and sorry. She mentally gave herself a shake. "I don't think that's going to work."

Jaden was surprised. "No? Oh. Uh, well, I guess I'll go on home then."

"That's not what I meant. I meant it won't work for you not to touch me." She moved closer and put a hand out to her.

Jaden took her hand and raised it to kiss her knuckles. "You need to tell me what you want, Sloane. Even if it's 'get out', I'll understand. We had a great night last night, but if that's all you want, then that's okay."

"What do *you* want, Jaden?"

Jaden pulled her closer and put her arms around her. "You want me to go first? Okay. I would like to take last night and see where it goes." She kissed her cheek. "But then I'm a romantic." It didn't mean anything Sloane knew. Kerry had spoken all the romantic words too. However, she couldn't keep her body from responding to Jaden. "So?"

Sloane laid her head against Jaden's shoulder. "I enjoyed last night very much. I'd like a chance to try it again too."

"Okay," Jaden's voice held a hint of a smile. "Not exactly a declaration of undying devotion, but I'll take what I can get." She kissed her cheek again.

"I'm sorry, Jaden. I didn't mean it like that."

"Don't worry," she chuckled. "It was one night. We'll see where it goes from here." She released her. "But promise me you'll send nude pictures of you if I go to prison."

Sloane's heart clutched in her chest. "If that happens, I'll send you pictures that'll make you come in your striped pants," she swore.

Jaden laughed and released her. "Maybe you should practice some of those poses right now." She started unbuttoning her own shirt and Sloane helped her eagerly. When the last button gave way, Jaden shrugged it off her shoulders and Sloane immediately put her hands on her breasts. Jaden sucked in a breath when Sloane flicked her tongue over a nipple, making it tighten and swell. She felt the rush flow through her and welcomed it when it landed between her legs. She cupped the back of Sloane's head and urged her on, arching into her mouth.

Sloane spent some time on her breasts, alternating between them both until Jaden finally eased her away. "My turn," she said. "Get undressed."

When they were both naked they kissed, hands moving, searching, touching. They made it to the bed and fought each other for control of their lovemaking.

"You were too fast last night, babe," Sloane said in a rush. "Let me have some fun."

Jaden gave in. "You're the boss."

"Oh, yes," Sloane breathed. "You have a fantastic body, Jaden." She put her lips on her neck and began an agonizingly slow and sensuous trail of kisses down her torso. Jaden was writhing on the bed, aching for her touch, her own hands touching Sloane wherever she could reach.

"Sloane," she groaned in frustration. "You're making me crazy."

Sloane circled Jaden's belly button with her tongue then lifted her head, her hair tickling Jaden's sensitive areas. "Are you wet, babe?"

"Oh God, yes!"

"Maybe I should check." Sloane eased a hand down her belly until her fingers raked through moist pubic hair. Jaden arched off the bed as Sloane pressed a palm against her and she began moving against it immediately. "No so fast, babe." Sloane lifted her hand away and Jaden moaned piteously. Sloane turned and kissed her, tongue probing. Jaden sucked it deeper into her mouth. Sloane was losing control. Everything she did to Jaden only served to excite her too. "Baby, you make me so hot," she whispered as she lay on top of her again. "Tell me what you like."

"I like it when you tease me," Jaden admitted. "I like it when you make me wait." She cupped Sloane's breasts in her hands, flicking the nipples with her thumbs. Sloane moaned. "I like it when you show me how much you like what I'm doing to you too." She tried to capture a breast in her mouth but Sloane pulled away.

"I need to feel you, Jaden," she said a bit breathlessly. "I want to feel you, taste you, and I want to make you come."

"Oh yes. That's good. I need your hands on me. Come on, Sloane, touch me."

Sloane eased down Jaden's body until she was kneeling between her legs. She pushed her knees apart and softly laid a hand on her. She was rewarded when Jaden jerked at the first touch. "Hold off, baby. I want to play a while," she whispered. She caressed the inside of her thigh, edging ever closer to her center. When she couldn't hold herself back any longer, she slid along the length of her softly. She was slick and soft and her clit stood at attention. She stayed away from it, knowing Jaden wouldn't be able to refrain from climaxing if she touched it.

You're so wet." She positioned her hand and pushed two fingers into her but only a short way. "God, you feel so good." She leaned up to place a soft kiss on her lower stomach. "Do you want more, baby?"

"Yes!" Jaden had to concentrate not to force herself down on Sloane's hand.

Sloan pushed into her in one swift motion but then just held it there, not allowing Jaden to start the climb. "Not yet." She slowly withdrew her fingers until she was totally out.

Jaden groaned and whined. "Sloane..."

"I love touching you." She was massaging her folds as she spoke, still avoiding her clit. She bent her head and put her mouth on her, sliding her tongue the length. Jaden instantly pushed against her. She backed off a bit but then pulled the hard clit into her mouth for a quick suck. Jaden lifted off the bed, straining. Sloane thought she was ready to go off without her so she settled her mouth on her and began a steady rhythm, working her up to the top. Jaden's legs began to quiver and she had her fingers buried tightly in Sloane's hair. The climax hit her hard and Sloane wrapped her arms around her thighs and held on.

"Inside me," Jaden panted in a strained whisper.

Sloane raised her head, slid into her quickly, and felt her spasm against her fingers. "Can I move?"

"Yes." Her voice was rough.

Sloane loved how Jaden's muscles captured her fingers and pulled them into her, milking them for her own pleasure.

"Yeah, that's it," she panted again. Her legs were still straining and Sloane could feel her gushing all over her hand. It was incredible. When her legs finally fell limply to the bed and her spasms had stopped Sloane stayed inside her, moving slowly just to keep feeling her.

"Sloane," Jaden moaned softly.

She reluctantly slid completely out of her and climbed up the bed to take Jaden into her arms. "Oh babe, that was great," she whispered. Jaden rested her head against Sloane's shoulder, unable to speak yet. Sloane's heart absolutely swelled with...love? Could it be love so soon? She held Jaden tighter and kissed the top of her head. "So good, Jaden."

After many minutes, Jaden finally stirred. "Jesus!" she mumbled. "You're going to kill me, Sloane."

Sloane grinned, feeling on top of the world. "You said you like it when I make you wait," she reminded her.

"Oh man, remind me not to talk to you when I'm naked."

Sloane laughed softly and rubbed a hand over her

shoulder and upper back just to be touching her. "But that's one of the things I like," she said. "I like to talk during sex. I like to communicate."

"I'm a dead woman then," Jaden moaned. She lifted a hand to Sloane's breast and let the weight of it settle in her palm. "What else do you like?" She rolled the nipple between thumb and forefinger. Sloane took in a quick breath as she squeezed and pulled. "I know you like this hard." She tugged even harder and Sloane gasped. "Do you like everything hard?" She kept the nipple between her fingers and turned her head to let her teeth scrape over the other one. Sloane's quick intake of air told her all she needed to know. Jaden rolled on top of her and kissed her softly. "You do like soft kisses though." She kissed her again while continuing to fondle her breasts and she could tell Sloane was aroused. "Do you like my hands on you?"

"Yes."

"Do you like my hand inside you?" Jaden kept up a steady massage of her breasts as she talked and she'd straddled her, moving just enough to let Sloane feel her continued wetness.

"I...Yes" Sloane was breathing heavily now.

"You want me to fuck you." It wasn't a question. She bent and bit a nipple just hard enough to make Sloane want more. "So do I."

"Touch me," Sloane urged her.

Jaden slid between her legs and put her mouth on her. Sloane made a noise between a moan and a whimper. Jaden quickly drew her clit into her mouth and Sloane's hips began pumping. Just as quickly, she lifted her head. "Not so fast, honey." She pulled her knees up and laid her wide open.

"Oh, God...Jaden." Sloane was panting in anticipation.

"Just relax, honey," she said as she massaged the length of her and teased her opening. Sloane rolled her hips and groaned in frustration until Jaden pushed hard inside her and ran her thumb over her clit. "You're so wet, lover," she said as she twisted her wrist. "Do you want more?" she crooned to her. "Like last night?"

"Oh God, yes!" Sloane cried out. "Please, Jaden."

Jaden added a third finger knowing Sloan wanted it just as she had the night before. Sloane arched her hips and pushed against Jaden's hand immediately and Jaden began a steady stroke in and out, watching Sloane's face transform as the tension built in her center. Her thighs were quivering and straining and Jaden knew she was getting close. She slowed the pace to keep her from going over the edge. Above her Sloane groaned.

"Babe...I'm so close."

"I know, lover. I can feel you." Jaden ran a soothing hand over her soft belly. When she felt her relax again, Jaden put her mouth on her and began working her clit. It wasn't long before Sloane's thighs were clamped tightly against her head as she lost it in a mind-blowing orgasm.

Everything went red and then there was total blackness as all the blood left to gather between her legs. She was gone, out of this life, floating in glorious euphoria. When she came back to her body, she was wrapped in Jaden's arms, her head resting in the crook of her neck, being soothed and held gently. There was a sheet covering the bottom half of them and Jaden's leg was between hers. Her limbs felt like dead weights and she struggled to move.

"You're so wonderful," Jaden was whispering in her ear. "So beautiful."

"Uh."

"God, Sloane, you make me feel so…" Words failed her and she kissed Sloane on the top of her head.

"Uh," Sloane said again. She finally got her arm to move and lifted her hand to Jaden's cheek.

Jaden kissed her palm and nuzzled against her hand. She couldn't believe how Sloane made her feel. She had never met anyone who captured her so totally so quickly. "Are you okay, honey?"

"Uh huh," she managed.

"Get some sleep," she murmured in Sloane's ear. "We both need some sleep."

When Sloane awoke the next morning, the bed next to her was empty. She pulled the pillow to her and inhaled Jaden's scent. This was crazy, she thought. How could she be this far-gone so quickly? She rolled to a sitting position and stood up. She needed a shower. She groaned as she went into the bathroom. She was sore everywhere, her legs, her back, and her sex.

Jaden was sitting at the table drinking coffee and reading the paper when she entered the kitchen. She immediately felt better. Jaden stood and smiled at her. "Good morning."

"Good morning," Sloan gave her a loopy smile in return.

Jaden went to the cupboard and poured Sloane a cup of coffee. She set it on the table as Sloane took a seat.

"Thanks."

"You're welcome." Jaden kissed her on the back of her neck before taking the seat opposite her. "How are you this morning?"

Sloane fought to keep the grin off her face. She reached across the table and took Jaden's hand. "Sore."

"Uh..."

"Just sore, not hurt," she said firmly.

"Shall I kiss it and make it better?"

Sloane's hand tightened in Jaden's and she blinked slowly as the rush shot through her. Jaden watched her eyes turn from chocolate to dark chocolate in a split second. Before she could answer, her cell phone rang and she withdrew her hand to pick it up. Jaden got up and refilled her cup as she answered.

"Hello...I'm sorry. I shut it off when we got on the plane yesterday and I forgot to turn it back on until this morning...No, I don't know where she is...We got off the plane and picked up our cars and that's it...They kept her phone...I'll be in soon. I'm still tired from everything...Okay, see you then." She ended the call and set the phone back on the table. "Coach has been trying to call you," she said.

Jaden sighed. "To tell me I've been let go, no doubt."

"You don't know that for sure," Sloane protested, not wanting it to be so.

"Well, I'm playing the odds on that one," Jaden said. "Why did you tell her you didn't know where I was?" Jaden looked into her coffee cup when she said it.

"To give you a chance to do whatever you want," Sloane said. "If you want to go somewhere or call someone first you can. They can't get in touch with you until you want them to right now."

Jaden looked up and smiled.

"What? Did you think I didn't want her to know you were here with me?"

Jaden shrugged. "Maybe. I'm a suspect in a murder. I wouldn't have blamed you."

"You were a suspect last night too, and the night before that."

"Well, being with me is one thing. Having other people know you've been with me is something different."

"Not to me. I don't normally care what other people think of me. Life is too short for that." She smiled across the table at her. "What are you going to do today?"

"I guess I'd better get a new phone."

"And after that?"

"I think I'll call this beautiful woman I know and see if she'll have lunch with me."

Sloane knew she was blushing. "I hope your woman says yes."

"So do I."

Chapter 11

After Sloane had told both John and Stan everything that had happened while they were in California and Portland, she was finally able to get to work. She had updated the web site from her laptop, but a ton of pictures needed organizing and cataloging. She hadn't bothered to stop in the coach's office on her way in so she wasn't surprised when Georgia Tate appeared in the office.

"Hey, Sloane."

"Hey." She looked up from where she was working.

"So, how did it go in Portland? Was it bad?"

Sloane sighed and picked up her coffee cup. "Let's get some coffee."

They picked a table in the empty break room and sat silently for a moment. "How is she doing?"

The question surprised Sloane. "She's the prime suspect in a murder," she said. "She's just glad to be out of jail right now. But I do think she's waiting for them to come get her." Coach Tate rubbed her forehead and

Sloane began to notice signs of stress. "She's got a lawyer now and that'll help."

"She didn't kill anybody, Sloane," Georgia said quickly. "You don't think she did it, do you?"

"No." Sloane took a sip of coffee but never took her eyes off the coach. "I can't believe she'd even think of doing something like that. I'm certain she didn't kill Kendall Paxton."

"You're certain?"

"We made up a time line and there wasn't more than an hour and a half to two hours that she didn't have an alibi for." Sloane kept her gaze on Georgia. "Plus I don't think she could kill her ex-girlfriend and go back to the hotel and go to sleep. Do you?"

"No."

Sloane took a deep breath and forced herself to ask, "Have they fired her? Is she off the team?"

Georgia nodded wearily and rubbed her head again. "Yeah. Donald Sutter called me yesterday."

The bottom dropped out of Sloane's stomach. She knew it was probable but had hoped against all odds. "She didn't do it, Georgia. How can they let her go when she didn't do anything?"

"There's a clause in her contract that says if she's involved in anything that brings negative attention to the organization the team can let her go." She shook her head. "She doesn't have to actually do anything herself."

"That is insane!"

"I know. It's business, Sloane. If anything impacts the bottom line in a negative manner it's a basis for releasing her from her contract."

"Jesus!" Sloane ran her hands through her thick hair in exasperation, lifting it up off her neck before letting it fall back into place. A new thought occurred to her. "What about your job, Georgia?"

"They haven't made a decision yet," she answered and Sloane knew where all the stress was coming from.

"Oh Georgia, I'm so sorry."

"It's out of my hands now," she said. "I vouched for Jaden. I was the one who kept telling them we needed her. They're within their rights to demand my resignation."

"All because a rich bitch California brat got herself killed?" Sloane's voice was full of disbelief.

"Yes, it would seem so." She gave a short bark of laughter. "Even dead she's still causing trouble."

"Has Jaden called you yet?"

"No. I don't think she will either."

"Why not?"

"If she calls her agent first, which is what I'd do, she'll know she's out of a job already. And she's smart enough to know there is nothing I can do about it."

"Yeah," Sloane nodded. "I guess so."

"We were on our way to the title this year behind her, Sloane. We would have gone all the way."

"She's good," Sloane nodded absently, not thinking about the team but about Jaden herself.

"No, Sloane, she was great," Georgia said with heat. "I can't believe we've lost her because of something that bitch of an ex-girlfriend did. What a fucking waste!"

Jaden browsed through the cell phone selection at a local electronics store without much interest. She had the feeling that as soon as she bought a new phone it would bring everything bad back into her life. She finally just chose one and went through the process of de-activating the old one and activating the new one. It rang before she could exit the store. She sighed and decided to ignore it. She was tired of being on the defensive. She didn't have control over much these days but she could decide whether to answer her phone. She started her truck but kept it in park for the moment. She needed to call Stan and let him give her the bad news first. She left a message on his voice mail and he called her back before she could call the attorney Sloane had set her up with.

"Christ, Jaden, where the hell have you been? I've called every police station between here and California!"

"Nice to talk to you too, Stan," she answered. "I'm fine, thank you."

"I'm sorry," he rushed to apologize. "I've just been frantic looking for you. I called everybody I could think of."

"The police took my phone, Stan. I just now bought a new one." She was going through the console of the truck as she spoke and finally found the card. *Keith Braden, Attorney at Law*. "Write this down, Stan. My new attorney's name is Keith Braden. If I should abruptly disappear again he'll know why." She gave him the numbers and then asked the important question. "How much of my contract was guaranteed?"

"You'll be fine money-wise," he told her. "You were past the incentive clause so they'll have to pay you for most of this year and you already have the up-front signing bonus. They can't take that back." He said this with some satisfaction since he had negotiated the contract. "They'll take a hit on their salary cap for next year unless they make a deal and buy you out."

"Okay, good." She thought about it for a moment. "Which way are they leaning?"

"They're not saying yet. It's still early, Jaden. They just made the decision."

"Okay," she conceded. "I'll think about it. I'm going to call this attorney now and see what's going to happen. I'll let you know what I find out."

"Okay, great. Keep in touch from now on," he ordered gruffly.

"I will. Oh, by the way—I didn't do it."

"I never thought you did, kid."

Next, Jaden made an appointment with her new attorney for later that afternoon and finally called the only number she had really wanted to all day. Sloane.

"Sloane," she answered and Jaden could tell she was concentrating on her work.

"Jaden," she responded in the same way.

Sloane's tone changed immediately. "Hello."

"I have a new phone."

"Different number?"

"I thought about it but it was just too much trouble to change everything."

"Where are you?"

"I'm close to downtown. Are you free for lunch today?"

"I can manage that," she smiled into the phone. "Are you picking me up?"

"That might not be the best idea right now. Why don't you meet me at Sparky's, say one o'clock?"

"Okay." Sloane wanted to say more but was aware of the two guys in media within hearing range.

Jaden chuckled, knowing her dilemma. "I'll see you then, sweetheart."

She was at a small booth along the side wall in Sparky's when Sloane arrived. She stood and waved at

119

her, then waited until she had taken a seat opposite her before sitting again. "Hi."

"Hi," Sloane smiled. She was instantly happier.

"How's work today?"

Sloane looked at her in wonder. "With everything that's happening to you, that's what you want to know?"

"Yes," she laughed.

"Work is fine." Sloane picked up a menu and studied it briefly before putting it down. When she had, she found Jaden staring at her. "Have you decided what you want?"

"Oh, yeah," she answered softly and there was no mistaking her meaning.

Sloan felt the heat climb her cheeks. "Stop that," she hissed but she was smiling.

"Now, you don't really want that, do you?" Jaden asked with a rakish grin Sloane was sure she had perfected on countless other women in the past.

"What are you going to eat?" Sloane asked, trying to keep her voice calm.

"Your name does not appear on this menu," Jaden said and tossed it aside with a flip of her hand while her gray eyes never left Sloane's face.

"You are...out of your mind." Sloane tried to hide her blush by turning her head and looking away. Fortunately, for her, their waitress appeared then and they ordered. "Have you talked to anyone today?" Sloane asked as they ate.

"I talked to Stan. I talked to Keith Braden. I talked to you." She smiled again. "I saved the best for last."

Sloane ignored that last comment. "Tell me what you found out."

"I have an appointment with Keith this afternoon. He said he's been in contact with the LAPD and he'll tell me everything then. He says to tell you hello, by the way."

"And?"

"And Stan says I'm in good financial position and they may want to buy out my contract." She held up a hand as Sloane started to speak. "Then I called a beautiful woman and asked her to lunch and she said yes. So, all in all, my day is going well."

"You're impossible," she said with a sigh. She briefly squeezed Jaden's hand across the table. "I'm so sorry this stupid organization can't see past the end of its nose. You didn't do anything! How can you be so calm about it? I'd be so pissed. I am pissed!"

Jaden shrugged. "It's business, Sloane. Sure, I'd love to have been able to stay with the team, but it's a fact of life in this kind of business. I knew that going in."

"What will you do?"

"First, I'll concentrate on not getting arrested for murder."

"Do you have any ideas about that?"

"No. I've been gone too long to know what kind of shit she'd gotten herself into. It could be anything." Her gray eyes were sad when she looked at Sloane. "It's such a waste. She wasted so much time, so much of her life!" She averted her eyes until she got control again. "She had everything going for her and she just...fucked it away." She heaved a sigh full of regret, resignation, and remorse. She didn't think she'd ever feel quite the same about anything now. Everything had changed. She tried to move on, at least in front of Sloane. "I'm surprised the Dallas paper hasn't picked up on it yet."

"Me too," she nodded. "Be careful when you go home. They might be camped out on your doorstep."

"Can I stay with you if they are?" The teasing tone was back in her voice.

"Yes," she smiled. "You know you can."

The smile disappeared. "We haven't talked yet."

Sloane tried to keep her expression neutral while her heart rate accelerated in response to the irrational fear flooding her body. "No, we haven't," she said carefully.

Jaden looked at the clock on the wall and reluctantly sighed. This conversation always seemed to come up at the worst times. "I need to get to my appointment with Mr. Braden." She laid money on the table for the check. "Really, Sloane, I'm sorry. We need to talk but can we do it later?"

"Yes, of course," she agreed but suddenly wasn't sure she wanted to talk about it at all.

"Thanks. I'll call you after I meet with Braden."

"Please do."

Jaden slid out of the booth. She wanted to kiss Sloane but contented herself with a touch on her shoulder as she passed.

Sloane pushed the food around on her plate once Jaden had left, the sunshine suddenly gone from her world.

Keith Braden, attorney at law, turned out to be a young, energetic, fit looking man with short hair. Jaden liked him immediately. They spent two hours together exchanging information and forming a plan of action. At the conclusion, Jaden wrote him a check and he promised to keep her informed.

Back on the street, she felt a sudden loss of purpose. She thought the team was probably done practicing by now. Not that she could go anyway. She wondered if Sloane was done working. She sat in her truck and thought about everything she had learned from Keith Braden. Someone was definitely setting her up for

Kendall's murder. They just hadn't been very thorough. That was good for her.

Keith found out the LAPD had found a cell phone near Kendall's body. The call log showed a call from the cell phone the PPD had found in her equipment bag. The clincher had been her name scratched in the dirt. On the surface that would have been enough to arrest her for murder. The problems started popping up when they realized both phones were brand new disposable ones sold in any convenience store and there was only one call sent from Jaden's phone and only one call received from Kendall's phone. If they were brand new then how did Kendall receive hers? That was only one question they had to answer. They were checking the mail service and her home for any possible left over packaging to indicate Jaden had sent the phone to her in the mail.

The other thing was why Jaden would leave the phone there if she had killed her, and why keep the phone in her equipment bag where the police could find it? There were only a few smudged fingerprints on either phone so no match could be made. Would she have left the phone near Kendall's body but then thought to wipe the phones off? It just didn't make sense. The thing that sent them after her had also gotten them to back off. Her name. Her name, scratched in the dirt, was misspelled. Jayden, instead of Jaden. Wouldn't a former lover know how to spell her name? And that was the reason Jaden had been able to walk out of the Portland Police station. The LAPD was not forthcoming with information as to the time of death or how she was killed. She had given Keith the time line she and Sloane had worked up and hoped it would help clear her also. For now, there was nothing more she could do and she felt helpless.

She finally started the truck and turned for home. She

hadn't been home since they'd left for California, and while that was only four days ago, it seemed like a lifetime. She went through her apartment and straight into the shower. She emerged a short time later dressed in a pair of boxer shorts and an old faded and baggy tee shirt, her short dark hair still damp. She felt disoriented, disconnected, alone, and depressed. There had always been something to do until now to keep her going. Now there was nothing; no practice, no game to prepare for, nothing. She looked into her refrigerator and realized she could have a cheese sandwich or order out. She took a beer and went back into the living room. She flopped down on the couch and stretched her long legs out in front of her, slumping with fatigue. By the end of the beer, she had closed her eyes and gone to sleep.

Chapter 12

"Gilly, she should have called by now."

Gillian held the phone between her ear and shoulder while she dug out money to pay for a drink while smiling at a cute redhead across the bar. "She's probably out having a beer," she said, keeping eye contact with the woman. "Maybe she's with her agent, or still with the lawyer."

"Maybe," Sloane admitted slowly but was unconvinced.

"Sloane, are you getting in over your head?" Gillian turned her attention back to her phone call.

"Gilly, she said she'd call when she was done with Keith. It's been four hours."

Gillian gave a mental sigh. "Have you called her?"

"Yes. She isn't answering."

"Are you still at work?"

"Yes. I've got a lot of catching up to do from the trip. I didn't even get to practice today."

"I noticed." Gillian thought a moment but could find no solution. "Sloane, maybe she'd just out getting drunk. I know I would be if this were hanging over my head."

Sloane gave a frustrated grunt. It was obvious Gillian wasn't going to be any help. "Yeah, okay. I'll try calling her again." She hung up and leaned back in the chair at her work counter.

On the large monitor in front of her, she had displayed the candid shots she had taken on the bus the morning they left L.A. She had six photos up on the screen but she didn't actually see any of them. She was remembering how Jaden had acted that morning. She had been subdued after the dream the night before but she had been relaxed and had joked with Gillian. It was the first morning she had awakened in her arms. Her stomach did a little flip. She thought that might very well have been when she started falling in love with her. She picked up the phone again, scrolled down to Jaden's name, and hit the send button. She was about to hang up once again when a muffled hello sounded in her ear. "Jaden?"

"Yeah."

"Are you okay?"

"Yeah." Jaden sat up on her couch and blinked. The sun was getting low in the west but it was still light. Before nine o'clock then, she thought.

"Where are you?"

"Home." She realized suddenly what she had done. "Shit! I was supposed to call you. I'm sorry. I fell asleep on the couch."

Sloane's voice changed immediately, getting light and soft. "That's okay. I was just worried about you."

"I'm fine." She cleared her throat. "I like Keith Braden. We had a good meeting this afternoon."

"Can you tell me about it?"

"I guess. He didn't say not to anyway." She stood and stretched. "Do you want to come over?" she asked and then hastily added, "Or we could meet somewhere."

Sloane wanted to see her but knew if they met for drinks, they'd never get to talk quietly. "I can come to your place. I'd like to see it."

"Okay, good. Uh, Sloane?"

"Yes?"

"Can you bring something to eat?"

"Yeah," she laughed. "I can do that. I'll be there soon." She hung up smiling. She then quickly chose two photos from the group on her screen and put them in place and hit the publish button to update the web site. She disconnected the flash drive and dropped it in her pocket to take with her. There were some shots she thought Jaden would like.

She was ringing the doorbell an hour later after picking up burgers for both of them. It was getting dark. Jaden opened the door immediately and let her in.

"Thanks." She took the bag of food from her. "You are a life saver."

"I got everything on it since I didn't know what you liked." She followed Jaden into the kitchen and waited while she got out plates and napkins.

"Beer or Coke?"

"Coke."

She took two cans from the refrigerator and handed one to Sloane. "It's kind of small in here so how about eating in the living room."

"Sure." They settled around the small coffee table and dug in. "You like living here?"

"It's okay," Jaden shrugged. "I was in a hurry. I hate living in a hotel and I rented this without really looking around. It'll do until the lease runs out."

Sloane thought about that. What would Jaden do now that she was out of a job? Would some other team want her to play for them? Some team far away? Would she leave here forever? She put the rest of her burger down, unable to swallow around the lump in her throat. *Don't make her think about how much she's lost*, she thought. "Tell me what Keith said today."

Jaden did and soon Sloane was smiling. "That's great! I knew there had to be something wrong when they let you go in Portland."

"And thanks for making me do that alibi time line thing. It just might be the clincher." Jaden felt better than she had since leaving Portland. "Thanks for staying with me in Portland too, Sloane, and getting me a lawyer and hell, for everything."

Wild horses couldn't have kept me away, Sloane thought. "You're welcome, again. Coach Tate arranged for me to stay behind. I'm glad I was the least valuable person on the trip."

"I'm glad she thought so anyway." Jaden got up to clean up the remains of their meal. When she returned from the kitchen, Sloan was relaxed against the arm of the couch, one leg up and one still on the floor. She reminded Jaden of a cat, lithe and beautiful, sensuous and smooth. She stood in the doorway a moment watching, memorizing her. "Did you talk to Gilly today?" she asked as she entered the room and broke the spell.

Sloane shifted on the couch and motioned for Jaden to join her. "Yes," she said when she sat down. "She said practice was quiet and Coach Bob wasn't even there." She took Jaden's hand in hers. "They all missed you. It seems you've made some friends here."

"I miss them too," Jaden admitted. "After I left Keith's office I didn't know what to do with myself. It was weird.

I'm so used to having some place to be, something to do, you know?"

"I know. It must be hard on you," she agreed. "Georgia came in to talk this morning. She's afraid of losing her job too. She was hoping you'd call her, I think."

"There didn't seem to be much use in talking to her," Jaden shrugged. "I know it wasn't her decision. If DSG has any sense at all, they'll keep her. Bob Winslow can't coach this team. No one respects him enough."

"Hey, I brought some photos of the trip to show you." Sloane abruptly changed the subject. She dug the flash drive out of a pocket and held it up.

Jaden chuckled. "Are there any photos of you in there?"

"No," she giggled. "No one gets their hands on my cameras."

"Well, maybe I'll look at them later." Jaden leaned close but kissed Sloane instead of taking the flash drive.

Sloane immediately melted, her mouth welcoming Jaden's tongue. They quickly descended into moans, groans, and searching hands. When they parted for breath, Sloane put a hand on Jaden's chest to keep her at bay. "Jaden, we should talk," she gulped.

Jaden looked into her eyes and didn't try to get past her hand. She knew Sloane was right so she pulled back into a sitting position and allowed Sloane to do the same. "Yes, okay," she nodded. "You're right."

Sloane straightened her blouse and pushed her hair back from her face. She forced herself to take a calming breath before turning back to Jaden. "It's been...shall we say a bit tumultuous lately."

"Yes," she sighed. "That would be an apt description."

"Do you think we might be getting a little ahead of ourselves?"

Jaden's heart twisted in her chest. *Was this the kiss off?* She tried to see the situation from Sloane's point of view. "I suppose that's possible," she acknowledged even as her heart was breaking. "I don't blame you if you're...if you want to..."

Sloane had wanted her to say no, they were meant to be together. Now she was forced to eat her own words. "I'm not saying we should stop seeing each other," she said in a rush.

"What *are* you saying?"

Sloane reached out to put a hand on her arm, arms that had rocked her world. She took in a breath. "I'm saying there are so many things happening and neither one of us knows what or how this will end." She looked into eyes that were tinged with hurt. "You might go play for a team in New York or something."

Jaden nodded. "And you'd be left here alone. Is that what this is all about?"

"You have to admit it's possible."

"Yes, it's possible," she nodded. "I wish I could say differently." She sat closer and put her arm around Sloane's shoulders. "I don't know what's going to happen. I might be done playing ball. Maybe no team will touch me after this."

Sloane leaned into her, comfortable with the way they fit together. "That's not likely, Jaden, and you know it."

"Do you want to end this now, before it gets too hard to do so?"

Sloane's eyes filled with tears and she was glad Jaden couldn't see them. *Would that be the best thing? Could it get harder to have her leave than it was right now?* She tightened her arm around Jaden's stomach. She made a decision, right or wrong. "No, Jaden, I don't want to end it now. And just so you know, I don't want to end it at all."

Jaden pulled her tightly against her and kissed her neck. "Neither do I."

"Are you sure?" Sloane's voice was muffled against her chest.

"Yes, lover, I'm sure. Very sure," Jaden said softly in her ear while nibbling on the lobe. She held her tightly against her and ran a hand up through Sloane's silky hair, letting the strands slip through her fingers. "Sloane," she murmured as she began a slow exploration with her mouth.

When she pushed her down on the couch, she was already reaching for the buttons of her shirt. She paused to pull the shirt over her head. Sloane was struggling to get out of her blouse but Jaden leaned in to kiss her, stopping everything.

Her mouth is so soft, Sloane thought as her lips were devoured. *How could I have even thought about giving this up*?

Jaden kissed down her jaw and along her neck, heading ever lower. She spent a long time on Sloane's cleavage while Sloane moved with increasing urgency beneath her.

"Jaden." Sloane had her hands in Jaden's hair. "Let me get out of these clothes."

Jaden slowly raised her head and gave her a smile. "Okay, honey. Do you want to move into the bedroom?"

"Yes, that would be nice."

Jaden got up and helped Sloane off the couch. She removed her shirt and bra both on the way into the bedroom. Next to the bed, Jaden stepped close and put her hands on her waist, opening her pants. They kissed again while she slid the zipper down and hooked her fingers under the waistband of her panties. "I need you to be naked," she whispered and bent to push both off her hips. "You are so beautiful." Jaden dropped to her knees and put her hands on Sloane's hips before kissing her belly. Sloane put her hands in Jaden's hair, her knees threatening to give out. Jaden steadied her with an arm around her thighs and nuzzled against the tangle of curls between her legs.

"Jaden," Sloane warned in a rush of breath. "I can't stand up much longer."

Jaden stood and moved her onto the bed never allowing her to be free of her touch. When she lay in all her glory, Jaden stripped off all her own clothes but her eyes never left Sloane. "Oh, honey, you don't know what you do to me," she whispered as she covered Sloane's body with her own.

I could say the same for you, Sloane thought with a gulp.

Jaden kissed her again and settled a thigh between her legs, pressing into her center. Jaden couldn't get enough of Sloane's kisses.

Sloane finally pulled away for air and pushed a hand between them to squeeze Jaden's breast. "Jaden," she panted, "you're driving me crazy. I need to touch you."

Jaden lifted her torso and held herself over Sloane, giving her free access. Sloane's touch was sweet torture. Jaden's skin burned where her fingers made contact and all she wanted was more. She couldn't keep control when Sloane touched her. She was a strong, independent woman who turned to putty in an instant. If Sloane ever learned how much power she held, Jaden was a goner. Her nipples tightened and she ached to have Sloane's mouth on her.

"Sloane," she whispered.

"Yes, baby?" Sloane answered absently while continuing to fondle her.

"Lover," Jaden tried again. This time her voice betrayed her need.

Sloane stilled her hands and let Jaden's breasts rest in her palms. She raised her eyes slowly to Jaden's. "Do you need something, baby?"

"Slone, honey, please," Jaden whined. "I need..." She faltered as Sloane once again captured a nipple between thumb and finger.

"You need more?" She teased. "Would you like to see how much of your breast will fit into my mouth? Is that what you'd like?"

"Sloane, you're killing me."

"Well, we can't have that." Sloane gave her a slow, sensuous smile. "Would you like to bring yourself up here a little?" She let her tongue rest on her bottom lip. Sloane felt her wetness against her stomach as Jaden lifted herself forward, straddling her torso until a breast brushed against her mouth. When Sloane took the offering Jaden sucked in a breath and threw her head back, eyes squeezed tightly shut. She fought to breathe and thought she could quite possibly come just from this.

Sloane lifted her head. "Hold on, babe," she said. "I'm not ready to let you come just yet." She held Jaden above her with hands on her ribcage until Jaden was breathing more easily. "That's better," she murmured.

"You destroy me," Jaden gulped.

"You seem a little...um, anxious tonight. Perhaps we should take a little break."

"Or we could do it fast," Jaden countered. "You know, the first time, just to take the edge off."

Sloane gave her a smile. "Oh, you want it fast?"

"Yes, please," she huffed.

"Then come up here, babe, and let me give you a mustache ride."

Jaden felt the mother of all rushes race through her and land between her legs. She closed her eyes again to deal with it and when she opened them, she was staring into Sloane's dark chocolate eyes. "Come on, baby, I want to give you what you need." Jaden maneuvered herself up Sloane's body until she was in position above her face. "Yeah, baby. Come here."

Sloane took her by the hips and pulled her down.

Jaden reached for the headboard and held on. It was over quickly but no less forcefully. Jaden came with a vengeance, gripping the headboard so hard the wood creaked beneath her hands. When she could, she fell to the bed and collapsed. Sloane put an arm softly across her stomach. She was feeling a little satisfied with herself and smiled.

Jaden eventually covered Sloane's hand with one of her own and rolled her head to look at her. "Jesus!"

"Did that take the edge off, baby?"

Jaden smiled then chuckled, the chuckle turning into full-blown laughter. She rolled on top of Sloane and smiled down into laughing brown eyes. "You are so pleased with yourself, aren't you?"

"Yes."

"You have good reason," she said softly and bent to kiss her. Now that she could think clearly she slowly but steadily kissed her way down Sloane's body. Once between her legs she sucked and caressed Sloane ever higher until she was rigid and straining. From there, it was just a touch of her tongue to send her over the top. At the height of her orgasm, Sloane choked out Jaden's name.

Chapter 13

Dallas was scheduled to play Memphis that night and Sloane wanted to get the rest of her photos cataloged and filed so she'd be ready for the next group she'd shoot tonight. That meant getting to the office early. After the night of lovemaking she felt like just sinking back into bed next to Jaden but forced herself to get up. She quietly took a shower, got dressed, and left without waking her. She could pick up something for breakfast later, she thought as she got into her car. Rush hour wouldn't start for another hour and the streets were quiet. She rolled down the window and enjoyed the early morning fresh air until she parked in the stadium lot. She had to swipe her key card to unlock the door since it was before regular business hours and headed for the elevator and her office. The first thing she noticed was that the door to the media room was closed. They hardly ever closed it but she shrugged it off. She opened the door and flipped on the lights. The first and last thing she saw was that her workstation had been trashed. Then all she saw was black.

Jaden finished her work out with a series of laps in the pool. She might not have a job but she could still work out and stay in shape. She was an athlete and that was all she knew. Now she'd just have more time to do it. She took a leisurely shower and returned to her apartment. It was a short trip since the health club was a part of her apartment complex. Her cell phone was ringing when she opened the door and she hurried to answer it, hoping it was Sloane.

"Hello?"

"Jaden, it's Gillian."

"Hey, Gilly, it's good to hear from you."

"Yeah, uh, listen...there's been a break-in at the stadium."

"Really? What happened?"

"Sloane's in the hospital," she blurted out. "She must have surprised the guy. At least that seems to be what happened."

"What hospital? Where is she? Is she okay?" Jaden was in panic mode already. The air didn't seem to be getting into her lungs and she was having trouble breathing.

"I don't know," Gillian was saying. "All I know is what Coach said when she called. They took her to Baylor. I've been trying to call you ever since."

Jaden wasn't listening. She had stopped when she heard Baylor. "I'll be there in a minute," she said and closed her phone. She was already heading for the door. Rush hour was in full swing by now and Jaden fumed and cursed every driver that seemed intent on slowing her down. She finally turned off Gaston Avenue and into a parking lot. She was heading for the front desk when Gillian intercepted her.

"Jaden."

"Gilly, where is she?" Jaden grabbed her by the arm, a wild look in her eyes.

"She's in room 406. Come on, I'll show you the way." Gillian waited until Jaden had loosened her hand and then led the way to the elevator bank on the left. She gently massaged her upper arm where Jaden had held her in a vice-like grip.

"How is she?" Jaden asked as she followed Gillian.

"She has a concussion," she told her. "She was hit on the back of the head."

"What happened?" Jaden's whole body was shaking by now.

Gillian hugged her briefly. "She's going to be okay, Jaden." She faced the front again as the doors opened on the fourth floor. "This way." She led her down the hall to Sloane's room.

Sloane was lying in bed, unconscious. She looked so small and pale. Jaden's heart squeezed in her chest. *Oh God, please let her be okay*. She moved to the side of the bed and took her hand. It was warm but limp and she didn't stir.

"They said she woke up once, but I guess she didn't remember anything."

"Hey, Jaden."

She turned. Coach Tate was standing in the doorway, a cup of coffee in her hand. She looked pale herself. "Hey, Coach," she returned. "How are you?"

"I'm good," she nodded. She looked at Jaden's hand still holding Sloane's. "She's suffered a concussion."

"Yeah, that's why Gilly said. What happened?"

Georgia nodded toward the chair next to the bed. "Have a seat. Gilly, maybe you could get Jaden a cup of coffee."

"Yeah, sure." Gillian touched Jaden on the shoulder and gave her a gentle squeeze before leaving.

Georgia took the chair from the empty bed next to them and moved it closer. "The police seem to think someone broke into the building and she walked in on him. Or them."

"What did they steal?" Jaden wasn't listening. She was watching Sloane. Watching her breathe—in and out. Watching her eyes move behind closed lids. She moved her thumb over Sloane's wrist softly. She looked so helpless. Her eyes filled and she blinked rapidly to clear them.

"Jaden."

She realized with a start that Georgia was talking to her. "I'm sorry. What did you say?"

"I said I'm sorry about the whole L.A. thing. I'm sorry they cut you from the team. I argued with them but...well, they'd already made up their minds."

"It's business," she shrugged. "You did warn me." She looked over at her and tried a smile. "How are you doing?"

"I'm still here. At least so far. I don't know how long that will last. Like you said, it's business."

Gillian entered the room then and handed Jaden a cup of coffee from the machine down the hall. "Anything yet?"

"No." Jaden shook her head.

"The doctor said she could come around at any time or it might take longer." Gillian leaned against the wall and looked at Jaden. "She'll be okay, Jaden."

"I know," Jaden nodded. "I know. She has to be."

The doctor said she's in good health and that will help," Georgia added.

"Why did this happen?" Jaden asked.

"They think she surprised the thieves and they knocked her out," Georgia said.

"So what was so valuable they had to hit her so hard?" Jaden asked in frustration.

"That's the thing," Georgia said. "It looks like they hit the media room first. Sloane's workstation was trashed. They broke her monitor, took the external storage drives, and bashed the hell out of her computer. She must have got there about that time because that's as far as they got. They must have gotten out of there fast after that."

"Why was she there so early anyway?" Gillian idly wondered. "Didn't they say Coach Winslow found her when he came in?"

"Yeah," Georgia nodded. "He said he went in early to work on some scouting reports on Memphis for tonight's game. He said he saw her when he got off the elevator. He called 911."

"Why start with the media room?" Gillian asked. "That makes no sense."

"It does if they were after stuff they could sell quickly. Her cameras are missing along with the storage drives. Those are things that were easy to carry." Georgia stood up. "We need to get going. I've called an early meeting before practice and now this." She looked at Jaden.

"I'll stay here with her," she said quickly. "Don't worry."

"I'll call you later, Jaden," Gillian said as she left. "Keep her safe."

"I will. Thanks for calling, Gilly." When they were gone, Jaden could finally do what she had wanted to do since entering the room. She leaned over the bed and kissed Sloane on the lips. "Hey, honey. It's me, Jaden. I'm right here with you. I hear you had a little excitement this morning. You surprised a thief, they tell me, and he conked you on the head." She raised Sloane's hand to her lips and kissed her knuckles. "I wish you had stayed in bed with me this morning, honey." She sat for a while just watching her and sipping coffee. "I realized how much you mean to me when Gilly called to tell me you were hurt." She rubbed Sloane's hand again. "I'm finding it hard to think about ever being without you in my life. I'm glad you decided you didn't want to end it yet. I know you're worried about me leaving but you don't have to be. I don't think..." She stopped, unable to continue through a throat that was closed with emotion. She brushed the tears away and contented herself with just watching her.

She was still there hours later when the doctor came in to check on her. "Hello. I'm Doctor Bronski," he introduced himself. "How is our patient doing?"

"She hasn't moved," she told him.

He smiled at her. "Don't worry. Her brain got bounced around inside her skull from the blow. That caused some swelling. That swelling needs to be reduced. That will take a little time. When it does, she'll wake up."

"Will she be okay? When the swelling goes down, I mean?"

"We have every reason to believe so," he answered. He checked Sloane's vital signs and made notes on her chart. "It's been said it helps if someone they know talks to them."

"I have been talking to her," Jaden confessed.

"Good." He replaced the chart on the end of the bed. "Keep it up. If she wakes up call the nurse and she'll let me know." He smiled at her again and was gone.

It was late afternoon before Gillian called. Jaden gave her a report on Sloane's condition, unchanged, and her own, waiting. "How was practice?" Jaden needed to change the subject.

"Pretty weird," Gillian admitted. "Everyone's spooked a little. It's like there's this black cloud hanging over us or something."

"I can imagine. Have you heard anything more about the break-in?"

"They aren't saying anything. Coach Bob was pretty shook up and Georgia wanted to get ready for Memphis tonight. It was a mess actually and we didn't get much done."

"How is Erin pitching?"

"She's okay. She hasn't quite got your control and she definitely can't throw the *smoke* but she's doing pretty well. My hand doesn't hurt though."

Jaden smiled for the first time that day. "Thanks, Gilly."

"Can I bring you anything? Something to eat maybe, or something to read?"

"No, you don't have to do that."

"I'm coming by before the game anyway," she said. "I'll stop and get you something to eat at least. You don't want to eat hospital food, do you?"

"Okay, thanks."

Jaden woke with a gasp. She had fallen asleep in the chair and her neck had a stabbing pain. She let go of Sloane's hand and stood slowly. She was stiff all over and hobbled away from the bed a few steps to stretch. It was very dark and very quiet. It must be the middle of the night. She used the bathroom and then went to the window to stare out into the night. There was just a sliver of moon but the lights in the parking lot gave off a bright glow. She yawned and let the curtain fall back in place. She should take a walk, she thought, to loosen up her muscles. She went back to the bed and picked up Sloane's hand again.

"Where did...you go?" It was a hoarse whisper.

Jaden gave a start. "I'm right here, honey," she said quickly. "How do you feel?"

"Head..." was all she got out before she slipped back into unconsciousness.

Jaden kissed her cheek. "Don't worry, honey, I'm not going anywhere. You just concentrate on getting better and I'll be right here with you." All thoughts of a walk were gone now. She needed to stay right here with Sloane. Somehow, she had gotten through to her and she knew Jaden was there for her. She sat down again. Those few words probably didn't mean all that much but Jaden's spirits were buoyed anyway. She clicked on the little light beside the bed and picked up the magazine she'd been reading earlier. She'd found it in the lounge area and, while a girlie magazine wasn't exactly her thing, it helped pass the time.

She was dozing again when the hospital came to life with the arrival of the new day. The first shift nurses sent her out while they tended to Sloane and she went down to the cafeteria for coffee that didn't come from a machine. Her eyes were gritty, her clothes screamed having been slept in, and she was starving. She got breakfast after remembering the nurses saying they would be giving Sloane a sponge bath this morning. She gulped her meal down and raced back up to the room. She didn't want to miss the chance that Sloane might wake up and be alone. She waited by the window while they finished up and then used the bathroom to scrub her face and try to refresh a little. It was a good thing her hair was short and she could finger comb it into some semblance of order.

"Hey there, sleepyhead," she said as she took Sloane's hand again. She was surprised when Sloane's hand curled into hers. "Feel like waking up yet?" She held her breath but Sloane made no further movement. "Guess not, huh? That's okay. I've got nothing but time. The team played last night. I don't know if they won or not though. Memphis isn't all that great but Dallas has been through some shit lately so who knows how they played. They all said to tell you to get well soon and they miss you." She reached up to kiss her cheek. "That's from Gilly. She said to give you a kiss but she gets your cheek. I'm the only one who gets to kiss you on the lips. Right?" Jaden smiled at Sloane knowing if the emotion was on your face it would show in your voice. "You can be the only one to kiss me too if you want. All you have to do is say the word. Not that I have women lining up to kiss me." She squeezed her hand. "I can't wait to kiss you again. I mean really kiss you. Have I ever told you how much I love kissing you? I do. I could kiss you all night long. But then I never get the chance because you always get impatient. Once you touch me, I lose, uh...control. I think you know that too and you take advantage of it. You are wicked that way. Then I get to touch you after and that's worth anything. I've never felt like this with anyone before, Sloane, not even Kendall. With her, it was always wild, frantic, and crazy. I thought that was love. Now...now I know it wasn't. It's so different with you. I can't believe we've only been with each other a short time. It seems like we've known each other a lot longer. I want to go to sleep with you every night and wake up with you beside me every morning. I want you to be a part of my life from now on." She felt Sloane's fingers tighten around her own.

"Are you proposing?"

Jaden jerked around to see Sloane's eyes open. "Hey, honey."

"Water," she croaked.

"Hold on." She filled a glass part way from the pitcher and inserted the bent straw. "Here, just open your mouth a little and suck on this."

Sloane tried a giggle and settled for a smile. "Suck on this?" She sipped some water, cleared her throat, sipped again. "Thanks."

"How do you feel?"

"Headache."

"Just be still and I'll let the nurse know you're awake." Jaden kissed her on the cheek and hurried out to the nurse's station. She was back in a minute. "They're going to call the doctor and let him know you're awake." She was all smiles as she sat beside the bed again.

"Can I sit up?"

"I don't think that's such a good idea. You've had a head injury."

Sloane tried to raise her head and immediately felt the bile rise into her throat, her stomach roiling in protest. Jaden was at her side. "Please, Sloane, stay still." Sloane thought she needn't worry about that. She wouldn't be lifting her head again anytime soon. "Honey, please." Jaden's voice was pleading.

"Okay," she whispered. They were quiet for a few moments.

"Do you remember anything about what happened?" Jaden asked.

"No," she said after a pause to think about it. It was too much trouble at the moment. "The only thing I remember is leaving your apartment to go in early this morning. What happened? Was I in an accident?"

"Yesterday."

"What?"

"Yesterday morning. You've been out for over twenty-four hours, Sloane."

She frowned. Her head pounded. "What happened?" She was confused now.

"You interrupted a thief at the stadium." Jaden kissed her hand. "He hit you on the head."

"I don't remember anything." She started to shake her head but stopped when the wave of pain hit. She closed her eyes and swallowed repeatedly to keep the nausea at bay.

"The doctor should be along pretty soon, hon. Hang in there, okay?"

"Yeah," she croaked, her eyes tightly shut. "Talk to me," she said after a while.

"Okay. The thief was in the media room when you got there. He must have heard you coming. When you went inside, he hit you on the head and knocked you out. He trashed your computer and broke your monitor. And he stole your storage drives and your cameras." She stopped to collect herself. Sloane could have died from such a blow to the head. "It seems Coach Winslow got there first and found you. He called 911."

"Stuff isn't worth that much," she muttered.

"Nothing is. Just relax and try to sleep, okay? The doctor will wake you when he gets here."

"Kay." Her voice was weak and she dropped into sleep.

Jaden prayed she'd be able to wake up again. She was standing in the hall outside her room when Gillian got off the elevator.

"Hey, what's going on?"

"She woke up," Jaden grinned. "The doctor's in with her now."

"That's great!" Gillian gave her a hug. "Does she remember anything?"

"No, nothing. She thought she'd been in an accident."

"Well, maybe she will in time."

"Maybe. It doesn't matter. Hey, did you guys win last night?"

"No," Gillian shook her head. "We were holding our own until the last inning and then they rallied for three runs and we couldn't catch them." She blew out a frustrated breath at the memory. "We didn't have any energy. We were, I don't know, going through the motions. You know?"

"Yeah," Jaden nodded.

"So far, Georgia is still our coach. I'm going to hate to see what happens if they fire her."

"That'll be the end of things for sure," Jaden said. "No one is going to follow Winslow."

"You got that right. He's been a basket case since you got arrested. He can't handle the extra stress of sole coaching responsibilities."

"I wasn't arrested."

"Yeah, well, whatever. All I know is that everything has been crazy since that trip."

"You can't blame this on me," Jaden protested. The door to Sloane's room opened then and the doctor came out. "How is she?" she asked without preamble.

"She's doing very well, all things considered. She's still feeling a little dizzy so I want to keep her here for another day. I'll check on her again tomorrow and we'll re-evaluate her condition then." He gave them both a smile. "You can go back in now."

Sloane was propped up slightly with pillows behind her shoulders. She gave them a smile when they entered. "Hi Gilly."

"How are you feeling?" Gillian went to the bed and kissed her on the cheek. "It's good to see you awake."

"I feel much better," Sloane told her but was careful not to move her head. She smiled at Jaden and raised her hand. Jaden took it and settled into the chair she had occupied for the past day and a half.

Gillian took note but smiled at Sloane. "Are you able to remember anything?"

"No, not yet."

"One thing you have to look forward to," Gillian grinned, "you'll get all new equipment out of this."

"That'll be a fun shopping trip," she agreed with a grin. "But I hear I've lost all the storage drives too."

"You'll get new ones," Jaden put in quickly. "It'll be fine."

The door suddenly opened and a man in a brown suit came in. He was a big guy, around 6'3" and 240 pounds. His hair was sandy brown and thinning on top and cut very short. His suit pants were wrinkled around his crotch as if he'd been sitting much of the day. His eyes were brown but kind and his nose was slightly flat. He reached to brush away his jacket to show them his police badge and the gun on his belt. "Ms Ellison? I'm Detective Tillis from the Dallas Police Department. May I speak with you privately, please?"

Jaden opened her mouth to protest but Sloane squeezed her hand and then dropped it. "Of course. Ladies, can you give us a few minutes?"

Out in the hall Gillian and Jaden made their way down to the lounge. "So, Jaden," Gillian said after making sure they were alone in the room. "Want to tell me what's going on between you and Sloane?"

"Come on, Gilly."

"I'm serious, Jaden. What's going on?"

"Gilly, that's between Sloane and me."

"You know I like you but I love her." She saw the look on Jaden's face. "No, not like that. I'm not *in* love with her."

"So, what's the problem then?"

"She deserves the best."

"And you don't think I'm good enough?" Jaden's voice was incredulous. "What? You think I'm a predator or something? You think I'm just using her?"

"It's not that!" Gilly paced in front of her, hands deep in her pockets. "She needs someone who's serious about her, that's all, someone who'll be good to her."

Jaden stared at her as she continued her pacing. "I must be missing something, Gillian. It's great you're a good enough friend to want to see her with someone that's good for her. But, I gotta tell ya, you're out of line here."

Gillian's shoulders slumped and she stopped pacing to stand in front of Jaden. "She's been hurt before, Jaden. I just don't want to see that happen to her again. Okay?"

"Shit, Gillian!" Jaden stared at her for a moment. "She's not the only one who's ever been hurt, you know."

"God damn it! I didn't mean it that way!" She flung herself down in the chair next to her. "Just forget it, okay? Just forget I said anything."

"How the hell do you expect me to do that?" she asked. "What's going on?" Gillian sat staring across the room. "Were you two together at one time?"

"No," Gillian sighed. She leaned forward, forearms on her knees, head hanging down, staring at the floor. "I knew her...ah, ex."

"And?" Jaden asked when she didn't continue.

"And she was the love of Sloane's life back then." She leaned back in the chair again, resigned to telling the story, knowing full well she shouldn't. "Do not tell her I'm the one who told you this story. Please." Jaden just looked at her. The gap in the bridge between them hadn't yet been repaired. "Okay," she nodded. "I knew her when she first started dating Kerry. That was her name. They were...good together. At least it seemed so at first." Gillian was staring into space, remembering. "Kerry was good looking, successful, had a good job; everything a woman could want. She and Sloane had been dating for about six months and Kerry treated her like a princess. Sloane was so happy."

"What changed?"

"Kerry changed," she said flatly. "She got Sloane wrapped around her little finger and moved her into her apartment. I guess that's when it all started to go to hell. I wasn't seeing as much of her back then because she was always with Kerry and I was doing other things. But not long after she moved in Kerry started staying out at night, drinking and bar hopping with the boys. When Sloane wanted to know what was going on, she got...abusive."

Jaden stared at her in shock. "Physically?"

"Yes. Well, physically, mentally, and emotionally. She told Sloane she belonged to her and she'd damn well do whatever Kerry wanted her to do."

"Jesus!" Jaden gulped.

"She ended up breaking Sloane's wrist. That's when she called me. I picked her up from the hospital and took her back to my place. I wouldn't let her go back there alone. I knew Kerry would try and sweet-talk her into coming back to her. I didn't trust her. Meanwhile, Kerry was out drinking and chasing another woman. We got her clothes and stuff out of the apartment when she was working."

"Wow."

"It's not over yet. Sloane reported the broken wrist to the police and got a restraining order against her, but she was stalking her anyway. Sloane said she saw her all the time but could never have gotten the police there in time. I told her to report it anyway so they'd have a record of it." She held up a hand to stop Jaden from commenting. "Not long after that the woman Kerry had been seeing called the police on her, or maybe it was the neighbors. We were never sure. Anyway, they arrive and find the woman bruised and bleeding. They arrest Kerry, find the complaint filed by Sloane and she goes to jail."

When it was clear she was done Jaden took a deep breath. "I've never hit a woman in my life. Not even Kendall, and God knows she could piss off the Pope. Violence is not part of loving someone." She took a moment. "I haven't...been with Sloane very long but I do care for her. More than is reasonable for such a short time really. I hope she cares for me as well. I think she does but we haven't talked about it." She touched Gillian's arm. "I would never hit her, Gilly."

"It's not just that. She hurt Sloane in every way imaginable," Gillian told her. "She made her feel stupid and ugly. She told her she didn't deserve to be loved. She told her all she was good for was fucking and she wasn't even very good at that. She used her...sexually...to dominate her."

"Oh my God." Jaden closed her eyes in pain.

"She had Sloane's head all screwed up, Jaden. And it took a long time to get her back."

"Gilly, you can't possibly think I'd do that to her."

"No, Jaden, I don't, but I didn't think Kerry would either. You know?"

"Yeah, okay," Jaden nodded. "I don't know what I can tell you."

They sat in silence for a while. "Anyway, that's why I wanted to know."

Jaden nodded absently. "I understand." They sat for a while longer, neither one of them knowing what more to say. Finally, Jaden got up. "Maybe we should go back."

Sloane was alone when they returned. She clicked off the TV. "I thought maybe you guys left."

"No way," Gillian laughed. "I just got here."

"Jaden, have you been home yet?"

"Uh, well...no."

Gillian looked sharply at her. "You've been here since they brought her in?"

"Well...yeah." Jaden shifted from one foot to the other. "She was unconscious. I didn't want to leave in case she woke up. I didn't want her to be all alone if she did."

"Jaden, my God, that's been two days!" Sloane cried. "Go home and get some sleep. In your own bed this time."

"I will in a little while. First, tell us what the cop said."

"He just wanted to know what I remembered; if I heard or noticed anything."

"Did you?" Gillian asked.

"No," she answered regretfully. "The last thing I remember is leaving Jaden's apartment to go in early to work."

Jaden carefully avoided looking at Gillian. "You didn't even remember going into the building?" Gillian asked.

"No."

"Did he say anything else?" Jaden asked.

"Not really." Sloane yawned and then laughed. "I've been asleep for almost two days; you wouldn't think I'd be tired."

"I saw your car in the lot last night," Gillian said. "Would you like us to take it home for you?"

"Oh, that would be great, Gilly. Thanks."

"Okay, then here's the plan. Jaden will come with me and we'll go get your car and take it home. Then I'll bring her back here to get her truck."

"Sounds like a plan to me. The keys are probably in my bag here in the bottom drawer."

Jaden retrieved them and looked at Gillian. "Okay then. You ready?"

"Yeah, let's go."

"Hey." Sloane was looking at Jaden. "Not so fast."

Jaden smiled and moved to the bed. Without hesitation, she bent and kissed her.

"That's better," she smiled. "Go home tonight and get some sleep, okay?"

"Okay." Jaden couldn't keep from giving her a peck on the forehead. "I'll be back tomorrow morning."

"See you then."

They waited for the elevator together in silence and Jaden wondered if Gillian would comment on the kiss. She didn't say anything until they were in her car. "She spent the night with you, huh?"

"Yes. And I've spent the night with her before."

"You work fast."

"No, it's not like that. It just kind of happened with us." Gillian was silent. "I truly care for her, Gilly."

"She seems to care for you too," Gillian allowed. She sighed. "I guess there's nothing I can do about it."

"No, you can't," Jaden said, but kindly. "This is something between us. I can't guarantee we'll be together forever but I can guarantee that I won't abuse her in any way. I promise that. Besides, didn't you once tell me you'd like to see her with someone again?"

"Yeah," Gillian agreed. That had been before this whole murder situation and the police and everything. Couldn't Jaden see how that changed things? "Well, just remember what I told you, okay?"

Jaden smiled. "I'll remember."

"Hi, Gilly. Everything go okay?" Sloane asked when Gillian returned to her room.

"Yeah. Your car is sitting in your spot at your apartment."

"Did Jaden go home?"

"Yes." Gillian sat beside the hospital bed. "It looks like you two have something going on."

Sloane smiled. "Yeah." The smile got bigger. "We do."

Gillian smiled back at her. "You don't think you're moving a little too fast, do you?"

"I know, Gilly, I know. I can't help it."

"Is it serious?"

"It's too soon to tell but right now it's going very well."

"You're not in over your head, are you?"

"No, Gilly. She's good to me."

"Yeah." Gillian said it without any inflection in her voice.

"I mean it. She's not Kerry."

"I know. I like Jaden too. I just like you more and it seems like she's getting to you."

"I don't know what it is, Gilly, but I can't be around her without wanting to touch her."

Gillian knew when she had lost a battle. "Just be careful, okay?"

"I'm trying," Sloane said but she was smiling. "Now, tell me about the game."

Gillian gave her an account of their loss the previous night, adding how the team was being affected by everything. They all sent their best wishes. Sloane was yawning again by the time she finished. "You should get some sleep." Gillian stood up. "Would you like to stay with me for a few days when they let you out of here? It'd be like old times."

"I'm sure it would be."

"But you're going to stay with Jaden."

"Yes," she answered. "But thanks for offering, Gilly."

"You know I'm here for you whenever you need me." She turned for the door. "Get some sleep."

Jaden let herself into Sloane's apartment the next evening and dropped her bag just inside the door. It was quiet so she walked into the bedroom to find Sloane asleep on top of the covers. She brushed a strand of hair off her face and tucked it behind her ear. She was so beautiful it made Jaden's heart ache.

Sloane stirred and opened her eyes. She smiled up at Jaden. "Hi."

"Hi. How are you feeling?"

"I'm fine," she yawned.

"Why don't you take a nap and I'll just putter around here for a while?"

"No," she said with a pout.

"No?" Jaden carefully stretched out on the bed next to her, put her hand under her shirt, and rubbed soft circles on her belly. She loved the feel of Sloane's skin under her hands. "Maybe just a little nap?"

"Not as long as you're doing that," she said with a lazy smile.

"Oh, so it's my fault then?" Jaden laughed.

"Yes."

"Well, in that case, I guess I should stop touching you."

"I don't think that's the problem," Sloane said quickly.

"Then I should keep doing this?"

"That would be for the best," Sloane agreed. She lifted her shirt and urged Jaden's hand higher. Jaden smiled and moved her hand up until it rested just beneath a beast. She brushed her fingers over the swell but refrained from anything else. "Maybe just a bit higher," Sloane said in a hushed whisper.

"I don't think the doctor would like it if you were to get, um, excited."

"I won't. I promise."

Jaden couldn't help herself. She laughed out loud. "Sure."

Sloane had the decency to laugh with her. "I'll try really hard not to then. How about that?"

Jaden slid her palm up to cup her breast because she couldn't resist. "I think this is about as far as we can go."

"Oh man," Sloane groaned.

Jaden very carefully pulled Sloane into her arms until her head rested on her shoulder. "How about if we just lie here quietly for a little while? I just need to hold you."

"That would be good," she mumbled against Jaden's neck. She put her arm across her waist and a leg over her thigh, essentially using Jaden as a body pillow. Jaden had never felt anything so right, so good, or so natural. Soon Jaden felt Sloane's limbs grow heavy as she drifted off to sleep. She smiled and let herself sink into sleep with her.

Chapter 14

"Listen up." Coach Tate addressed the team grouped outside the dugout. "The L.A. police have sent a detective down here to talk to us." She waited for the murmurs to die down. "His name is Detective Maxwell and he's going to be conducting interviews this afternoon. So, starting with our batting order, would each of you please see the detective. He's sitting behind home plate. When you're done, join practice. And," she added as they began breaking up, "please tell him what he needs to know and do it as quickly as possible." She sighed as she watched them disperse. She looked forward to the day when this would all be over and they could get back to playing ball again.

"Maybe this will be the end of it," Gillian said under her breath.

"I don't know," Georgia shook her head. "He didn't seem like he was...excited. You know, like he was about to arrest the killer."

"Well, that's good, right? It means he's not here to put the cuffs on Jaden or anybody else."

"Jaden didn't kill that woman."

"We all know that," Gillian agreed. "We just need to convince him of that."

"I don't think it'll help her any. I mean, it won't get her job back. Don Sutter doesn't change his mind very often and he sure as hell doesn't like admitting he may have made a mistake."

"She'll end up playing for somebody else then." Gillian grimaced. "I don't look forward to that."

"Neither do I."

When it was Gillian's turn, she joined Detective Maxwell in the seats behind home plate. He was jotting something on a fresh sheet in his notebook. "You're Gillian Banks, correct?"

"Yes."

"What can you tell me about Jaden Hawke and Kendall Paxton?"

"Nothing. She didn't talk about her."

"Never?"

"Never."

"When you were in L.A. did you go to a bar called Lucille's after the game?"

"Yes."

"Was Jaden there?"

"Yes."

He refrained from sighing in frustration at her one-word answers. "Okay, why don't you tell me what happened from the time of the end of the game on."

"You want to know when and where I saw Jaden, right?"

"Yes."

"We all rode the bus back to the hotel. I left shortly after that for the bar."

"Were you alone?"

"No. Sloane went with me to the bar. Jaden hurt her arm in the game and she stayed behind to ice it down."

"So she was alone then?"

"Yes, for about an hour. Then she joined us at the bar."

"Do you know what time she left the bar?"

"No."

When he learned she had spent the night away from the hotel, he lost interest in her story.

"You should know that Jaden was in pain that night. She hurt her arm during the end of the game and was still in pain the next day." Gillian stood; ready to leave. "If Kendall Paxton was killed by anything that required strength, then you should look at someone else, because she couldn't have done much damage that night or even the next."

"Thank you, Ms Banks."

By the time he interviewed every player, they were well into practice. He stood up and caught the attention of Coach Tate. "I need to talk to someone named Sloane. Her name has been mentioned by several players."

"She's our photographer. I'll call her and see if she can join us." Georgia made her way to the dugout and her cell phone. She dialed Sloane's number in her office and she answered on the third ring. "Sloane, we have a Detective Maxwell from the L.A. Police Department here doing interviews. Can you come and talk with him?" She listened for a second before hanging up. She stepped up to the backstop and gave Detective Maxwell a thumbs up.

When Sloane came onto the field, Georgia pointed to the detective and she went to sit with him. "I'm Sloane Ellison."

"Ms Ellison, I'm Detective Maxwell from the Los Angeles Police Department."

"Yes, I know. Are you here to arrest Jaden?" She sounded relaxed but her stomach was in knots.

"That would depend on what information I get while I'm in town." He flipped to a new page in his notebook. "Tell me about the night after the game in L.A."

Sloane went through the time line of the evening, filling in the spaces left by Gillian's absence. She detested telling him about Jaden having a nightmare but she knew being awake in the middle of the night gave her a more complete alibi. Detective Maxwell made notes as she talked but didn't comment until she finished.

"Thank you, Ms Ellison. Can you think of anything else that might have any impact on this matter?"

"No. That's all I know. Except I know she didn't do it."

"I'll take that into consideration," he smiled kindly. "Can you tell me where she might be today? I haven't been able to interview her yet and she doesn't seem to be at practice."

"She doesn't play for Dallas anymore," Sloane told him with a bite to her voice. "They let her go when you guys had her taken into custody in Portland."

He pondered that a moment. "So, does anyone know where she is now?" He might have to re-think things if she'd fled.

"She's probably around town." Sloane would not tell him she was probably at her apartment, since that's where she'd left her that morning. "Do you want me to call her for you?"

"Yes, thank you."

160

Slone reached into her pocket and pulled out her cell phone. Jaden answered and Sloane filled her in on the situation. She closed the phone and turned back. "She'll be here soon. Can I get you something while you wait? A cold drink, maybe?"

"That would be great."

"Follow me then. We'll go back into the office and get out of the heat." She led him back upstairs and into her office. She introduced him to John and Stan and led him to a spare chair next to her work counter.

"What happened here?" he asked. "Are you doing some spring cleaning?"

"I wish that were true. A few days ago, I walked in on a burglary. They stole my cameras and drives and trashed almost everything else."

"I'm sorry to hear that. Do you have any idea who did it?"

"No. They knocked me out and I still don't remember anything about it."

"And all they got was your cameras and drives? That seems stupid."

"Those cameras were expensive! And I can't replace the photos."

"If you were going to commit a robbery why would you target this place?" he asked. "And why target this particular office and your particular work station?" He looked at her. "See what I mean?"

Sloane nodded slowly. "Yeah, I see what you mean. I guess." She frowned.

"How about that cold drink?"

"Oh yeah, sorry. Let's go into the break room and see what we have." She raised her voice. "John, Stan, when Jaden shows up would you please send her down to the break room?"

"Jaden's coming here?"

"Yes."

"Cool," Stan grinned.

Sloane led Detective Maxwell down to the kitchen and found him a soft drink in the refrigerator. She took one for herself and they sat at one of the small tables.

"Do you think she'll show?"

"Of course," Sloane answered.

"Why 'of course'?"

"She said she would."

He nodded but didn't say anything. He had no recourse. He didn't have an arrest warrant for her and couldn't force her to talk without her attorney present. He was in doubt that Jaden was guilty of murder anyway, but he needed to dot all the i's and cross all the t's. His investigation in L.A. turned up evidence that Kendall had been killed between three o'clock and four o'clock in the morning. It seemed at that time Sloane was with Jaden in their hotel room, talking about some dream she'd had. Alibis weren't all that great when it was just one other person giving it, but without proof Sloane was lying he had to accept it. However, several things just didn't add up either. He sipped his drink and regarded Sloane Ellison, a beautiful woman by anyone's standards. She had that come-hither look that was very alluring. She reminded him of a movie star in one of those old movies where the leading lady was beautiful but totally unattainable to the ordinary guy. He was thinking Ingrid Bergman in Casablanca when Jaden came through the door. Sloane smiled at her but her eyes never left Detective Maxwell. He stood as she approached and held out his hand. He couldn't have said why. Jaden hesitated but shook his hand in the end. He stood over six feet tall by several inches and she looked up into his eyes for a hint of what to expect. His face betrayed nothing. His brown eyes were clear and there was just a hint of upturn at the corners of his mouth. He was clean-shaven and his haircut was standard police issue—short. He waited until she took a chair before sitting down again. He knew she was gay but she was still a woman and his mother had taught him to use good manners. He sized her up during this silent interaction and had to admit he liked what he saw. She looked him straight in the eye and had a firm handshake. She gave the unmistakable impression that she was ready to meet him head on and to bring it. He detected no fear of him in her manner.

"Should I have my lawyer here?" she asked as she sat down.

"You're welcome to call him if you want but all I really want to do is fill in some blanks."

Jaden looked him in the eyes for a long moment before leaning back in her chair. "Okay. Go ahead."

He looked at Sloane. "I'd like to talk to her in private if I may."

"Of course." She got up and left without another word.

"Ms Hawke, I got a recounting of events on the night Ms Paxton died from all your teammates."

"Yes?"

"Now I'd like to hear what you have to say about it."

"What would you like to hear? The part where I didn't kill her or the part where someone is trying to frame me for it?"

"Why don't we start with what you did after the game until the next morning?"

Jaden blew out a big breath and her eyes lost focus as she remembered. She told him about hurting her arm at the end of the game, icing it down at the hotel and for how long, sitting at the bar with Gillian, going back to the hotel and going to bed, then waking up from a dream and getting sick, straight through the night omitting only what the dream was about.

He made notes as she told the story and knew hers matched pretty well with every other interview he'd conducted that afternoon. And he read her body language as telling the truth. He sighed internally. It left him with no suspect at all. "One thing bothers me about all this," he said as he closed his notebook.

"Only one thing?"

"Well, one thing in particular. If someone wanted Kendall Paxton dead why go to so much trouble to frame you for it?"

"I have no idea," Jaden shook her head. "We dated when I was in L.A.," she admitted. "Hell, the entire country knows about that, but she was into a lot of things back then. If you remember, she was busted for drugs at one of her famous parties. Maybe it has something to do with that."

"That was a long time ago," he said. "Why wait this long to kill her? Were you there that night?"

"No. I was long gone by then."

"I'll look up the report on it but unless you had something to do with it there probably isn't going to be any connection."

"I wasn't even in L.A. that night."

"But people might have assumed you were," he mused. "I seem to remember the listing of some famous names that were hauled in that night. Movie stars, rich and famous kids of political leaders in the state, the whole gamut of celebrities."

"Yeah," she nodded. She had read the tabloid accounts along with the rest of the country. "But I wasn't one of them."

"There might be some thinking you got out before they came in." He was baiting her and she knew it.

"Anything to keep a story going," she offered. "I wasn't there."

"Maybe," he agreed. "But still, what's the connection to you?"

"I don't know. It's been a long time since I've seen her so this doesn't make sense."

He sighed out loud this time. "That's just it. It really doesn't make any sense." He reached into his coat pocket and withdrew a manila envelope. He slid it across the table to her. "This is yours."

She upended the envelope and two cell phones clattered onto the table. The red one was hers, the other one was the one they had found in her equipment bag. She picked up the red one and flipped it open. The battery was dead. She had the service shut off when she bought her new phone, but she could at least retrieve some of the phone numbers she had stored in it. She was aware of the big detective watching her. She put the phone in her pocket before looking at him. "That one isn't mine."

"So you've said."

"It's the truth." She slid the large envelope under the phone and slid it back across the table in front of him. "Give it back to its owner...when you find him."

Coach Winslow interrupted them when he came into the break room. He stopped short when he saw them. His features hardened for just a second before he recovered. Jaden was surprised. She hadn't thought Coach Bob cared for her at all so his seeming anger at seeing her interviewed by Detective Maxwell was surprising, to say the least. He stood in the doorway for a moment, unsure what to do.

"Coach Winslow, this is Detective Maxwell from Los Angeles."

"Coach," Detective Maxwell nodded at him. Bob Winslow stared at him blankly. "I should interview you today. I've already talked to everybody else."

"Sure." He made no move and they all stared at one another for a moment.

"I'll bring him down to your office when we're done," Jaden finally said.

"Sure." Bob turned and left and Jaden and Detective Maxwell looked at each other.

"Is he normally like that?"

"You mean weird?" Jaden provided.

"Yes," he nodded. "He looked very unhappy to see me here."

"I don't really know him well. He hasn't exactly warmed up to me this season."

"Is he homophobic?"

"I've thought so but I'm not sure. He's never said or done anything and he's okay with others on the team, so I don't know what's going on. It doesn't matter now though."

"Yes, I've been told they released you from the team. I'm sorry about that. It seems unfair."

"Yes, it does," she agreed but her voice told him she was resigned to it.

"You can't change people's mind-set," he offered.

She nodded. "Can you tell me when Kendall was killed?"

"It'll be in the papers by the time I get back anyway. She died between three and four o'clock."

"How?"

"She was hit from behind by a two by four piece of lumber." He paused. "She probably never knew what happened."

"Where?"

"In the alley behind a bar called The Goose. She was found next to the dumpster. It was full of scrap lumber from a construction site down the block. We figure it was a crime of opportunity or maybe the killer just saw a different method and used it. We may never know."

"And a cell phone was there? Like this one?"

"Yes. It was in her hand."

Jaden looked at the table. "So it looked like her killer called to lure her out of the bar."

"Yes, except the only call on the phone was from this one." He lifted the cell phone from the envelope. "And the only thing this one was used for was to call that one." He waited for her to work it out.

"That would mean the killer wasn't very smart."

"Why do you say that?" He wanted to know how she thought.

"How do you explain the only calls on brand new phones, first of all? How would I get one of the phones to her? How would I be sure she'd have it with her and would answer it and why would I want to kill her anyway? Why now?"

"That's exactly why you aren't behind bars right now."

"I'd be pretty stupid to keep that phone, leave it in my own equipment bag, but wipe my fingerprints off it. I wouldn't have left the other phone with her either. Why? I could have just ditched both phones somewhere else."

"That was my thinking as well." He looked at her for another moment. "A lot of people knew you'd be in L.A. that night, but who would know you'd be out at a bar and thought you'd stay out all night? And most likely be without an alibi?"

"Jesus! Anybody could have thought that. I used to party hard back when I lived in LA. It wouldn't have been wrong to think I'd close a bar and keep going and maybe not have an alibi at all."

"There's something off here but I just can't put my finger on it."

"When are you leaving for L.A.?"

"Tonight. I'll make my report and we'll keep the case open, of course, but I'm at a dead-end right now. Her father is demanding an arrest and he's putting some pressure on the mayor."

"Try reminding him of all her past public mistakes and maybe he'll shut up," Jaden said. "He doesn't really want all that brought out again, no matter what he says. It's public image first with him." She sighed. "Do you still want to talk to Coach Winslow?"

"I might as well since I'm here. I've got time before my flight leaves tonight." They stood and started out of the room. "Tell me, do you think Sloane Ellison would have dinner with me?"

Jaden smiled back at him over her shoulder. "You can ask, but she actually plays for the other team, if you know what I mean."

"She's a lesbian?"

"Yes sir, she certainly is."

"Damn, she's so...enticing."

Jaden chuckled as they passed her office. Yes, that was exactly what Sloane was—enticing. "Yes, she is that." She stopped at the coach's office. "Detective Maxwell, it's been good talking to you. Have a safe trip." She offered him her hand.

"Thank you, Ms Hawke, and good luck to you."

Jaden left him there and went back to Sloane's office. John looked up when she entered. "She left a few minutes ago," he said. "She said she was getting a headache and wanted to lie down."

Jaden spun around with a wave of thanks and headed out. If Sloane was sick, she needed to be there with her. She drove as quickly as she dared and was soon knocking on her door. She was just about ready to knock again when she heard movement on the other side of the door. "Sloane, it's me." The lock was turned and Jaden pushed the door open. Sloane was pale and looked ready to fall down. Jaden put her arms around her and held her tight against her. "You should be in bed," she whispered in her ear.

"Is that a line?" She managed a weak laugh.

"No, I mean every word of it." Jaden bent and lifted her into her arms and carried her into the bedroom. The bed showed signs that Sloane had been there when Jaden knocked on her door. She placed her tenderly on the bed. "I'm sorry I made you get up. John told me you weren't feeling well and I wanted to check on you."

"S'okay," Sloane mumbled. Her eyes were already closed and she had a palm against her head. It was obvious she was in pain.

"Can I get you anything?" she whispered. She knew that with a headache like this, sound was greatly enhanced.

"No."

"I'm going to stay here for a while, okay? I'll make sure no one interrupts you again."

"'Kay."

Jaden eased out of the bedroom and closed the door softly behind her. It worried her that Sloane was having such a bad headache again. She wondered if she should call the doctor. She hated that Sloane was in such pain and she wasn't able to help her. She noticed Sloane's laptop computer on the coffee table and opened it. She'd do a little research while Sloane slept.

She found that having continued occasional headaches was common with a concussion and the knot in her stomach finally eased up. She got up to check on Sloane and found her asleep so she returned to her computer. She checked the bookmark file, found the one for the team, and pulled up the site.

Sloane had done a good job. The page was very professional and Jaden smiled with pride. She clicked through several pages. Sloane hadn't been able to update the site since her concussion and Jaden's name and photo were still listed. She stared at it for a long moment. She had liked being part of the team. She'd made friends and had thought that maybe she'd gotten past the whole California thing finally. She had been looking forward to the season and hoping she could help Dallas make it to the finals this year. She closed the site. No use in thinking about that now.

She needed to start thinking about what to do for her future. Where could she play? Would any team even want her now? Did she want to play somewhere else? The thought of leaving Sloane was unbearable. Without conscious thought, her heart had given itself to Sloane already. How had this happened so quickly? It scared her to death. She knew first-hand what could happen when you let your heart make decisions. She never wanted to go through that again. She resolutely typed in the URL for the team in Denver. Maybe she'd like cooler temperatures and thinner air. It was beautiful in Denver she knew. She checked out the names, numbers, and E-mail addresses of the owners as well as the coaching staff.

She did a copy and paste, and sent it to her own E-mail address. Then she did the same for the teams in San Antonio and Houston. Finally, just in case everything went to hell, she got the pertinent information for the team in Chicago. Chicago was at least a thousand miles away. If Sloane made it clear she wasn't interested in anything long term, a thousand miles might be enough distance between them. She hoped. She shut down the computer and went into the kitchen for a cold drink.

Thinking about the future was making her restless and edgy. Maybe she should just call her agent and tell him to find her a spot somewhere. He had already called her about that but with everything still up in the air about Kendall's death neither one of them had thought it was a good time to pursue it, but maybe now it was time. Detective Maxwell had all but told her she was no longer a suspect. Maybe that would open some doors. She gulped more of the soft drink and leaned against the kitchen counter, head down, thinking. She jumped when the phone rang. Sloane's cell phone was on the kitchen table. She debated answering it but it went to voice mail before she could make a decision. She picked it up and read the number. It wasn't one she recognized. *Don't be stupid*, she told herself. Sloane knew a lot of people. She put the phone down again just as the doorbell rang. She hastened to the door before it rang again. It was Gillian and Jaden opened the door to let her in.

"Hey, Gilly. Sloane's sleeping."

"Sleeping?" Gillian looked at her with a knowing smile.

"Not that," Jaden told her quickly. "She has another headache."

"Is it serious?" she asked anxiously. "Should we take her to the doctor?"

"No. She'll have these for a week or so. It's natural. She went to work today and probably overdid it."

"Yeah, I saw her talking to the cop from L.A." Gillian helped herself to a soft drink from the refrigerator and they settled at the kitchen table.

"Did he talk to everybody?"

"Yep. He'll probably want to see you too, I'm sure."

"I've already had my turn," Jaden told her. "Sloane called and told me to come to the stadium unless I wanted him knocking on my door. I left him with Coach. John said Sloane left with a headache and I came over here to make sure she was okay."

"So what did he say to you?"

"He agreed that I would have had to be supremely stupid to have killed her and left the clues that were there."

"Does that mean you're off the hook?"

"Yeah, pretty much so," she smiled.

Gillian's whole body relaxed and she laughed in relief. "That's great!"

"You didn't think I did it, did you?"

"No," she grinned. "But that doesn't mean they weren't going to arrest you!"

"Yeah, I was worried about that too," she agreed.

"When are you coming back to work?"

"Uh, I don't think it's going to work like that, Gilly."

"You don't think they'll want you back?"

"It's going to be up to Don Sutter. He's the one who cut me and he's the one who'll have to renew my contract."

"And he won't want to admit he jumped the gun," Gillian was nodding.

"That, plus it's still out there that I was the original prime suspect. If they don't find the killer, people will suspect I'm guilty and they just couldn't prove it. Bottom line, my presence on the field means a drop in the gate receipts."

"The bottom line rules."

"Amen," Sloane said from the doorway.

They both looked her way and they both smiled. Jaden looked into her eyes and was relieved to find them clear. She stood and held out a chair for her. "Can I get you something to drink?"

"Thank you." She kissed her on the cheek and sat down. "Ice tea would be nice." She looked at Gillian as she sat down. "Hey, Gilly."

"How are you feeling?"

"I'm much better now. I just needed a little nap." Jaden set a glass of tea in front of her and resumed her seat at the table. "How was your talk with Detective Maxwell?"

"Mine was kind of short," Gillian offered. "All I could tell him was when I saw her at the bar. Then I had to confess I stayed out all night."

Sloane raised an eyebrow. "Oh yes, now that you mention it, with whom did you spend the night, Gilly? Give us the details."

Gillian grinned but looked away. "It was nothing. We just went dancing at another bar and then she took me to a party she knew about."

"It must have been some great party," Sloane said casually, "because, if I remember correctly, your shirt was inside out when you got back to the room."

Jaden burst out laughing as Gillian turned a nice shade of pink. "Busted!"

"Look who's talking," she muttered, trying to deflect the attention away from herself.

"What was her name, Gilly?" Jaden grinned.

"Susan." Gillian couldn't keep from smiling at the memory.

"Was she the brunette or the blonde?"

"She was definitely a blonde," Gillian laughed.

"A natural one, I take it?" Sloane dug deeper.

"Oh yes, most definitely a natural," Gillian agreed. "And that's all I'm going to say so stop asking."

Sloane squeezed her hand across the table. "We didn't expect you to reveal anything more than that, honey. I hope you had a good time."

"Of course she had a good time," Jaden snorted. "Her shirt was on inside out!"

"And who was holding whom in bed when I got back to our room?" Gillian turned the tables on her.

"Enough!" Sloane laughed. "That's the end of it. But, just for the record, nothing happened with us that night."

"Yeah, but..."

"That's it. No more. Let's move on to something else."

"Are you hungry?" Jaden asked. "I could go get us something to eat." Her tone was warm and caring, as always when dealing with Sloane. It suffused Sloane with a glow and calmed her very soul.

"I could eat something," she admitted. "How about it, Gilly? Hungry?"

"Sure. I can always eat. What are we having?"

"Pizza? Chinese? Mexican?"

"Oh, Mexican sounds good," Sloane smiled. "Let's have that."

"Mexican food coming up," Jaden nodded. "What does everybody want?"

Chapter 15

"Why don't you get ready for bed? I'll clean up the kitchen," Jaden offered. Gillian was gone and it was late.

"I'll help."

"No, I'll do it," she insisted. "Go on to bed."

"Jaden?"

"Yes?"

"Will you stay with me tonight?"

"Sure I will."

"I'll be waiting for you then."

"Go on to sleep. I'll be here. I promise."

Sloane put her arms around her from behind and kissed her on the neck. It sent the now familiar electric shock down Jaden's spine. "I'll sleep when you're beside me."

"I'll be right there," Jaden promised. She cleaned up their take out dinner, assembled the coffee pot and set the timer for the morning perk. She went through the apartment checking that the door was locked and turning off lights. She was quiet when she entered the bedroom but Sloane was not asleep. She was in bed but the small light on the bedside table was on. "You should be asleep."

"I'm not sleepy," she smiled from under the covers.

Jaden sat on the edge of the bed and ran the back of her hand along her cheek softly. "How do you feel?"

"I'm fine," she insisted. "Why don't you get out of your clothes and get in here?"

"Slone, you're still suffering from a concussion. You need your rest."

"I can't rest until you're beside me." It was a plea.

"I'll be back in a second. Just let me brush my teeth first." She returned from the bathroom wearing a tee shirt and boxers and got into bed next to Sloane. Sloane turned into her immediately and Jaden realized she was naked under the covers. When Sloane kissed her, Jaden, as always, melted into her. She felt Sloane's hands burn a path under her shirt up her stomach to cup her breasts. She tore her lips away, gasping for air. "Damn it, Sloane." She trapped her hands against her body and stopped her. "Please stop."

"Stop? Oh no, baby, there's no stopping."

"Sloane," Jaden warned. She held both of Sloane's hands in hers. "You need to rest tonight."

"I had a power nap this afternoon." Sloane quit struggling to free her hands and kissed her instead. In seconds, Sloane was sliding on top of her. They broke apart for air only to come together again immediately. Sloane pulled Jaden's tongue into her mouth deeply then expelled it only to suck it back inside. Her hips began a similar motion and soon they were rocking together. Sloane stopped finally, gasping for breath. "Baby, I need to feel your skin against me." She pulled at Jaden's clothing and when Jaden was naked, she turned them so she was on top. Jaden took over and slowed things down a bit. Her hips rolled against Sloane's center and she groaned into her mouth. She tore free and covered Sloane's breast, sucking as much as she could before allowing it to slide out until only the rock hard nipple was captured. She sucked it hard. She bit it. She pulled on it and it was driving Sloane crazy. She had her hands buried in Jaden's hair, holding her to her breast while she arched her back into it.

"Jesus, Jaden! I need you inside me. Please."

Jaden shifted and ran a hand down her stomach. She could feel Sloane's muscles jump and quiver under her fingers. She slowed to a stop at the moist curls between her legs. Sloane whimpered like Jaden knew she would. She sucked harder on her nipple to distract her and the whimper turned into a gasp. Jaden turned her attention to Sloane's other breast and let her fingers brush through the curls and along her slick folds, parting the lips and freeing the pool of desire to coat everything. Sloane jerked and lifted her hips. Jaden moved a caressing hand along the inside of her thigh. Sloane groaned again and her hands in Jaden's hair tightened almost painfully. She returned to Sloane's center and rubbed over the bundle of nerves that were straining for her touch. Sloane's knee jerked up and her pelvis pumped against her thumb. Jaden backed off and let her fingers slide through the folds, up and down, coating her fingers. She positioned her fingers against Sloane's opening and bit down on her nipple at the same moment she entered her and drove deep inside.

Sloane's cry was loud and torn from her lips without conscious thought. She couldn't breathe. She couldn't think. She could only feel.

Jaden drove deep again while pulling hard on her nipple. She was frantic to possess this woman, all rational thought wiped out by her own need. She continued to pound into her and suck on her breast, the pace increasing as she demanded more and more of her.

Sloane was higher than she'd ever been; her body tight as a bowstring. She was shaking and jerking as her orgasm continued to build, sending fiery streaks of need up through her legs to her core.

Jaden dropped her other hand between her legs and manipulated her clit with her thumb. It only took two strokes before Sloane flew over the edge and into the universe filled with stars and darkness. Jaden let up on her clit but continued to stroke into her as the violent spasms claimed her fingers again and again. She lost count of how many waves crashed over Sloane before she was done. Jaden stilled her hand and gave the breast under her mouth gentle licks and kisses as she waited. Sloane's head was back, eyes closed, mouth slack as she slowly came down. It took a long time. She planted one last kiss against the still erect nipple and sat up. Sloane didn't move. Jaden's fingers were still buried deep inside her and she very slowly inched out, earning a small moan from Sloane's lips and a jerk of her leg. Jaden loathed to be disconnected from her but finally did extract completely and moved up to lie beside her, gathering her in her arms. Sloane was limp, boneless in her lassitude. When she realized Sloane was asleep, she dropped a light kiss on her head and eased out of bed.

In the harsh light of the bathroom, she suddenly realized how out of control she'd been. It caused a shot of fear to race through her. What had gotten into her? She had felt a crazy need to possess her completely. She'd wanted to fuck Sloane, to take her and make her beg for more. Only when Kendall was at her wildest did she so totally lose it like that. Gillian's story about how Sloane's ex-lover had treated her in bed came back to haunt her. She could not bear the thought she might be guilty of the same offense. Tears of shame pooled behind her eyes. She pulled on her boxer shorts and searched for her tee shirt. She must have dropped it on her way into the bathroom. She found it next to the bed and sat down to pull it over her head.

"Baby?" Sloane's voice was soft and sleepy and it made her jerk.

"Go back to sleep, honey," she whispered. She felt Sloane's hand on her back.

"Baby?" she said again.

Jaden steeled herself and turned to face her. Sloane's face was slack with satisfaction and sleep. She was so beautiful it took her breath away. "Go back to sleep, honey," she repeated.

"No." Sloane caressed her softly. "Jaden?"

Jaden turned back to face her again. "Sloane, I'm..." Sorry seemed so inadequate and she searched for some word that would convey the depth of her feelings.

"Come here," Sloane commanded, her voice getting stronger now as she woke.

Jaden looked for any possible way out but found nothing to save her. She leaned up the bed and Sloane circled her arms around her neck and pulled her down on top of her.

"Honey," Jaden protested.

"What?" Sloane kissed the crook of Jaden's neck and sucked the soft skin into her mouth. "I love the way you taste."

"Honey," she tried again. "I'm sorry."

"No, baby, I'm sorry." She moved her lips over Jaden's shoulder, kissing and nipping. "I'm sorry I fell asleep." She let her teeth scrape across her shoulder. "I plan on

making it up to you though. I promise it'll be worth it."
She hooked her thumbs under the waistband of her boxer
shorts. "Why are you wearing these again?"

"Sloane please let me apologize for what I just did to
you."

"Apologize?" Sloane's head snapped up, "for what?"

"I...lost control. I'm so sorry." Jaden couldn't look her
in the eye. "I'll never hurt you again," she promised.

Sloane stared at her wide-eyed. "What are you talking
about?"

"I totally lost control," Jaden said again. Her voice was
full of anguish. "I just wanted to fuck you."

Sloane pulled her down against her and locked her
arms around her. "Oh baby, you're so wrong. I don't know
where this is coming from but you're wrong. I loved what
you did to me. I wanted it, baby. I love that you lost
control." She kissed her mouth hard. "Please don't be
sorry."

"But I thought..."

"You thought what?" she demanded. "You thought
you were hurting me because I was screaming your
name? And when I had multiple orgasms you thought I
was in pain?" Sloane's mouth turned soft and she
caressed the back of Jaden's head. "Oh baby, that was the
most satisfying sex I think I've ever had." She kissed her
softly before pushing her away a little. "I have a
confession to make."

"What?"

"Sometimes I get out of control too. Tonight was one
of those times." She smiled up at her. "It worked out
great that the night you want to fuck my brains out
happens to be the night I wanted you to do just that."

Jaden searched her face but found nothing to contradict her words. "You're not just saying that, are you?"

"If I didn't like it I would have stopped you."

"Would you have been able to?"

"Yes," she nodded. "I've learned how to take care of myself." She looked into Jaden's eyes. "Who told you?" Her voice was suddenly flat. Jaden started to shake her head in denial but Sloane stopped her with a finger to her lips. "Gillian is the only one who could have told you so don't bother to deny it."

Jaden slid to the side and sat up. Next to her Sloane did the same. "Okay, so Gilly told me a little about your...ex."

"She had no right to do that," Sloane said with a bite to her voice. "When did she tell you?"

"While you were in the hospital. She was, ah, concerned that we were sleeping together."

"So she thought she could scare you off with a story about how an ex-girlfriend roughed me up?"

"I don't think she wanted to scare me off." Jaden chanced taking Sloane's hand in hers. "She's just concerned about you. She's afraid I'll hurt you in some way." She rubbed the back of Sloane's hand. "And tonight it hit me that maybe she was right. I've never...been like that with anyone before, except Kendall, but you're nothing like her."

Sloane curled her fingers into Jaden's hand. "She had no right," she repeated. "I love her, but she shouldn't have told you something like that." She sighed. "The truth is, I like sex and sometimes I like it fast and hard like tonight." She ran her free hand up and down Jaden's arm. "There is a huge difference between rough sex and abusive sex though."

"I promised Gillian I wouldn't hurt you," Jaden whispered.

"You aren't capable of being abusive, Jaden. It just isn't in you." She turned into Jaden's shoulder. "Tonight was fantastic, babe. Please don't ever hold yourself back." She kissed her collarbone. "And for future reference, wanting to fuck me is a good thing."

Jaden lifted her arm and put it around her shoulders, drawing her closer. "Are you going to rat me out to Gillian?"

"Not if you don't want me to. I should though. She makes me so mad sometimes."

"You can't blame her," Jaden said and kissed the top of her head. "We have been moving kind of fast. At least it probably seems that way to her."

"Why wait?" she countered. "If you see something you want you should go after it, right?"

Jaden laughed. Her heart was light once again, the shadows gone from her soul. Sloane still wanted her in her life. "Sloane," she murmured. "You are so wonderful."

"Ah babe, how is it you know exactly the right thing to say?"

Because I love you, jumped to Jaden's lips, but she held the thought. It was too soon for that. "It's easy with you," she said instead.

Sloane wasn't listening. She turned into Jaden and while one hand squeezed and fondled one breast, her mouth covered the other one. "Come on, babe, lie down—but get naked first."

Jaden pushed herself down on the bed until she was flat. Sloane followed and straddled her hips. Jaden couldn't take her eyes off Sloane's breasts just inches above her. Sloane leaned forward slightly, teasing her. "You are definitely a breast woman," she laughed. Jaden hopefully opened her mouth and let her tongue rim her lower lip. "Oh, no you don't," Sloane shook her head. "Once you get your mouth on me I'll lose your interest in anything else." She rocked her hips against her. "And while I love having your mouth on me, I want to taste you this time. I want to make you feel as great as you just made me feel." She leaned forward and kissed Jaden softly. She had learned Jaden loved to kiss. The kiss lasted until neither one of them could breathe. And as they kissed, their bodies began surging against each other.

"Oh, baby, I love how you feel against me." Sloane cupped Jaden's breasts in her palms, her thumb and forefingers rolling her nipples into hard points of need. Jaden's pelvis lifted to make contact with her and she leaned back to enhance the friction, making Jaden grunt. Sloane shifted to the side and placed a thigh against Jaden's sex urging her to use her leg for her pleasure while she watched her face transform into a mask of want and need. Jaden was breathing hard now and Sloane leaned forward to put her mouth on her breast, flicking the nipple with her tongue. Jaden's thrusts against her leg became faster and more frantic and Sloane quickly pulled away from her.

"Sloane," Jaden gasped.

"Not so fast, baby," she murmured. "I want this to last a little longer." She continued her attention to Jaden's breast and let a hand roam over her flat, hard stomach. Her hand drifted closer and closer to the tangle of moist hair between her legs. She lifted her head from her breast and looked into Jaden's eyes. "You okay, baby?"

"Yes," she gulped. She was struggling to maintain, as she knew Sloane wanted her to.

"I love the way your skin feels under my hands. So soft." She caressed a hand over her hip and up her side.

She watched Jaden swallow hard and smiled. "Do you want me to touch you now, baby?"

"Yes. Please."

"Do you know how much I love to touch you?" Sloane's voice was breathy. She slid a hand back down her side and across her stomach before finally dipping into the wetness waiting for her. Jaden hissed above her. "You're so wet. I love how you get waiting for me." She slid a finger on either side of her clit and pumped a few times before leaving it for her opening. Above her Jaden clenched her jaw. Sloane slid down her body until she was between her legs. She opened her up and ran the flat of her tongue up through her slick folds. Jaden groaned. "You taste so good." Sloane flicked a pointed tongue over her clit and Jaden's hips jerked. Sloane lifted her head to see Jaden's fists clutching the sheet and her neck taut with strain. She entered her and began a slow in and out, savoring the sound, smell, and feel of her. "Oh baby," she whispered, "I love being inside you." She kept up the rhythm but raised her body so she could kiss Jaden's belly. Her skin was so soft and Sloane continued to brush her lips over her, kissing and nuzzling. Soon she felt Jaden's muscles tighten and looked up at her face. "Babe, don't come yet." She slowed the pace and backed off a bit. Jaden groaned above her in frustration. "Look at me, Jaden." She finally did but it was with effort. "Hold off if you can." Jaden whimpered this time. Sloane increased the speed and pressure again but slid down between her legs. She could feel Jaden tense and begin to strain.

"I'm...so close," Jaden panted, her voice pleading.

"Come for me then, baby. Come in my mouth." Sloane captured Jaden's clit between her lips and sucked hard, using her tongue to push her over the edge.

Jaden's climax hit her with the force of a tidal wave. She lost all thought as well as her breath. Her entire existence was reduced to the sensations between her legs. She was unaware she was shaking still, minutes after the wave hit. She didn't know she was babbling incoherent words. She couldn't know what a jumble of raw nerves she had been reduced to. She couldn't hear, see, or think anything for many minutes. The first thing she felt when she became aware of her own existence again was Sloane's breast beneath her head. Then she felt Sloane stroking her back, soft and soothing. She drew in a deep, shuddering breath.

"Baby," Sloane whispered above her and pressed lips to her forehead.

"Uh."

"Mmmm." Sloane smiled and rested her cheek against the top of Jaden's head. "Are you okay?"

"Uh."

Chapter 16

Jaden sat alone in the outfield bleachers watching the Dallas Metros beat the Ohio Cougars by one run. It was the bottom of the fifth inning. She was anonymous here, just one more fan among hundreds. She was still ducking the inquisitive press. The news that Jaden was no longer a suspect in Kendall Paxton's death was reported in the L.A. papers and picked up by the one in Dallas. Why they wanted to talk to her now she had no idea. What could she say except I told you so?

She caught sight of Sloane roaming the sidelines taking candid shots of everyone. She had rented a camera until she could get her equipment replaced. She smiled. She was so beautiful. By the seventh inning, Dallas was leading by three runs and Sloane had worked her way around to the visitor's dugout. It wasn't long before Jaden saw one of the Ohio players chatting her up. Her stomach clenched. She didn't like it and had to restrain herself from standing and making her way down to the dugout. *You don't have exclusive rights to her*, she told herself.

She's free to do whatever she wants. She clamped her jaw shut and stared across the field at them, chatting and laughing. She didn't see the end of the game. In fact, she didn't see anything else until Sloane moved away from the opposing dugout and the too friendly player. She tried to relax her shoulders and neck and took a few deep breaths. She realized the game was over only when everyone around her stood and started leaving. She mixed with the crowd as they headed for one of the exits. She was almost out when her phone rang. She smiled when Sloane's number showed up on the read out. "Hello?"

"Hey."

"Hey yourself." Jaden could hear the smile in Sloane's voice and her heart lifted.

"Would you like to meet me at Sally's for a drink?"

"Sure."

"Great. The game is over and I'll leave as soon as I can."

"I'll be waiting."

Jaden was on a stool at the end of the bar when she saw Sloane walk in. She glanced around the room before catching sight of her and Jaden took the opportunity to watch her. There was just something about her that got to Jaden. She felt something in her very core. Sloane threaded her way through the crowd to her. Jaden wasn't certain what to expect but Sloane put an arm around her neck and reached up to kiss her.

"Hello."

Jaden smiled and drew her closer. "Hi. How is your head tonight?"

"I'm fine." Sloane rolled her eyes but smiled. "I could use a drink though."

Jaden raised a hand to the bartender and soon a fresh drink was placed in front of Sloane on the stool next to hers.

"We won tonight—against Ohio."

"I know," Jaden nodded.

"Were you there?" Sloane asked in surprise.

"Yeah, I snuck into the outfield. They played well tonight."

"They did," she agreed.

"Where was Coach Winslow tonight? I noticed Ellen Stewart coaching first base."

"I'm not really sure. I heard he had a family emergency. He's been gone ever since that cop from L.A. was here."

"I didn't know he had any family."

"He's never said much but I know he has a daughter. He doesn't talk about a wife though so I'm guessing she's an ex."

"He's an odd duck," Jaden mused.

"That he is," she agreed. She let a hand drop to Jaden's thigh. "Will you go with me to a bar-b-que tomorrow?"

Jaden was startled at the abrupt change of subject. "Uh, I guess."

"You guess?"

"What's going on?"

"Georgia is having some people over tomorrow."

"As in Georgia Tate? Coach Tate?"

"Yes." Sloane rubbed along her thigh. "We're just going to cook out and have a few beers. Will you come with me?"

Jaden looked at her but her mind was on the hand on her thigh. "Why do you seem nervous about asking me?"

she asked after finally wrenching her mind away from her leg.

"Well, it is Coach Tate. I wasn't sure you would want to socialize with her."

Jaden pondered that a moment. "Okay. I'll go with you."

"Are you sure?"

"Does she know you're bringing me?"

"Yes. I told her as soon as she invited me and said to bring a date."

"And what did she say to that?"

"She was glad," Sloane assured her. "I think she would like to see you."

"I'm sure we can find something to talk about," Jaden nodded.

Sloane gave her a look. "You're going to be nice, aren't you?"

Jaden laughed. "Yes, I'll be nice." She sipped her beer. "I saw you taking pictures tonight. How is the camera working out?"

"It's a great camera! I'll hate having to give it up. I'll be able to get a really good one but I rented the best and I'm already spoiled."

"Did you get some good photos of the Ohio team tonight?" Jaden tried to keep her voice casual.

"Yes," Sloane answered in a tone that told her she hadn't been casual enough. "Did you want to see them?"

"No," Jaden shook her head.

"Then what?"

"I just thought one of them might have caught your eye."

Sloane sipped her beer and looked steadily at her. "That's what you thought, huh?"

"Well," she hedged. She was definitely feeling stupid and foolish now. "It looked like maybe that was what was happening."

"So you were watching me talking to the Ohio players."

"Well, uh, yeah. I guess so."

Sloane's hand was back on her thigh and now it went higher and closer to the vee between her legs. Jaden held her breath. "And you thought maybe I was what? I was arranging to meet her later? I was getting her number? What were you thinking, Jaden?" She moved her hand to trace the inseam of her jeans.

"I was..." She lost focus as Sloane's hand rubbed against the center seam of her pants. She unconsciously pushed forward against her.

Sloane took pity on her and withdrew her hand to put it back on the bar. Beside her Jaden released a breath a bit shakily. "You were what?"

Jaden was still unfocused. "What?"

Sloane shook her head but was secretly pleased that Jaden was both jealous and easily aroused by her touch. She took a drink and smiled.

Jaden regained control of her mind and touched Sloane's hand on top of the bar. "I'm sorry if I sounded jealous."

"You're forgiven."

"Hello Sloane."

Sloane jerked around on her stool and Jaden looked up in surprise. A short, stocky woman with spiky hair stood next to Sloane, a smile on her lips that didn't quite reach her eyes. Jaden took an instant dislike to her and her impression was confirmed as she felt Sloane stiffen.

"What do you want?" she asked harshly.

"I just wanted to say hello."

"Now say goodbye."

"Aw come on, Sloane. I don't want anything except to be friends."

"No." Sloane was forceful in her denial.

"I've changed. I've been to anger management classes and I'm better now." Her voice was soft and easy. She looked across to where Jaden sat and something unpleasant flickered in her eyes and then was gone. "Aren't you going to introduce me to your friend?"

"No. Go away and don't come near me again. I swear I'll get another restraining order against you."

"For what?" She feigned hurt. "I haven't done anything. I'm just trying to make amends, that's all."

"Hell, a TRO ain't anything," Jaden snorted a harsh bark of a laugh. "I'm suspected of murder in California." She guzzled some beer. "They got to prove it first though and I got this little place down in Mexico where no one will ever find me." She gave her an evil grin. "I'm just killing time until they decide to come for me." She guzzled the last of the beer and thunked the bottle down on the bar hard. "What jail you been in?"

"County."

Jaden snorted, shook her head derisively and turned back to the bar, dismissing her. Sloane took her cue and she also turned away, leaving her ex-lover, Kerry, standing alone and feeling small. When Jaden draped an arm over Sloane's shoulder possessively and let her hand cup her breast she left.

"I think she got the message," Sloane said a few minutes later.

"I know. I saw her leave through the back door." Sloane turned to her and raised a brow. "Well, I was enjoying the, uh."

"My breast in your hand?"

Jaden laughed. "Yeah." She removed her arm and bumped Sloane's shoulder with her own. "I'm going to assume that was your ex-lover unless you have multiple restraining orders out there."

"That was her," she nodded. Then she began laughing, deep belly laughs that shook her whole body and threatened to overwhelm her. Jaden joined in and soon they were both helpless. Eventually the laughter trailed off and finally subsided into just an occasional giggle.

The bartender put two beers in front of them with a big grin. "On the house, ladies. I like to see people having a good time. It's good for business."

"Thank you." Jaden made a mental note to leave him a big tip when they left. She tipped her bottle to clink against Sloane's. "Here's to ex-lovers."

"Hear, hear," she giggled and looked away quickly before it got out of hand again.

"Hey guys." Gillian slid onto the stool next to Sloane.

"Hi Gilly," Jaden greeted her while Sloane kissed her on the cheek.

"What's going on? Anything happening in here tonight?"

They both started laughing again. "You just missed it," Sloane said. "Kerry just left a minute ago."

"What? I didn't know she was out of jail yet."

"She is," Sloane nodded.

"What did she do?" Gillian was ready to go after her.

"Calm down, Gilly. She's gone and I don't think she'll be back."

"Why? What happened?"

"Jaden put her in her place," Sloane said with pride. She took Jaden's hand and put them both on top of her thigh. "She thought she was tough until Jaden informed her she was a murder suspect and let her know she was a very small fish in a very big pond."

Gillian looked past her to Jaden. "Who would have thought being a suspect in a murder would come in handy."

"You use whatever tools are at your disposal," Jaden shrugged.

"I must say, you sure seem to live in interesting times."

"Yeah, unfortunately, I do."

"We beat Ohio tonight," she told her. "I only wish you were sitting on the bench beside me. Or better yet, out on the mound."

"I was there—watching."

"Oh man, that must really suck," Gillian shook her head.

"Yeah, well," Jaden shrugged.

"Who are you taking to the cook out tomorrow, Gilly?" Sloan asked to change the subject.

"I asked Pam if she wanted to go with me."

"Who's Pam?"

"She's a hottie I met a few weeks ago," Gillian laughed. "She was down at the Rawhide bar one night and we started talking."

"How hot is she?" Jaden asked, then, "Ow!" as Sloane's elbow connected with her ribs. "What I meant was that I hope you have a good time."

Gillian laughed at her discomfort and got a glimpse of the easy dynamic they shared. Maybe they were good for each other after all. She was about to say so when a hand slid over her shoulder and a breath blew over her ear. She turned to find a petite redhead behind her. "You made it!" Gillian took her hand and brought her around beside her. "Sloane, Jaden, this is Pam Daniels. Pam, the beautiful one is Sloane and the ugly duckling beside her is Jaden."

"Hey," Jaden protested but grinned and held out her hand to Pam. "Nice to meet you."

"Nice to meet both of you," she smiled. "Do you play ball with Gillian?"

"No," Jaden answered before anyone could fumble for an explanation.

"I'm the team photographer and web master," Sloane told her.

Gillian had ordered drinks and when they arrived, she handed one to Pam and said, "Let's see if we can get a booth."

The four of them settled into a booth along the wall and Sloane leaned against Jaden's side, her hand on her thigh once again. They spent a couple of hours talking and getting to know their new friend. Jaden finally asked Sloane to dance when the DJ played a slower tune. They smiled at each other as Jaden gathered her into her arms and they began to sway to the music as naturally as if they'd been dance partners for years.

"I like Pam," Sloane said into Jaden's ear as they circled the floor. "Don't you?"

"Yeah. Gilly seems to really like her." She brushed her lips over Sloane's ear and felt her react with a slight tremble. She smiled to herself. "Of course it's Gilly so I wouldn't get too attached to her yet."

"I don't know. I think this one is different somehow."

"Yeah?" Jaden wasn't interested in Pam at the moment, because holding Sloane in her arms was taking up all her attention. She was slim but Jaden could feel the muscles in her back and shoulders. She was strong from the constant hauling of all her equipment and from hours of holding a camera at the ready for that one instant opportunity for the perfect shot. She knew from experience that Sloane had strong legs. In fact, she had wonderful legs, but her breasts were the crowning attribute that made everything else come together in a beautiful body. At least as far as Jaden was concerned. Sloane was right when she'd said Jaden was a breast woman. She felt Sloane's breasts now pressing into her own chest. She shifted her body slightly and savored the feel of them rubbing against her. Sloane had her arms around her and Jaden could feel her fingers brushing through the soft strands of dark hair on the back of her neck. It was a sensual touch and Jaden's breathing sped up a little. "Uh, Sloane?"

"Yes baby." Sloane pulled back in the circle of her arms and gave her a slow, knowing smile. "What do you need?"

"Can we go soon?"

"We can go whenever you'd like." Sloane pushed her pelvis against Jaden and watched her eyes. The eyes always gave her away. "Are you ready now?"

"Oh yeah, I'm ready," Jaden managed in a rush.

"Good, because so am I." She took Jaden's hand and led her from the dance floor back to their booth. "We're going to take off, kids. Have a good time and we'll see you both tomorrow at Georgia's."

"See you there," Gillian nodded.

Jaden and Sloane stopped short in the parking lot, both of them having forgotten they'd arrived separately. Sloane laughed when she saw the look on Jaden's face. She pulled her next to her car and leaned her back against the door. She kissed her softly and ran a hand down to trace the contour of her leg when it joined her body. Jaden made a noise that was meant only for her ears.

"Let's see," Sloane mused as her hand continued its exploration. "We can leave one car here and get it tomorrow or we can each go to our own apartments." Jaden grunted at that suggestion as Sloane knew she would. "Okay, then one of us get some clothes from their own apartment and meet the other one. How does that sound?"

"Okay," Jaden managed to get out as she felt Sloane's hand slide between her legs.

"I'll go home and you go get your stuff and meet me there. Okay?" She pushed against the center seam of Jaden's jeans and then cupped her. "This is just in case you forget why you're going through all this trouble. You know, in case you change your mind about staying with me and stand me up tonight."

"No, no way," she gulped. She just barely managed to keep her hips from jerking into Sloane's hand.

Georgia Tate lived in an upscale neighborhood in north Dallas amid tall oak trees and quiet streets. It was a two-story brick on a large wooded lot with a pool. They could hear splashing and yelling before they even got to the front door. They rang the bell and a good-looking woman opened it. She was Sloane's height but carried more weight. It looked good on her. She had dark brown hair done up in a French twist at the back of her head and eyes that were the same color. She had a smile on her face and looked like it was probably always at the ready. She threw her arms around Sloane and gave her a hug. When they parted she turned to Jaden. "And you must be the famous Jaden Hawke." She hugged her too and Jaden felt herself being squeezed as if they were old friends. "I'm Mallory Wendt."

"Infamous would probably be more like it," she murmured when the woman let her go. "Nice to meet you, Mallory. Thanks for inviting me." Jaden was glad Sloane had told her all about Georgia and Mallory on the trip over.

"Come on in. The rest of them are out in the pool." She led them inside and Jaden took a moment to take in the beautifully decorated foyer as they passed through the house and entered the kitchen. It positively gleamed with care and she knew someone in the house liked to cook. She set the bag of groceries she'd carried in on the granite island and sniffed.

"Something smells wonderful."

"Thank you. I'm just making something for dessert. You didn't have to bring anything, you know. Didn't Georgia tell you that?" She shot a look at Sloane.

"Yes, but Jaden made me bring some things anyway."

"You can't just show up at a house party empty handed," Jaden protested, "Especially if you've never been there before. I wanted to make a good impression on the host." She smiled and Sloane saw Mallory succumb to Jaden's charm. "And maybe she'll let me have a second helping of the fabulous dessert she's making."

Mallory took Jaden's arm. "We'll see about that," she said with a smile. "Why don't you go on out to the patio and see what fun everyone is having. There are drinks in the coolers so help yourself, or you could go swimming. I hope you brought your suit." She was leading her out the back door as she spoke leaving Sloane to fend for herself. When she returned, Sloane raised an eyebrow at her. "So, you like my girlfriend?" she asked.

"Whooeee girl, what's not to like?" Mallory fanned her face with her hand and laughed. "She's hot!"

Sloane laughed and hugged her again. "She is, isn't she?"

"Most definitely. Georgia never said anything about what she looked like."

"That's because they're both on the butch side," Sloane commented. "And that's what we like about them, right?"

"Right," she nodded. "How's all this affecting her? Is she handling it okay?" Mallory moved about the kitchen tending to her baking and Sloane helped herself to a drink from the refrigerator and sat at the counter to keep her company.

"She's okay," she nodded. "At least I think she is. She doesn't talk about it too much. She didn't do it, of course, but still..."

"It has to be stressful," Mallory said. "This isn't like getting a speeding ticket." She poured the contents of her mixing bowl into a large pan and slid it into the oven. "I can't imagine what it must be like for her."

"Yeah," Sloane nodded. "She lost her job, she's been accused of murdering a former lover, she's been held in jail, she's been hounded by the media." She sighed and thought that maybe she hadn't been attentive enough to what Jaden had been going through. "I need to give her more support."

"Honey, it looked to me like she was pretty happy with you. It's probably the one bright spot in her life right now." Mallory regarded her for a moment. "How do you feel about her? I mean, is it just fun and games with you or is it more than that?"

"It's more than fun and games," Sloane said vehemently. "I really like her, Mal."

"Do you know how she feels?" She was busily cleaning up the kitchen, but when Sloane didn't answer, she stopped and looked up.

"I think she feels the same," she nodded. She thought back to the previous evening and how Jaden couldn't keep her hands off her. She smiled.

"I see," Mallory laughed.

Sloane blushed but laughed with her. "Yeah."

"Well, let's go outside and see what they're all up to."

Everyone was in the pool and there was a fierce water polo game in progress. Sloane shook her head at them. "Why is it always a competition of some sort?"

Mallory laughed. "I don't know but it always seems to be. I don't think they can help it." She raised her voice. "Time to get the food on, Sweetheart."

Georgia turned her attention to the deck and Jaden promptly scored on her. "Thanks Mallory," she laughed.

"No fair!" Georgia sputtered. She returned her attention to Mallory. "Betrayed by my own lover."

"Ain't it always the way?" Jaden gave her no sympathy.

"Time to cook," Mallory called, ignoring her complaint.

Georgia pulled herself from the pool and the rest of them resumed the game. Jaden followed her out and grabbed a towel. "Can I give you a hand with anything?" she asked.

"Sure." When they were both dry they assembled the tools of cooking on the grill and Georgia fired it up while Jaden put the plastic cloth on the table and carried out all the covered dishes and utensils. Mallory was busy with the dessert and Sloane was making the salad. They both paused when Jaden went in and out.

"Lord, Sloane," Mallory remarked finally. "She could be a run way model."

"Yeah, I know," she agreed, her eyes still on the door Jaden had gone through.

"Maybe you should tell her to put something on before I spontaneously combust."

Sloane laughed, her chest swelling with pride. "Better not let Georgia hear you saying that," she warned.

By the time the salad was mixed and the dessert was cooled the rest of the women were out of the pool and drying off. Sloane grabbed a cover-up from Jaden's bag and took it to her. It was like a large terrycloth tee shirt that reached down to mid-thigh. "Put this on before you cause trouble," she whispered.

Jaden laughed, thinking she was kidding and loving her for it. "You're so sweet." She pulled it over her head and brushed a quick kiss on her cheek. "Thanks."

There were five couples altogether and by the time the meal was over and they were enjoying Mallory's fabulous dessert they were all laughing and joking with each other. Jaden earned additional points with Mallory when she urged Sloane to enjoy the pool while she helped clean up the patio and do the dishes.

"Jaden, I didn't intend for any of my guests to work," Mallory chided her.

"I don't mind. You went through a lot of trouble for all of us so this is a small thing for me to do." Jaden smiled and began filling the sink with hot soapy water.

"Wouldn't you rather be with Sloane?"

Jaden laughed lightly. "It won't take me that long to do the dishes!"

Mallory grabbed a dishtowel and together they had everything done in record time. "Jaden, you're the best,"

Mallory said when they were finished. "Sloane is a lucky woman."

"Naw, I'm the lucky one." Jaden dried her hands and tossed her head toward the back yard. "She's special."

"It's nice to know you realize that," she grinned. "We think so too."

"Don't worry," Jaden told her. "I know it and I'll try to be worthy of her."

"Wow. I've never heard it put quite that way before."

Jaden laughed and put an arm around her shoulders. "Come on, let's go make someone jealous."

Of the group, only Georgia was not in the pool. She and Jaden had both changed into dry clothes before eating and now Georgia was busy restocking the coolers with beer, water, and soft drinks. "Hey," she said gruffly. "That's my woman you've got your arm around."

Jaden drew Mallory closer. "What are you going to do, fire me?" They both froze until Jaden laughed. "Oh, lighten up you guys. It was a joke."

"Shit, Jaden, you scared me," Georgia said.

"Aw hell, Coach, it wasn't your fault. I know that." Jaden took a beer and settled on the patio. "I'm going to be sorry to leave this team though."

"Fuck!" Georgia spat out. "Don Sutter is an idiot!"

"Maybe, but he's the idiot that's in charge." Jaden took a drink and waved a hand, dismissing the subject. "Let's not spoil this wonderful party. You have a great home, Coach, and a wonderful woman as well."

"Quit flirting with her," Georgia mock growled at her.

"Don't worry, sweetheart," Mallory kissed her on the cheek before sitting next to her. "She's working on being worthy of Sloane right now."

Georgia grinned. "Worthy, huh?" She was nodding now. "That might take some doing."

"I know," Jaden agreed.

"Will you go to another team?" Mallory asked hesitantly.

"That depends," Jaden shrugged. She didn't really want to talk about that right now.

"On what?" she persisted.

"On whether any other team will have me," Jaden grinned and willed Mallory to drop it.

"She'll get more than one offer," Georgia told Mallory with assurance.

"Well, shit, that's not fair!" Jaden raised an eyebrow. "I mean, it's not fair that you didn't do anything but lose your job anyway, and then some other team benefits from it. That's not right."

Jaden shrugged but had to laugh. "I guess I see your point."

"Hell yes, she's right!" Georgia growled. "I hate the thought of you playing for another team."

"Don hasn't hinted at replacing you, has he?"

"No, not yet." She drank some beer. I'm pretty sure I'm safe until Bob comes back at least."

"Yeah, I heard something about a family emergency?"

"I don't really know anything about it." Georgia shrugged. "Don called and said Bob had called him saying he had an emergency and he'd be back as soon as he could."

"Sloane said she thought he had a daughter."

"Yeah," Georgia nodded. "He showed me a picture of her once. Pretty."

"How pretty?" Mallory asked.

Georgia choked on a mouthful of beer and Jaden laughed. "Mal, she's Bob's kid!" Georgia protested while trying to suppress a laugh. "She doesn't even live here!" She leaned over and kissed Mallory's cheek fondly. "She's in California so maybe that's where Bob is." She kissed her again and laughed. She knew Mallory wasn't really jealous.

"Did he see her when we were there?" Jaden asked.

"I don't know. Bob and I don't really socialize," Georgia admitted.

"What do you think of Pam?" Jaden asked. She didn't want to talk about the team any longer.

"She seems really nice," Georgia said.

"Not exactly the kind of woman Gillian usually shows up with," Mallory observed.

Jaden laughed. "That's putting it mildly. She's a bit tame compared to some I've seen her with."

"Maybe she's slowing down."

"Remember, it's Gillian we're talking about," Georgia grinned.

"Oh yeah, I forgot. She's probably just taking some down time then." They all laughed.

"What's so funny?" Sloane had gotten out of the pool and now stood dripping next to them. She grabbed a towel and began drying off. Jaden's eyes were locked on Sloane's body as she did. Mallory laughed silently at her while Georgia answered.

"Just commenting on Gillian's date today."

"Pam's really nice. I like her," Sloane said. She wrapped the towel around her waist and squeezed the water out of her hair. She looked at Jaden and smiled when she caught her staring at her breasts.

"So do I," Mallory agreed. "I think she'd be good for Gilly too."

Sloane sat beside Jaden and took a sip from her beer. "We'll have to wait and see." She leaned back in her chair and sighed in contentment. "It's great of you two to have us over today. Thanks."

"Any time," Mallory said. "You're always welcome."

The evening wore down eventually and they all began to leave. Mallory put her arm around Jaden as they walked out to the car. "Please keep in touch, Jaden, wherever you go. Would you do that? I'd hate to think you'll go off and find another whole family."

"Aw, don't worry, Mallory, you'll always be my friend. I promise."

"Good." She kissed her on the cheek and released her to get in the car with Sloane.

"Damn, Jaden," Georgia exclaimed. "Can you not keep your hands off my woman?"

Jaden looked across the seat past Sloane and laughed. "Hey somebody has to do it."

"Thanks again you two, for such a great day. I'll see you tomorrow, Georgia." Sloane put the car in gear and drove off.

Jaden put a hand casually on Sloane's thigh and rubbed lightly. She'd been separated from her for most of the day and she felt the need to re-establish their connection. "They have a great house," she commented absently.

"Yes, they do. What did you think of Mallory?"

"She's great. They both made me feel very comfortable. Mallory seems to fit with Coach like they were made for each other, don't they?"

"Yes," Sloane nodded. "I can't think of either one of them without the other." She drove slowly home and conversation fell off into a comfortable silence until they arrived at Sloane's apartment. "Are you hungry?" she asked.

"No, I'm still stuffed." Jaden laughed and kissed Sloane on the cheek. Then she kissed her on the neck and then her ear. Sloane closed her eyes and wilted a little under the onslaught of Jaden's mouth and tongue. Jaden wrapped her arms around her and pulled her close enough so their breasts and thighs were touching. Sloane buried her face in Jaden's neck and her breath ratcheted up a notch. "I've missed touching you today," Jaden murmured into her ear as they kissed again.

"You're never satisfied, are you?" Sloane laughed lightly against her neck.

"You satisfy me," Jaden swore while her lips and tongue trailed a path along her jaw and down her throat to nibble where her pulse beat in a quick rhythm.

Sloane closed her eyes and reveled in the sensual feeling racing through her body at the hands of this woman. "I missed you too," she whispered.

Jaden kissed her way back up to her mouth and claimed her lips again. Sloane made a noise in her throat and Jaden pressed against Sloane, matching all body parts along their lengths. Sloane buried her hands in Jaden's thick, dark hair and held her tight in an increasingly passionate kiss. Jaden dropped her hands to grip Sloane's ass, massaging and kneading the firm flesh. As their tongues slid against each other, she reached lower and bent at the knees to pick Sloane up. Sloane curled her legs around Jaden's waist, and without breaking their kiss, Jaden walked them into the bedroom.

"Jaden," Sloane whispered on a moan as they tumbled onto the bed. "Oh God."

Jaden wanted to just tear Sloane's clothing from her body and ravage her but forced herself to rein her urges in and slow down. Her raspy breathing betrayed her need, however, and Sloane quickly pulled the shirt over her head along with her sports bra. She cupped her breasts and offered them to Jaden, who immediately covered them with her own hands. She rolled the nipples into hard nubs and Sloane felt herself grow heavy with need. "You're so beautiful," Jaden whispered. She bent to flick her tongue over her left nipple and Sloane arched up into her. She grazed her teeth gently across it and she was rewarded when Sloane moaned.

"Jaden," she hissed, as she felt her breast being devoured. "Jaden."

"Yes, lover? Do you want something?" Jaden teased her right nipple with a thumb and forefinger, her lips rolling and pulling still on her left one.

"I need to feel you," Sloane whimpered. "I need your skin against me."

Jaden rose up and got out of her shirt quickly. Sloane's hands were instantly on her, cupping and holding her. Jaden held herself still for her but ran out of patience quickly. She lowered herself to Sloane's lips and pushed her tongue into her mouth softly, slithering over her tongue and searching out every inch of her. Sloane moaned against Jaden's mouth. She was on fire. Every inch of her strained for release. The blood pounded in her head and rushed between her legs. She throbbed with need and unconsciously rolled her hips, seeking friction.

Jaden moved against her until she knew Sloane was climbing too close to the peak. She rolled to the side and Sloane groaned in frustration. Jaden quickly slid a hand down the front of Sloane's shorts and through her slick folds. Sloane jerked at the first touch. "I need you naked," Jaden said with a growl in her voice. Sloane lifted her hips and Jaden peeled the shorts and underwear together down her legs and tossed them to the floor. She took a moment to look at her. She was so perfect. She positioned herself between her legs and breathed deeply of her scent. It got into her and made her blood boil.

"Babe, let me feel you," Sloane urged. "Please." Jaden rolled off her just long enough to kick her own shorts off. "Oh yeah," Sloane sighed. "That's good."

Jaden put a thigh between Sloane's legs and pushed tight against her center. At the same time she slid along Sloane's thigh and let her feel how wet she was herself. "Oh God," Sloane moaned. "You feel so good." Jaden leaned down and captured a nipple between her lips again and Sloane ran her fingers through her hair, holding her against her breast. Her hips were rolling rhythmically against Jaden and she felt the crest moving along her spine, flowing like liquid fire in her veins, building with each thrust. Jaden's own wetness coated her thigh adding to the fire and the mouth at her breast brought the blaze roaring to life. She was being assaulted from so many place she couldn't seem to separate them. They blended to form one giant coil of need within her. She was unaware she was moaning until Jaden covered her mouth in another kiss.

"Not yet, honey," she whispered against her lips. "I want my mouth on you." She kissed her again before positioning herself between Sloane's legs. She kissed the inside of her thigh once and Sloane brought both knees up, opening herself completely to her. Jaden wasted no more time and quickly entered her knowing she was ready. Sloane pushed against her hand, driving Jaden deeper into her. "Hard," she rasped. "Harder." Jaden complied and drove deeper, harder, and faster. Sloane gasped and thrust back at her just as hard. Jaden could feel Sloane's legs quivering as they came together again and again. Sloane was grunting on each thrust and she was rapidly approaching a climax. Jaden let up and she whimpered and reached for her immediately. "I need...Baby, I..." She held back a sob. She was so close and so fragile. "Please," she begged. Jaden put her lips around her engorged clit and sucked hard. Once. Twice. Three times and then Sloane was gone. She cried out her name as she bucked against her face. Her legs were stiff and tight, muscles clenched. Jaden wrapped her arms around her thighs and rode the wave with her, keeping her lips glued to the source of her pleasure.

She let her go only when Sloane's body was finally limp against the bed. Jaden pulled herself to a kneeling position and hung her head, fighting her own orgasm. She was so close, she couldn't hang on and she finally straddled Sloane's thigh, quickly bringing herself to a climax. She collapsed on top of Sloane then and rested her head against her shoulder, panting and still clenching. Sloane curled her arms around her, making her feel warm and protected. It was a feeling she was just getting to know. She liked it.

Chapter 17

Sloane quietly left her apartment and drove to the stadium. Jaden had still been asleep this morning and she had wanted to let her stay asleep. She looked so peaceful and Sloane's heart swelled with love for her. She grabbed her laptop and made her way up to her office. She was anxious to get new equipment but so far, they hadn't heard from the insurance company. She was grateful she had the web page hosting software on her laptop so the team web site would still function normally. She tried not to think about how many photos she'd lost.

John was busy on the phone at his desk when she entered their office and she waved a greeting to him as she passed by. She booted up her computer and went in search of coffee. The team was scheduled to play in Minnesota in two days and they were leaving tomorrow afternoon from DFW International Airport. She usually liked traveling with the team and especially to a cooler climate but this time, she wished she could stay home. Jaden was the reason. She poured a cup of coffee and leaned against the counter to take a sip. She missed Jaden already and wondered how that could be. Sloane had been sexually active for many years but had never had any woman affect her quite this way. It was absurd, she thought. But she knew it was more than the incredible sex they shared. It was much more than that. Her thoughts strayed back to Jaden sleeping in her bed and she smiled.

"Do I need to guess why you have such a silly grin on your face?" Georgia reached past her and poured coffee into her cup. Sloane could feel heat warm her cheeks and ducked her head. Georgia laughed at her discomfort. "How is she?"

"Fine," Sloane nodded.

"Mallory really liked her," Georgia remarked. "She thinks she's gorgeous."

Sloane's cheeks warmed again. "She is."

Georgia laughed and turned to leave. "Practice starts in an hour so I need to get some stuff done."

"Have you heard anything from Bob?" Sloane walked with her down the hall.

"Nothing." She shook her head and continued past Sloane's office. "If he doesn't get his ass back here soon I'm going to go nuts. I don't have time to do everything."

"See you later."

Jaden parked her truck in the lot at the stadium and entered through the side door. The security guard just nodded to her as she turned to the field. The team was already practicing and she hung on the top of the fence to watch. She missed this so much. She was going to ask Sloane out to lunch but couldn't resist the thwack of bats striking balls and the shouts of her former teammates.

"Jaden!" She jerked in surprise at her name. Erin Coe was standing at the end of the dugout and motioned her over.

Jaden moved in her direction. "Keep it down, Erin. I don't know if I'm even allowed to be here."

"Sure," she whispered. "But can you help me?"

"What do you need?"

"I'm having trouble with my riser. Can you take a look and just tell me what I'm doing wrong."

"Sure." Jaden looked around and located Georgia before hustling down to the bullpen. She worked with Erin for twenty minutes before Lindsey Jones, the catcher, abruptly stood up behind the practice plate. Jaden figured she'd been caught and she turned around to find Georgia coming up behind her.

"It's my fault," Erin said immediately. "I asked her to help me."

"What's the problem?"

"My rise ball, but I've got it now," she rushed to explain.

Georgia looked at both of them for a moment. Okay. You and Lindsey go relieve Gillian and Susan now."

Jaden waited until the two players jogged past before speaking. "Sorry, Coach. I was just watching and she asked me to help. I shouldn't even be here, I know."

"I'm sure it's hard on you, Jaden," Georgia nodded. "Dickhead Don rescinded your contract but I don't think he said you couldn't come to the park. Don't let him see you but other than that I don't care." She sighed. "What a fucking mess he's caused."

"Thanks, Georgia." Jaden knew it was Georgia she was talking to and not her coach.

"Don't mention it." She started back to practice. "I'm sure Sloane would like to see you," she teased over her shoulder.

Jaden laughed and walked toward the main building. The guard in the lobby also just nodded to her as she took the elevator to the second floor. Sloane was busy working on her computer when Jaden walked in. She greeted Stan and John and Sloane turned at the sound of her voice. She smiled and watched her cross the room. She raked her eyes over Jaden's body and felt the now familiar catch in her breathing. "Hello."

"Hi. Are you busy?"

"Not too much," she answered. "What are you up to?"

"Well, I slept in this morning," Jaden grinned. "It seems I was very tired."

"Yeah?"

"Yeah." She leaned her hips against the counter and crossed her ankles. "And I thought I'd ask a beautiful woman to lunch."

"How nice for you," she laughed.

"What do you think her answer will be?"

"I think she'd be a fool not to say yes."

Jaden tried to stay busy to keep her mind off Sloane's absence. It was not something she was used to having a problem with. She noticed the flash drive on her kitchen counter and plugged it into her computer. If she couldn't see Sloane then she'd look at her work. She tensed when she realized it was the photos from their trip to L.A. but clicked on the drive anyway. There were photos of the hotel, the field, the L.A. team, the scoreboard and everything in between. She got to the last few photos and knew they were taken the morning after she'd had the dream and finally Sloane had given her the strength to tell someone the story. Ever since Sloane had come into her life, the dream had faded away. She would be forever grateful to her for that. She smiled when she got to the end and saw the photos of Coach Winslow loading bags into the storage compartment of the bus. His expression was oddly fierce, like the bags were his sworn enemy. She remembered how horrible he had looked that morning at breakfast. They had all thought he'd been out all night. Maybe having to load the luggage was making his hangover even worse. The last photo on the drive was of Georgia coming out of the hotel with a scowl on her face. Until she had gotten to know her, Jaden had thought that was her permanent look. She knew better now. She thought both coaches looked like they were more than ready to get out of town. She clicked back to Coach Bob and sighed. If Don fired Georgia, the team was done. She kept staring at the photo and it finally sunk in that it was her own equipment bag he held in his hand. She laughed. Maybe that was the cause of his demeanor. He hadn't made a secret of how he felt about her. For being a homophobe, he had certainly picked the wrong vocation. Everyone knew professional softball teams were rife with lesbians. She leaned back in her chair and sighed. What the hell had Kendall done to get herself killed? Was she holding out on a drug dealer? Did she flaunt her affair with someone's wife and then was killed in a rage outside a lesbian bar? Maybe she jilted a lover and the lover followed her outside to the alley. Jaden knew Kendall could evoke strong feelings in women. Maybe she finally pissed off someone who had no self-control. No, that was wrong. This had something to do with her, but how could that be? She had been gone a long time so why kill Kendall now if it involved her? She rubbed her head. This was giving her a headache. Her phone rang then and she scooped it up quickly, hoping it was Sloane. It wasn't. It was Stan, her agent.

"Jaden, it's Stan."

"Hey, Stan," Jaden answered. "What's up?"

"I just got a call from Denver. They're probing for information about your availability the rest of this season."

"Yeah?" Jaden's heart rate increased. "What did they say?"

"They seemed interested in what price range you were going to be in." He laughed. "When they talk about price right off the bat it usually means they'd like to have you but they don't want to seem too eager. You know, it might increase your price if you thought they would pay. Anyway they want you up there for an interview and a work out tomorrow."

"Wow. That didn't take long."

"The word has gotten around by now and we should be getting calls from other teams soon too," he said confidently.

"Not L.A., Stan," she said immediately. "I won't play there."

"I know that, Jaden," he soothed her. "I wouldn't do that to you. Anyway, I just wanted you to know that the negotiations have begun and we'll see what happens next."

"Thanks, Stan."

"Hang in there, kid. You'll come out of this in good shape. I'll keep in touch."

Jaden hung up and sat for a moment contemplating the meaning of it all. Denver wanted her. Well, that wouldn't be the end of the earth. Right? It wouldn't be that far from Dallas. Not that far from Sloane. Her heart clutched. *Away from Sloane. How could she be away from Sloane? How could she even think of being away from Sloane?* She rationalized that they could still see each other. It would be hard during the season but after that, they would have all of the off-season together. It didn't even sound good in her head, so how would it sound when she had to tell Sloane? She wasn't looking forward to it.

Chapter 18

Sloane was busy sorting photos into folders on her laptop when the security guard in the lobby called her office extension. It seemed a detective from California was on the line wishing to speak to her.

"Hello?"

"Ms Ellison, this is Detective Maxwell."

"Yes sir, how are you?"

"I'm fine. I've been trying to get in touch with your coaching staff but I keep getting voice mail."

"Georgia is probably not in yet."

"I really wanted to talk with Bob Winslow."

"Oh. Well, he's, uh, on leave right now."

"Is he sick?"

"No. He had a family emergency."

"Do you know how I can get in touch with him?"

"I can give you his cell number," Sloane offered and wondered what was up. "Can I have Georgia call you when she gets in or maybe someone else can help you?"

"No. I was just finishing up some of the paperwork on the Paxton case and realized I never got to interview Mr. Winslow."

"Oh. I wish I could tell you when he'll be back but I'm not even sure where he is."

"It's okay," he assured her. "I've left a message on his phone and I'll call him on his cell. I'm sure he'll call when he can. Thanks for everything."

"You're welcome, Detective. Can I ask if you've made any progress?"

"I'm afraid not. We're still analyzing the physical evidence and we're hoping something will come from that."

"Thank you and good luck."

Sloane sipped a glass of white wine at the bar and waited. She had left the stadium later than normal and Jaden agreed to meet her at the bar. She came in the back door a minute later looking like a movie star on the red carpet. Sloane felt the same pull she always did whenever she first saw her. A part of her melted each time.

Jaden smiled as she spotted her. She was stunning in her faded jeans and tight white shirt. It took Jaden's breath away. She stopped at the far side of the dance floor and just looked at her. Sloane smiled back at her and all the pieces of her world settled into place. Jaden held out a hand and waited. Sloane slid off her stool and walked across the dance floor putting a little extra sway in her hips. Jaden smiled and took her in her arms and they swayed together in time to the music.

"I missed you today," Jaden whispered.

"Umm, that's nice. I missed you too."

"What did you do today?" Jaden smiled and waited for the answer knowing Sloane was just waiting for their first kiss.

Sloane's eyes were on Jaden's lips as she answered. "I sorted photos and updated the web page." She unconsciously licked her lips.

Jaden could feel her body humming against her own and as much as she liked having Sloane on edge, she was in the same state herself. She slowly lowered her head and they kissed softly. The tension eased instantly and they smiled into each other's eyes as they parted. "Nice," Jaden breathed.

"Very," Sloane answered.

"So, what else did you do while I was waiting to see you again?"

"I decided I need to replace some of the photos but I wasn't able to get that far yet. And I chose Gillian for the spotlight player."

Jaden laughed. "I'm sure she was pleased to hear that."

"She told me to fill out the questionnaire myself," she grinned.

"You could," Jaden nodded. "You know enough about her. Oh, by the way, I found your flash drive the other day. It was the stuff you took on the L.A. trip."

"Oh yeah, I forgot about those." Sloane leaned back to look into Jaden's eyes. "Was there anything there that was...?"

"Was what?" Jaden asked. "Was too reminiscent of the worst day of my short life? Was a reminder of the trip where I was accused of murder?" She kissed the tip of Sloane's nose. "Was the beginning of a glorious affair with a stunningly beautiful woman?"

"Wow. That must have been a hell of a series of photos," Sloane laughed.

Jaden smiled. "It was." The music changed and they went back to the bar. Jaden ordered a beer and kissed Sloane on the neck just under the ear. She smiled when Sloane tilted her head to give her more access and promptly kissed her again. "Mmm, you smell good."

"Thank you." Sloane put a hand on Jaden's thigh and rubbed gently. "What did you do today?"

Jaden's pulse spiked momentarily. "I talked to Stan this afternoon."

"Your agent?"

"Yeah."

When she didn't go on Sloane looked her in the eye. "And?"

"Denver is interested in me."

"Oh." Sloane looked away quickly and her hand slipped from Jaden's thigh.

"It's probably nothing," Jaden quickly added. "Stan said not to make too much out of it."

"So what does it mean?" Sloane was amazed she could speak at all. Her throat was clogged with emotion and she felt unshed tears burning behind her eyes.

"I'll go to Denver for an interview and a work out." Jaden covered Sloane's hand on the bar with her own. "It's just the process, Sloane. It's not a big deal."

Not a big deal? A job interview in Denver was not a big deal? Sloane swallowed hard and tried to blink the tears away. *Maybe Jaden didn't think this was a big deal but she certainly did!* She slowly slid off the bar stool and stood up. "You may not think leaving is a big deal, Jaden, but I do. I thought we had something special. I'm sorry you don't feel the same way."

Jaden caught her arm as she started to leave. "Sloane, it's not like that! I do feel the same!" She tried to put her arms around her but Sloane pushed her away.

"I need to get out of here." She continued toward the door. "Please just leave me alone tonight." There were tears in her voice.

Jaden stood staring after her. *What had just happened? This was wrong. So wrong.* She needed to explain what she meant about it not being a big deal. *Sloane couldn't possibly think Jaden didn't care for her. How could she think that? This was just a work out, not a job offer. It didn't mean she was leaving; at least not yet.* She slumped onto the bar stool and picked up her beer. It took no time at all to drain it and signal for another. She dialed Sloane's cell phone but it went to voice mail and Jaden hung up. She downed another beer. What the hell was she going to do? She couldn't get the look on Sloane's face out of her mind. She'd been devastated. She thought Jaden didn't care about her. She had another beer and dialed Sloane's cell phone again. This time it went straight to voice mail. This was not something she could explain in a message. She hung up again.

Several beers later, she went out to her car and drove herself home, her heart breaking into tiny pieces with every mile. She tried calling Sloane several more times but it was obvious she'd turned her phone off. She finally left a message. "Sloane, please talk to me. I need to see you. I need to explain." She knew her voice was shaky but didn't care.

Sloane was determined to stay busy to keep from thinking about Jaden. She sorted every photo she had, filed them in folders, updated the web site and actually looked forward to the trip to Boston the next day. She needed to get away. She went down to the practice field and found Gillian in the bullpen.

"Hey Sloane," she called.

"Hey, Gilly," she answered. She looked around the field nervously checking but Jaden was nowhere in sight. "I need your info for the Spotlight Player section."

"I told you to fill it out yourself," Gillian laughed.

"Okay," she nodded. "I think I'll say something about how surprised your teammates are that you seem to have an actual girlfriend these days."

"What?"

"I mean instead of the pick-ups you usually do." She put a smile on her face even though she didn't feel it.

Gillian's mouth hung open in surprise until she saw Sloane's expression change to a scowl. She followed her gaze and saw Jaden at the fence. She looked back at Sloane. Something was definitely wrong. She raised a hand in greeting to Jaden but walked closer to Sloane. "Sloane," she asked quietly, "what's going on?"

"Nothing, Gilly." She said it too quickly and her lips began to tremble.

"No, there's something," Gillian insisted. She glanced back to where Jaden stood on the other side of the fence. She looked miserable and she never took her eyes off Sloane. "Come on, Sloane, tell me."

"I'll tell you later," she said. "I just don't want to talk to her right now."

"Aw hell, Sloane," Gillian sighed. She didn't want Sloane to be hurt again.

"Don't worry about it, Gilly," Sloane said but her voice betrayed her.

"Shall I go tell her to get lost?" Gillian was angry. She had tried to tell Jaden not to hurt Sloane and this was exactly why.

"Stay out of it please." Sloane wiped her cheek. "It's just between us."

"Fuck, Sloane! What did she do?"

"I can't be here right now, Gilly." Sloane kept her eyes on the ground. "I just need some time, okay?"

"Sure." Gillian instantly backed off. She touched her arm gently. "You know I'm here for you, Sloane. Whatever you need."

"I know, Gilly, and I appreciate it." She swiped at her cheek again. "Maybe you can keep her from following me right now."

"You got it." Gillian stepped closer and hugged her. "Call me if you need anything."

"Thanks Gilly."

Jaden registered the fact that Gillian was heading her way but she kept her eyes on Sloane. She desperately wanted to hop the fence and go after her. But she knew all Sloane or Gilly had to do was make a complaint and she'd be banned from the park.

"Jaden." Gillian barked her name to get her attention.

"What?" Jaden barked back but her eyes still followed Sloane.

"She doesn't want to talk to you," Gillian said. She took in the red rimmed, bloodshot eyes and the look of utter exhaustion on her face and softened her tone. "I don't know what happened but she's just not ready to talk to you yet."

Jaden finally looked at her. "I need to see her, Gilly. I need to talk to her."

"I'm afraid not, Jaden." Despite being angry that Sloane had been hurt, she could see that Jaden was also suffering. "Just give her some time. We're leaving for Boston so maybe when we get back she'll be ready."

"Gilly, I need to make her understand!"

Gillian sighed. "Please, Jaden. You have to give her some space. Just let her have this trip first, okay? Maybe I can talk to her for you while we're gone."

Jaden ran a hand through her short hair in exasperation and despair. She knew she didn't have a choice in the matter. "Okay," she finally nodded. "I won't try to see her until you get back from Boston." She stepped back from the fence. "But please tell her I need to talk to her. It isn't what she thinks. I need to explain."

"I'll tell her, Jaden," she promised.

Chapter 19

Detective Maxwell took the evidence report of the murder scene from the Paxton case and read through it quickly. It took only a couple of minutes before his pulse quickened and he reached for his phone. While he waited for the connection to the Dallas Police Department to go through he re-read the report. Could it really be this easy after all? The call was answered and he turned his attention back to the phone. He asked to be connected to the detective assigned to the break in of the Dallas Metros stadium offices and was put on hold. When he finally got to talk to Detective Tillis, he told him the contents of the report and promised to fax a copy of it to him right away. By the time they ended the call Detective Tillis had started the process of getting an arrest warrant based on the information from that report. The Los Angeles crime scene technicians were able to pull fingerprints off the lumber from the dumpster that was used as the murder weapon. They were from Bob Winslow, coach of the Dallas Metros. He wiped the cell phone he put next to the body but he must have thought the lumber wouldn't hold a print.

In Dallas, Detective Tillis went through the incident report on the break in at the stadium again and had an idea. He called the security company for the stadium and requested a report on whose access cards were used from the day before the beak in through the day of the break in. By then the warrant was ready and he and his partner, Detective Dan Schmidt, went to pick him up.

The nondescript house was in East Dallas in an older neighborhood where lawns were mowed, bushes trimmed, and yards were free of abandoned toys. They approached the house from the side, being as quiet as they could. Detective Tillis took up a position on one side of the front door while his partner worked his way around the back. When he thought it had been long enough he reached for the weapon on his hip and with his other hand knocked on the door hard. When there was no answer, he knocked again even harder. Nothing. No sounds at all from inside. Detective Tillis tried the door. It was locked. "Dallas Police! Open up!" He waited but could feel the stillness of an empty house. He moved along the side and around to the back. Detective Schmidt was standing on the back porch to the side of the door. "I think it's empty," he said.

"Yeah, so do I." Detective Tillis holstered his weapon, as did Detective Schmidt. "There's a few papers on the driveway so maybe he's been gone a while."

"Let's check the mailbox too."

They were on the drive when the woman next door drove in. She stopped her car and got out. "Are you looking for Bob?"

"Yes Ma'am. Have you seen him?"

"Not for several days. He coaches for the softball team though and sometimes they're gone for days at a time."

"He's not with the team," Detective Tillis told her. "Can you think of any place else he might have gone? It's kind of important."

"Oh my, no. I don't know much about him. He kind of keeps to himself, you know. I'm sorry."

"That's okay, Ma'am." He handed her one of his cards. "If you see him or if you think of any place he might be, please call us."

Chapter 20

Sloane walked with Gillian to their hotel room and they both dumped their bags before heading back out to the team dinner in the hotel dining room.

"Want to tell me what's going on yet?" Gillian asked as they waited for the elevator.

"Not now," she shook her head. "Let's just eat dinner."

"Do you want to go out after that? Coach will probably give us a curfew but we'll still have time for a little fun."

"Maybe," she nodded. They got on the elevator. "Yeah, okay."

Gillian nodded but wasn't as happy about her decision as she thought she'd be. They went to dinner, chatted with all the other players and listened to Georgia give them a pep talk. When the obligatory curfew announcement came, they all groaned.

"Game time tomorrow is one o'clock," Georgia said above the noise. "The bus will be leaving for the field at ten o'clock. No excuses." She laughed at their continued groans. "Go on, have fun tonight."

Gillian and Sloane arrived at the bar along with several of the team members. They scattered around the tables and Gillian steered Sloane to a small table in the corner. "I'll go get us a drink." She went to the bar and returned with white wine for Sloane and a beer for herself. "This is a pretty nice place," she said as she took her seat next to Sloane. "I heard some women talking up at the bar about a dart league. That would be fun, don't you think?" She took a swig of her beer. "Maybe we can get a dart league going in Dallas." She looked at Sloane. "You know, in the off season."

"Yeah, that sounds like fun," Sloane nodded but there was no indication she'd even heard what Gillian had said.

"Sloane..."

"She's leaving, Gilly! And she said it was no big deal!" Sloane blurted out.

Gillian sat back. "So that's what this is all about?"

"Yes." Sloane sniffed and kept her eyes on her wine glass.

"Where is she going?"

"Denver." She could barely choke it out and fought hard to keep the tears away.

Gillian was quiet for a minute, thinking it through. "What happened?"

Sloane told her about Jaden having an interview and work out in Denver through stutters and stops, trying to hold on to her emotions, but she broke when she got to the part where Jaden viewed leaving as no big deal.

Gillian put her hand over Sloane's and laced their fingers together. "I'm sorry, Sloane." She squeezed her hand. "Are you sure that's the way she feels?"

"That's what she said." She used her free hand to wipe her eyes. "Oh God, Gilly, I really thought we had something special. And she says it's no big deal!"

Gillian put her arm around her and hugged her. "Sloane, I talked to her at the field yesterday and she didn't look like she didn't care. She was desperate to see you."

"It's what she said, Gilly." Sloane sat up and put her head in her hands. "I can't believe I got suckered again!" She wiped her eyes again. "That's it, Gilly. I'm done. No more women."

"Oh, Sloane." Gillian stood and took her hand, pulling her up. "Come on. Let's go back to the hotel. We'll talk about this and figure it out."

"Shit, Gilly, I've had it."

Back in their room, they both sat on one bed, their backs against the headboard. "Sloane, I know you're hurt but I promised Jaden I'd give you a message."

"What?" Sloane asked listlessly.

"She said she needs to see you. She wants to explain."

"Explain what?" she snapped. "Explain how I mean nothing to her?"

Gillian held her again as fresh tears ran down her face. "Well, maybe this is for the best, Sloane," she said finally. "I mean, let's face it, she's not exactly the clean cut all American girl. She was involved with Kendall Paxton and we all know what kind of lifestyle that was. She must have been going to wild parties all the time out there. It was all booze, drugs and orgies with the rich and famous. You had to have known that. She's probably bored down in dull old Dallas."

"What the hell are you talking about, Gilly?" Sloane stopped crying to glare at her.

"Come on, Sloane, you know she's probably looking for a little more action in her life. She probably isn't the kind to stay monogamous anyway."

"That's bullshit, Gillian!" Sloane moved away from her. "She didn't want all the parties out there. She hated all that."

"She's probably been seeing other people here." Gillian pushed her a little more. "And sitting around with nothing to do now is going to give her plenty of time to hunt, if you know what I mean."

"You know that's not true!" Sloane got up from the bed and turned to face her. "She stayed with me because she..."

"And when they accused her of killing Paxton you were there to help her and she took advantage of you." Gillian nodded as if to herself. "She didn't even have to work to get you into bed with her."

"That's absurd, Gillian, and you know it."

"Well, that would fit the character you've given her, Sloane. If what I said isn't true then you tell me what kind of a person she really is."

"She's kind and considerate, Gillian. She hated the life Kendall lived in L.A. and that's why she left. She went through hell with her and still has..." She stopped before revealing too much. "And she couldn't have known I would be there for her in Portland. She couldn't have known Kendall was going to be killed." She paced across the room. "And remember, someone tried to frame her for that. She never even got crazy because of it. She never once took it out on anyone."

"So what are you saying?"

"I'm saying you're wrong about her, Gilly."

Gillian nodded. "Maybe I am. Maybe you are too."

"What are you talking about?"

"The woman you just described couldn't be someone who would brush you off so easily as being no big deal." Gillian couldn't let her smile show just yet. "She wasn't involved in Kendall's murder. She sat by your hospital bed for two days straight even though you were unconscious and didn't know it. She never took out her frustrations on anyone else. And…she must have done something right to make you love her."

"Damn you, Gilly," she sobbed.

"Yeah," she nodded. "I know."

Sloane sank down on the bed next to her again. "You are a shit."

"Yes," she nodded again. "Now, can we talk about what Jaden said and what she actually meant?"

"Yes," she said through tears.

"Okay then." Gillian took her hand and entwined their fingers. "First of all, Jaden lost her job. That's huge, Sloane, especially since it wasn't even her fault. That must feel so unfair."

"Yes," she sighed, "it must."

"And she has to work. You know that, right? It's not like she could just get a job in an office or something."

"No," she shook her head. "That would kill her."

"Yes, it would. Her agent got her a work out in Denver. That's his job, Sloane." Gillian squeezed her hand. "He probably didn't want to get her hopes up so he told her it was no big deal and not to get too excited yet."

"Yeah, maybe," she nodded.

"So she was probably trying to tell you the same thing. She didn't want you to…"

"Do exactly what I did—jump to conclusions." Sloane sighed heavily. "God, I'm such an idiot!" She sniffed again and wiped at new tears.

Gillian hugged her tightly. "It just blind-sided you, that's all." She smiled. "I think you can be sure she feels the same about you as you do about her."

"Do you really think so?" she asked hopefully.

"She looked like hell when you wouldn't talk to her, Sloane," she told her. "She looked like she hadn't slept at all."

"What should I do, Gilly? I feel awful."

"Maybe you should call her and let her know you're talking to her and you'll see her when we get back tomorrow."

"Yes, I should definitely do that."

Gillian got off the bed. "I'm going down to the bar for a drink. Please don't be in the middle of phone sex when I get back."

Jaden hoped she didn't look as bad as she felt as she changed into her cleats. The coaching staff of the Denver Gold Dust waited on the field for her. Her head pounded from lack of sleep and the constant emotional turmoil she'd been in and she knew she'd appeared distracted during her interview. She needed to put her personal problems aside and focus on this work out. She picked up her glove and walked onto the field. She spent the necessary time warming up and then nodded that she was ready. She threw a few half speed pitches to the assistant coach crouched behind the plate. Her arm felt good and she was able to relax a little.

"Okay, Jaden, let's see some heat."

Jaden smiled to herself. She wasn't going to show them the *smoke*. She didn't need it to get a contract and if she didn't get this job, she didn't care. She did put some heat on the next few pitches though and saw the assistant coach wince. They worked her for over an hour, testing her control and speed and types of pitches she could throw. At the end, she was tired beyond belief. They thanked her and sent her back to the airport with no indication of their intentions. She was used to the game and thought nothing of it. As soon as she was in the cab on her way to the airport, her thoughts went automatically to Sloane. *Sloane*. Once again, her heart clutched in her chest at the mere thought of her. She had hurt her and it didn't lessen her own pain knowing it had been a misunderstanding. She couldn't bear the thought that Sloane was in pain. She ground her teeth in agony. She had to talk to her! She had to make her understand. She was so tired she couldn't think straight. She hadn't been able to sleep since Sloane walked out on her.

She settled into her seat in the rear of the plane for the short hop down to Dallas and clicked her seatbelt in place. It took a supreme effort to wait patiently while everyone boarded when all she wanted to do was get to Sloane. She needed to see her, talk to her, and touch her. God! She needed to touch her so badly! And that's what she thought about during the trip instead of getting some much needed sleep. She thought about how she felt the first time she saw her, how her eyes lost focus when they were making love, how her body responded to Jaden's touch, and how she made Jaden want to do anything to please her. *That's it*, she thought as they landed in Dallas. She would just stay in Dallas. She'd get a job and stay here with Sloane. It was so simple! Why hadn't she thought of it sooner? She relaxed for the first time in two days. Now all she had to do was tell Sloane.

She had to concentrate on the drive home just to stay awake. She set her bag down inside her front door and sat down on the couch to remove her shoes. It was the last thing she remembered until the doorbell woke her a short time later.

She didn't know how long it had been ringing but it stopped just as she sat up. Heavy knocking followed it. She was confused and barely awake and the banging was making her head pound again. She stomped to the door.

"What the hell do you..." she was violently thrown back into the apartment and landed on her butt. She quickly got to her feet. "Winslow?" She frowned in confusion. "What the hell are you doing here?"

"Shut up!" His eyes were wild and he stank, the body odor coming off him in waves. His clothes were dirty and wrinkled as if he had slept in them more than once and he hadn't shaved in days. He could have passed for one of the countless homeless people around downtown Dallas. All of that was nothing compared to the bat he was waving in front of her. "Just shut the fuck up, you stupid dyke!" Spittle flew from his mouth and he kept the bat moving in choppy strokes.

Jaden swallowed hard and felt the adrenalin rush as the fight or flight instinct kicked in. Flight was certainly her top priority but he was between her and the door. Something was very wrong here, she thought. *Drugs? Was he on something*? She glanced around for something to use as a weapon if she needed one. "What's going on, Bob?" she asked, and tried not to show how scared she was.

He took a home run swing and broke everything on the shelf above her TV. "What's going on?" His voice was shrill. "What's going on?" He laughed manically and the sound made Jaden's heart rate spike. "The little fucking doper of a queer wants to know what's going on." He swung again and sent her TV into a thousand pieces. Jaden knew she was in trouble now. Maybe her neighbors would hear the noise and call the police. "What's going on, *dyke*, is that you're finally going to pay for what you did in L.A." He swung through the air in front of her and she stepped back again. Maybe she could get to the kitchen and get a knife, she thought, or something to use as a weapon against him.

"I didn't kill Kendall!" she yelled at him, not knowing what he wanted to hear.

"Who cares about that bitch!" He had both hands on the bat and kept it moving in front of her with a malevolent gleam in his eye. "Nobody gave a shit when I killed her." He laughed at her shocked expression. "They didn't even come looking for her in that alley. Not one person missed her enough to look for her." The laugh was accompanied by the terror inducing maniacal look of a mad man. "And that was justice!" he screamed. "She didn't care about Julie! She gave her drugs until she couldn't think for herself. She told her she loved her. She never loved anyone!" He swung the bat and destroyed a floor lamp. "All she ever cared about was herself. She used Julie!"

Jaden began edging toward the kitchen as she realized he was totally insane. "Why me?" she asked to keep him talking instead of swinging that bat.

"You're the same! You were there—I know you were. You both lured her into the life of queers, drugs and booze. She was too screwed up to know any better, but did you care? NO!" He swung again and put a hole in the wall near her head.

Jaden took advantage of it and ran for the kitchen. He pulled the bat free of the wall and followed her. "You can't escape," he taunted. His bat cleared the counter of everything, shattering the glass coffee pot as well as several canisters. Jaden had managed to grab a knife from the chopping block, but she knew it was an almost useless weapon against the bat. She was frantically looking for a way out, but her brain wasn't functioning. Terror robbed her of rational thought along with her breath. She was going to die, she realized. He was going to kill her just like he'd killed Kendall. She was going to die before she had a chance to see Sloane. Oh God, she couldn't let that happen! She couldn't leave Sloane thinking she didn't love her! She gripped the knife tighter but she was sweating so much she could feel it slide in her hand. He gave an ungodly roar and swung the bat for the final blow to her head. There was no room to get away so she made the irrational decision to go toward him. If she was going to die, at least she could hurt him in the process. Instinctively she raised her left arm and felt the blow along her forearm as she lunged with the knife. The bat slid over the now broken arm and it would have broken her neck if his grip hadn't loosened as he fell back, her knife sticking out of his chest.

Chapter 21

Sloane thought about going home and calling Jaden first but instantly discarded that idea. She wanted to see Jaden as soon as possible. She hadn't answered Sloane's call, but since it had immediately gone to voice mail, her phone was turned off or it had lost its charge. She drove into the apartment complex and headed to Jaden's building but screeched to an abrupt halt upon seeing police cars and ambulances blocking the road. She pulled into a space at the building next to Jaden's and got out. She started toward the building with a growing dread in her chest. She began to run when she saw a stretcher being carried down the steps toward a waiting ambulance. She pushed through the knot of people gathered around the vehicles and was almost at the ambulance when she was grabbed from behind and pulled back.

"Let me go!" She struggled to get free.

"Ms Ellison?"

She whirled around to face Detective Tillis. "What happened? Where's Jaden?"

"Ms Hawke was attacked tonight," he told her quietly so no one else could hear.

She turned and was at the ambulance doors before he could stop her. Her heart stopped. Jaden lay strapped on the stretcher. There was a cervical collar around her neck and a compression cast on her left arm. She was unconscious, an oxygen mask on her face, and blood all down her left side. *Oh my God! No! Not Jaden! No, please no!*

"Ms Ellison, please stand clear." Detective Tillis caught up to her and took her arm. "Let them do their job." He pulled her back onto the sidewalk just as another stretcher was carried out. This one had a body on it that was completely covered with a sheet. Sloane stared in horror. Someone had died in Jaden's apartment tonight. She looked at Detective Tillis in a daze. She simply could not process what she was seeing.

"They'll take her to Baylor. We'll be going there as soon as we get a team here to handle the...apartment." He didn't want to say the words 'crime scene' to her.

"Who was..." she couldn't finish the thought.

"We'll catch up to you at the hospital," he told her. "Why don't you follow the ambulance and stay with Ms Hawke until then? I'll find you there, okay?"

"Yes," she mumbled, already moving. She didn't take a breath until she entered the emergency room. There were all manner of coughing, sneezing, and bleeding bodies scattered about the room but she didn't see any of them. She was focused solely on finding Jaden. She spent a great deal of time trying to answer questions from the admitting nurse that she didn't know the answers to until she was positively mad with worry. She wanted to scream in frustration but gathered the last shred of her self-control and grabbed the admitting nurse's hand. "I need to know where she is. Please." The tears brimming in her eyes threatened to fall and the nurse finally relented in her endless questioning.

"Surgery. Sixth floor."

She fairly flew down the hall and jabbed the elevator button repeatedly until the doors opened. She tapped her foot impatiently as the car labored upward. *Jesus! Jaden was in surgery! She had lain so still on the stretcher, so pale and helpless. How badly was she hurt? What were they operating on her for? What happened?* She was in full panic mode by the time she reached the sixth floor. *She can't die. Please, God, don't let her die!* She reached the nurse's station and tried to remain calm. Her insides churned and she thought she might be sick.

"Jaden Hawke," she managed to choke out.

The nurse checked her sheet. "She's in surgery. There's a waiting room just down the hall if you'd like to stay."

"Thank you." Sloane walked down the hall and found the waiting room empty. She sank into a chair and quickly bent from the waist to put her head between her knees. She was shaking uncontrollably. She concentrated on taking deep even breaths until she could think clearly again. She finally sat up. Gillian. She needed to call Gillian. Two words into the call she was sobbing. When she was able to get out that she was at the hospital, Gillian hung up. Less than an hour later she walked into the waiting room, wrapped Sloane in her arms, and held her. Sloane let go of the thin thread of control and totally lost it.

"Honey, can you tell me what happened?" Gillian asked when Sloane's sobs had run out of steam and her tears finally slowed.

"I don't know," she gulped. "When I got there they were putting her in the ambulance." She took a tissue from the box on a table and blew her nose. "Detective Tillis was there and he said she'd been attacked in her apartment."

"Attacked?" Gillian exclaimed.

"Gilly, there was a body there too. They brought a body out and put it into another ambulance. Somebody died."

Gillian stared at her in shock. "What? Who? Jesus, Sloane, what's going on?"

"I don't know, Gilly," she wailed. "All I know is that Jaden is in surgery and I don't even know why!"

"Okay." Gillian hugged her again. "Since we don't know anything we need to just wait and see what happens. Try not to think the worst, okay?"

"I'm trying, Gilly, I'm trying." Sloane dabbed at her eyes. "I can't stand the thought of her hurt, Gilly. I didn't even get to tell her I was sorry!"

They sat silently for a few minutes until Gillian asked, "Did you say Tillis was there? The same guy who was investigating who hit you on the head and stole your stuff?"

"Yes."

"What the hell does that have to do with Jaden being attacked? Why would a stolen property detective be at Jaden's apartment? Nothing makes sense here, Sloane."

"Ms Ellison."

Sloane jerked her head up. "Detective Tillis, what's going on?" She stood quickly and Gillian joined her.

"I'll tell you what I can." He waved at the doorway. "Would you like to go down to the cafeteria for a cup of coffee?"

"No!" Sloane looked panicked.

"Jaden is still in surgery," Gillian explained. "We'd like to stay close."

"Sure. I'm sorry." He sat in a chair at right angles to the couch they had been occupying.

"Please tell us something," Sloane begged. "Anything."

"Okay." He sighed audibly. It had been a long day and it wasn't over yet. "This is not for public knowledge." He looked at Sloane. "This somewhat involves you too."

"Me?" Sloane frowned in confusion. "What are you talking about?"

"We asked your security company to give us a run-down of whose access card was used on the day of the attack on you at the stadium."

"I don't care about that!" Sloane said in exasperation.

"You should. It seems someone entered the stadium that morning before you. An employee. We're certain now that that same person was the one who hit you on the head and trashed your office. We found no sign of a forced entry, if you'll remember."

"So?" Sloane was more than a little impatient now.

"The same person gained entrance to Jaden Hawke's apartment tonight and attacked her."

"Who was it?" she demanded.

"Bob Winslow."

"What? You must be kidding!" Sloane shook her head in disbelief. "Why would Bob need to knock me out? And why would he attack Jaden?" She paused. "Coach Winslow attacked Jaden?" She could not get her mind wrapped around that thought.

"I'm afraid so."

"Are you sure?" Gillian asked.

"Quite sure. His was the body on the stretcher you saw being loaded into the second ambulance," he said to Sloane.

"He's dead?" she asked in shock. "Bob Winslow attacked Jaden and now he's dead?"

"I'm afraid so." He waited, knowing it took time to process this much shocking information.

"Jaden killed him?" Gillian was the first to ask.

"It appears so. From the looks of the crime scene, it seems he went to her apartment and she let him in. He had a bat with him and absolutely destroyed the apartment. We're certain he was going to kill Jaden with the bat." Here he looked at them for a moment to judge whether they could absorb any more shocking information. "He killed Kendall Paxton the same way—with a blow to the head."

"Oh my God!" Gillian whispered. "Bob?"

"His fingerprints were found on the piece of lumber that was used as the murder weapon," he nodded. "The L.A. detective called here the other day to arrange for us to arrest him."

"Then why didn't you?" Sloan asked harshly. "Before he could try to kill Jaden?"

"We couldn't find him," he said evenly. "He hadn't been home in days and we were searching for him when the call came in about the attack. We recognized the name and went to investigate. We found him already dead."

"How?" Gillian asked.

"She must have gotten into the kitchen and grabbed a knife before he could kill her. She stabbed him in the chest."

"Jesus! She must have been terrified!" Sloane moaned.

"Hawke?" A green scrub clad doctor asked from the doorway.

"Yes!" Sloane jumped to her feet anxiously. Her heart thudded in her chest as she waited for the words that would define the rest of her life.

"She's out of surgery and in recovery," he smiled. "Everything went well. She should be moved to a room very soon."

"Doctor." Sloane's voice stopped him from leaving.

"Yes, Ma'am?"

"What was the surgery for? We don't know anything about what happened yet."

"Oh, I'm so sorry. She had multiple fractures of the left radius." He touched his arm to indicate where. "We set it and put three pins in to help it heal correctly. If there are no complications, she should make a full recovery. She also suffered a severe contusion of the neck. There is internal swelling in the trachea which is causing difficulty in breathing. She's been given an anti-inflammatory and we'll keep an eye on her condition. She'll make a full recovery although she might have a slight rasp to her voice for some time."

"Thank you, Doctor." Sloane was crying again as he left. Gillian hugged her close and cried with her while Detective Tillis stood looking on. When they parted, he came forward.

"Ladies, I need to go." He handed his card to Gillian. "Let me know if there are any changes please."

"Thank you." Gillian tucked his card into a pocket and plucked more tissues from the box. "She's going to be okay," she said to Sloane, more for her own benefit than hers.

"Yes," she nodded. She said a silent prayer of thanks. "Thank God."

Gillian and Sloane sat in identical chairs beside the hospital bed. Jaden was still unconscious. The upper part of the bed was elevated because of the injury to her throat. It made it easier for her to breathe. She had the oxygen cannula beneath her nose and her left arm was encased in a pristine white cast by her side. An IV drip was attached to the back of her right hand.

"She looks so helpless." Sloane whispered.

"She's going to be okay, Sloane." Gillian assured her. "Why don't you go get a cup of coffee or something to eat?"

"No," she shook her head. "I'm fine." She sighed. "How could Bob be so completely insane without anyone ever noticing anything?"

"I don't know," Gillian admitted.

"Why would he kill Kendall? He couldn't have even known her, and why Jaden? She's never done anything to him. I mean, it just makes no sense."

"Maybe Jaden can tell us something when she wakes up."

"Should we call Georgia?"

"Yeah, maybe I should," Gillian nodded. "She'd want to know."

"Yes. Why don't you go get some coffee and call her? I'll stay here in case she wakes up."

"Okay. Come get me though if she does."

Sloane sat quietly just watching and waiting. *She's alive. She's going to be fine.* She kept repeating it over and over in her mind, a mantra.

Gillian returned before long and handed Sloane a cup of coffee. "I left a message on Georgia's phone. She might not see it tonight though." She kissed Sloane on the cheek. "Should I even try to suggest you get some rest?"

"No. I can't leave until I know she's okay."

Gillian nodded. "That's the same thing she said when you were in the hospital."

Sloane gave her a shadow of a smile. "I remember. How could I have forgotten that, Gilly?"

"Don't be too hard on yourself, Sloane. I'm sure she'll be so happy to see you she won't even remember you were mad at her."

"God, Gilly, I almost lost her." Sloane sniffed and wiped at her eyes.

"But you didn't," Gillian said firmly. "Do you love her?"

"Yes!" she said instantly.

"It hasn't been very long."

"I know," she nodded. "I can't explain it, Gilly. The first time I focused my lens on her I knew she was special. It was during that press conference the first day of spring training. Remember? They wouldn't quit asking her about Kendall and she just shut down. I could see it in her eyes. It was so sad. I think I started falling in love with her then. She just stood there and let them yell questions at her about things that were none of their business."

"She is special," Gillian nodded. "But she thinks you're the special one."

"I don't know. I hope so." She rubbed her face vigorously. She was tired.

"Sloane, you're exhausted. Why don't you at least go take a walk, wash your face or something?"

The nurse came in then to check on her patient. "Yeah, okay." She stood and stretched. "I'm just going down the hall."

The nurse checked the bag and changed it out for a new full one. "She's doing very well," she said over her shoulder. "She'll be hoarse for a while but that should clear up. If she wakes up don't let her talk. Okay?"

Suddenly Jaden was awake and fighting. She grabbed the nurse by the arm and tried to swing the cast at her head. The nurse held on to her right hand to keep the IV needle from being torn out while trying to dodge the cast. Gillian was on her feet. Jaden was flailing with the cast but it was heavy. Her eyes were wild with fright. "Jaden, calm down," Gillian caught the cast in both hands and held on.

Sloane rushed back to the bed. She looked into Jaden's eyes and kept her voice calm. "Babe, calm down. It's me." Her eyes bored into Jaden's. She put a hand on her shoulder gently. "Baby, you're safe now. Please. You're in the hospital and we won't let anyone hurt you."

Jaden ceased struggling but was still rigid with residual fear. Her breathing was labored and they could all hear her struggling. Sloane put a palm against her cheek while continuing to hold her eyes. "You're safe. Come on; let this wonderful nurse take care of you. Just lie back and relax. Okay?" Jaden slowly relaxed against the pillow and Sloane took her casted arm and put it gently next to her, still holding her eyes. She was calmer but there was still a slight glaze in Jaden's look. Sloane leaned over and kissed her very lightly on the lips. "Get some sleep, baby. I'll be right here." She enclosed the fingers sticking out of the cast in her own and rubbed over them with her other hand. Jaden's eyes fluttered closed and she was unconscious once again.

"She's strong for someone still under the influence of the anesthesia," the nurse commented as she re-taped the IV line to her hand.

"She's pretty strong normally," Sloane nodded.

"She was attacked tonight," Gillian told her, "so she came up swinging."

"It happens sometimes," the nurse smiled. "And they almost always go back under just as quickly."

Sloane was asleep in the chair. It was early in the morning. Jaden woke slowly this time. She lay quietly, trying to figure out where she was. The ambient light from the hall way gave her a dim view of the room. Her head was fuzzy. When she noticed the cannula under her nose, she raised a hand to see what it was. She remembered then. She was in the hospital. Was she sick? She began taking inventory of her body parts. Everything seemed to be working except her throat hurt. She lifted her left hand and realized it was in a cast. A broken arm. *Okay*. She could deal with that. She looked at her right hand and saw the needle taped to her. *Hospital*, she thought, *so it must be an IV*. She needed a drink though. Her throat hurt. She put her right hand on the bed railing and pulled herself up.

"What are you doing?" Sloane rose and went to the bed. "You're awake."

"Yeah." It came out strangled and whispery and she raised a hand to her throat with a grimace of pain.

"Don't pull the IV out," Sloane said softly. She took her hand and lowered it to the bed again. "And don't try to talk. You hurt your throat." Sloane took her hand in hers and tried to keep the tears at bay. She kissed her softly. "Would you like some ice chips? They said you could have that instead of water." Jaden nodded. She wanted to speak so badly. Sloane held a couple of ice chips to her mouth and Jaden took them gratefully. Sloane moved to the window and opened the blinds. It was early and the sun was just beginning to show. Jaden's eyes followed her. When she turned back to the room, tears were visible on her cheeks. Jaden frowned and reached out a hand to her. "Don't," she rasped.

"Shhhh." Sloane stepped back to the bed and took her hand. "No talking." Jaden lifted her head and Sloane met her lips with her own. "Do you need anything? Are you in any pain?" Sloane brushed a hand through her hair. She just needed to touch her, to assure herself she was okay. Jaden shook her head no. She smiled up at her and Sloane felt her heart lift. Breathing became easy for the first time since she had seen Jaden on that stretcher. She offered more ice chips and Jaden took them eagerly. "Are you sure your throat doesn't hurt?" Jaden nodded but held her thumb and forefinger apart to show a little. "Anything else?" She shook her head. "Do you remember what happened?" Jaden paused and her eyes lost focus for a second as she thought back in time. Then her head jerked around to Sloan, her eyes wide. She opened her mouth but Sloane quickly put a finger against her lips. "Don't worry about it. He can't hurt you now." Jaden's hand squeezed hers hard and her eyes were frantic with the need to communicate. "The police know everything," Sloane reassured her. "Detective Tillis was here last night." Jaden's breathing was wheezing through her lungs and she labored against the pain. "Baby, calm down. Please. You need to let your throat rest. You're safe here." Jaden nodded and willed her lungs to slow down. She closed her eyes and forced her shoulders to relax. "That's it," Sloane encouraged her.

They sat calmly for a while and then the first shift nurses came on and the hospital came to life. They came to check on Jaden and shooed Sloane out of the room.

She went down the hall, got coffee from the vending machine, and stretched the kinks out of her body. She felt grimy and knew she needed a shower but there was no way she was leaving Jaden alone. She had a thought though and made her way down to the gift store. It was just opening. She bought a notepad and several pens and returned to the room. When she went inside, Jaden was sitting up and the IV had been removed from her hand. She also had a dark blue sling supporting her left arm. A cup of water was on the rolling tray table that had been pulled over the bed. She looked happy, gave Sloane a smile, and indicated she wanted a kiss. Sloane complied and the kiss was sweet and tender. Sloane held up the plastic bag. "I brought you something." Jaden's eyes lit up and she grinned. Sloane took out the notepad and pens and handed them to her. She was so excited she instantly grabbed them and quickly wrote her first note. She turned the pad so Sloane could read it. *I love you*. Sloane looked into hopeful eyes and started to cry. "I love you too, baby."

They kissed again and Sloane felt a little of the fire return between them. There was a discreet throat clearing behind them and the doctor came in.

"It looks like you're feeling much better this morning," he remarked with a smile. He checked her chart and asked her a few yes or no questions. "Well," he said when he was finished, "it appears you're doing very well. Other than your throat still being slightly swollen, that beautiful multi-colored bruise along your left jaw, and the cast, I'd say you're a very lucky woman." Jaden touched her face with raised eyebrows. "I'd like for you to stay here today so we can monitor the throat. I'll come by again later and if you're still improving maybe we can let you go home tomorrow." He finished making notes on her chart and slipped his pen into his shirt pocket. He smiled at her and left.

Jaden touched her face again and looked at Sloane. The question was in her eyes. "It's a bruise," Sloane told her. "Don't worry about it."

Jaden picked up the pen. *Is it big and ugly?*

Sloane laughed. She couldn't help herself. "No, baby, it's not ugly. You're beautiful. And strong and smart and the best thing I've ever seen."

Jaden grinned at her and wrote again. *I need to pee.*

"Let me help you." Sloane pushed the tray away and when Jaden slid off the bed, she put a shoulder under her arm and together they shuffled to the bathroom. "When you're done just knock on the door and we'll do this in reverse."

Jaden took more of her own weight on the return trip but was glad to get back into bed. Sloane watched her recover from the trip and was glad they had kept her for at least the day. She was still recovering from the effects of surgery. "Babe?" Jaden looked at her with a raised brow. "You said you remember what happened." Jaden frowned and nodded. "I think Detective Tillis will come by today." Jaden looked at her for a moment before writing a note and turning it for her to see. *Should I write down what happened?* Sloane looked into her eyes and nodded. "It'll make things easier, but if you can't then don't worry about it." Jaden sat back against the pillows and stared off into space. Sloane watched her anxiously. This could be a very intense thing for her to handle right now. Jaden then scribbled quickly and turned the pad for her to read. *Is he in jail?* Sloane dreaded this question, but she would not lie to her. "No." Jaden stared at her with raised brows in a silent question. "He's dead," Sloane told her and took Jaden's good hand in hers. Jaden looked away, processing this information, and she waited. Jaden was a mentally strong woman but this was way beyond ordinary. Jaden extracted her hand and put it to her forehead, closing her eyes. When she finally opened them again, Sloane saw they were glassy with tears. It tore at her heart. "He killed Kendall," she said forcefully. Jaden nodded that she knew. "He was going to kill you." She nodded again but looked away.

Sloane sat on the side of the bed, took Jaden's hand, and held it in her lap. "You defended yourself, baby. That's all. I would never have forgiven you if you'd let him knock your head off." Jaden's fingers squeezed hers and she gave a slight nod, but Sloane knew she hadn't made peace with it yet. It would take some time. "Shall I go for a walk and let you do this alone?" Jaden squeezed her hand again and nodded. "Okay. I'll go get a cup of coffee that doesn't come from a machine. Take your time." She stood up but bent down to kiss her. "I love you and I'm sorry I acted like a spoiled brat. I want to tell you all about it and I want to hold you, and kiss you, and beg you to forgive me. I want you to tell me I'm an idiot and that I don't deserve you. Then I want to make love to you until you can't move. And then maybe you'll begin to forgive me."

Jaden gripped her hand tight and shook her head, her eyes fierce. "No." It was still whispery and strained and Sloane kissed her again to keep her from saying anything else.

"No talking. I'll be back in a little while."

Sloane got coffee and toast in the cafeteria, and sat at one of the small tables. She realized she was hungry as she devoured the toast. She got another cup of coffee and knew she was probably burning a hole in her stomach. She glanced at her watch and picked up her phone. She didn't want to make the call to Detective Tillis. She wanted to just take Jaden home and keep her there, safe and protected. She hesitated on the last digit but finally pushed it and waited for the call to go through. She told him Jaden was writing the incident down on paper, but that she wasn't able to speak yet and wouldn't be for days. He said he would be there later and thanked her for calling. She had no sooner hung up when her phone rang. It was Gillian, saying she'd be there soon.

"Gilly, can you do me a favor?"

"Sure. What do you need?"

"Would you stop by my apartment and get some clothes for Jaden? Her stuff has blood on it and I don't think she should have to wear them home."

"Sure. Is the key in the same place?"

"Yes. Thanks, Gilly."

"No problem. See you soon."

Sloane returned to the room and found Jaden sitting in the bed with her knees drawn up and her head on her arm on top of them. The notebook lay on the rolling table. Sloane hurried to her side. "Babe?" She touched her arm. Jaden lifted her head and the look in her eyes told Sloane all she needed to know. She put her arms around her neck and pulled her into an embrace. "Oh, baby, don't feel bad," she whispered. "He was a killer." Jaden tightened her one arm around Sloane and nodded against her neck. Sloane held her, cradling the back of her head and letting her fingers slide through her hair. Jaden finally pulled away and Sloane let her go reluctantly. "May I read it?" Jaden nodded, but she wasn't looking at her. Sloane picked up the notebook and flipped it open. The first page said, 'I love you' still and Sloane let her fingers brush over the words lightly, smiling. Then she flipped through the pages until she came to Jaden's account of her attack. It was short, too short for the damage that it caused and would continue to cause in the months to come. She made a mental note to see if the hospital had a psychologist on staff that could spare a few minutes.

She sat on the side of the bed and read through the words that described the terrifying night. She blindly searched for Jaden's hand and entwined their fingers. When she was done, she turned to her, brought their hands to her lips, and kissed Jaden's knuckles. "I'm so sorry this happened to you." Jaden made a face and shrugged but she was squeezing Sloane's fingers. "Did he ever say who this Julie was?" Jaden shook her head. "She must have been someone he knew, maybe a relative." Slone tore the pages out of the book and folded them in half. She kissed Jaden on the cheek and stood up. "Tillis will appreciate this, I'm sure." She put the pages in the bedside drawer. "He said Bob was the one who trashed my office and stole my drives too."

Jaden's demeanor changed from sorrow at having taken a life to furious anger in an instant. She flashed back to sitting beside Sloane's bed in this same hospital as she recovered from her attack, a blow to the back of the head. She could have been killed! She swung her legs over the side of the bed and reached out to Sloane with her one good hand. Sloane moved between her legs and Jaden pulled her tight. When Sloane pulled back, she saw the tears threatening to spill from Jaden's eyes. She kissed her cheek. "I'm fine," she reminded her, reading her mind. "It's over now. Maybe Tillis can answer some questions when he gets here." Jaden hugged her once more then released her to pick up the notepad. Sloane watched as she began writing. When she finished she handed it to Sloane. She nodded as she read. *Who was Julie? Why did Bob Winslow link her to Kendall Paxton?*

And to her? Why steal Sloane's drives and smash her computer? And how did it all fit together?

"All good questions," she said to Jaden.

They were interrupted as Gillian entered with Georgia and Mallory close behind. They all came forward to hug her. Gillian carried a paper bag and handed it to her. "I brought you a present," she grinned.

Jaden looked inside and a big smile split her face. "Thanks." It was barely a whisper.

"Jaden!" Sloane said sharply.

Jaden looked guilty but couldn't keep the smile off her face. Sloane took the bag from her and handed the notepad back to her. "She's not supposed to be talking," she said to the others. She looked into the bag and saw Gillian had picked out some boxer shorts, jeans, and a dark shirt. No bra. She looked up to see Jaden looking at her hopefully. She held up the pad where she'd written, *shorts?* She nodded and pulled them out of the bag and handed them to her. With no modesty whatsoever she stood and stepped into them, letting the gown billow out around her. She sighed happily and hugged Gillian in thanks.

Sloane eased into the background as they all jabbered with each other and Jaden scribbled on her notepad in response. She was pleased with how these women cheered Jaden up and made her feel cared for. She felt herself relax for possibly the first time since parking her car at Jaden's apartment.

Lunch came and Jaden wrinkled her nose when she discovered mashed potatoes and Jell-O. They all laughed at her. Gillian touched Jaden on the shoulder. "I'm going to take Sloane down to get her something to eat. We'll be back soon." Georgia and Mallory elected to stay behind.

Jaden nodded and mouthed *thanks* to her before looking at Sloane and giving her a huge smile. Gillian took Sloane's arm. "Let's go sample the food in the cafeteria. I assume you haven't had anything to eat yet."

"I had some toast earlier," she defended herself.

"Uh huh," Gillian said dismissively as she pushed the down button for the elevator. They went through the line and took a table for two against the wall. "She looks like she's feeling much better," Gillian remarked.

"Yes," Sloane nodded. "And I think having all you guys show up really gave her a lift. Thanks for getting her underwear too."

"Yeah," Gillian laughed. "She really seemed to like that."

"She wrote down what happened yesterday." Sloane stopped to think back. Was it only yesterday that this all happened? It seemed like a week ago. "He talked about someone named Julie but she doesn't know who he was talking about."

"We may never know," Gillian mused.

"I'm just glad it's over."

"Me too. Did you get to talk to her about the two of you?"

"A little. I just told her I was sorry I was such an idiot." Sloane looked at her across the table. "She said she loved me." Her voice betrayed how she felt about that statement.

"Yes. I knew that," Gillian said with a smile.

"I *am* an idiot!"

"No, you're not," she told her. "You're just human. I guess you told her you felt the same way."

"Yes." Sloane felt her cheeks color. "I did."

"So she'll be staying at your place when she gets out of here then?"

"If she agrees," she nodded. "I don't want to assume and I don't want her to feel like I'm bossing her around."

Gillian snorted. "Like that's possible. She'd do anything for you, Sloane."

"I'd like to think that but we'll have to talk about stuff like that later, when she's healthy again."

"When is she going to be released?"

"Probably tomorrow. The doctor says if her throat is okay she can go home then." She looked down as her phone gave the chime for a text message. She opened it then looked at Gillian. "Detective Tillis is here."

They met Georgia and Mallory in the hall outside Jaden's room. Gillian stopped to speak to them but Sloane went inside immediately.

Detective Tillis was just finishing Jaden's account of the attack. He looked up as she came in. "Ms Ellison."

"Hello." Sloane looked at Jaden. She seemed calm. She sat in the chair next to the detective. "Do we know anything new?"

"Nothing yet." He re-folded the notepaper and slipped it into his pocket. "I'll start checking on this Julie person and maybe it'll give us a better picture of what he was talking about and why. Other than that, it would seem he had some connection to this Julie and she had some connection to Kendall Paxton. He must have believed Kendall told this Julie she loved her and then it went bad for some reason. He blames her for whatever happened to Julie because of it. And, by association, he must have blamed Jaden as well."

"You said he killed Kendall Paxton," Sloane probed.

"Yes. His fingerprints were on the lumber he used to hit her with. He had to have planned it in advance, but maybe the piece of wood was just there and he used it. He bought the two throw away phones and put the numbers in them and left one by her body so we'd go after Jaden."

"Didn't he think that only having the single number in each phone was going to be suspicious?"

"He would not have been thinking logically at this point, I don't think. He was a man obsessed with killing Kendall and framing Jaden. He might have had that very thought at the time though since he tried to write her name. He might have been in a panic at that point. He couldn't have known how actually killing her would have felt. Thinking about killing her, planning it, even obsessively, is not the same as the actual act. It would have had some effect on him." He paused to look at Jaden. "He probably put the second phone in your bag at some point during the trip."

Jaden suddenly sat straight up and grabbed the notepad. She wrote for several seconds before turning the pad toward them. *Photos!* It read and under that she had put, *Sloane must have a photo of him with the phone*. She was watching them with a questioning look.

Detective Tillis was nodding. "That makes sense," he said. "That would explain why he stole all the storage drives from you," he added to Sloane.

"I went through all my photos," Sloane protested. "I didn't see anything."

"That you know of," he countered. "And that's why he stole those drives—so you never would." He looked steadily at her. "You're very lucky, Ms Ellison. He could easily have killed you as well."

Sloane shuddered as the realization hit her. She'd been all alone in the building with a killer. Her eyes found Jaden's and the answering look she got told her it didn't matter now. She was safe. They were both safe. She inclined her head a fraction in acknowledgement. "What will happen now?"

"That depends on what we can discover about this Julie person, but I'd say it's pretty much over. We know he killed Kendall Paxton. We know he was the only one in the building with you when you were attacked. And, finally, we have his confession to Ms Hawke." He stood up. "Thank you for the statement. We'll have it typed up and you'll need to sign it."

Jaden nodded and shook his hand as he turned to leave. Sloane walked him to the door and Jaden leaned back against the pillows. It was over. She sighed and finally felt like she could relax.

Chapter 22

Jaden sat silently beside Sloane in the waiting room of the Dallas Police station. She brushed her fingers over Sloane's hand on the arm of the chair next to hers. Sloane smiled back at her and took her hand.

"It's okay," she whispered, knowing Jaden was tense.

It wasn't long before Detective Tillis came to get them. "Ms Hawke, Ms Sloane," he acknowledged them. "Would you please follow me?" He led them through the hallways until they came to his desk in a big open room full of other desks. He pulled up an additional chair so they could both sit down. "This is the statement you gave me in the hospital, Ms Hawke. Please read it over carefully and then sign it at the bottom."

"Did you find out anything more about Bob?" Sloane asked as Jaden read.

"A little," he nodded. "The Julie he talked about was his ex-wife. He evidently blamed Kendall for their break up when he found out she was in L.A. and had been seen with Kendall Paxton. When Jaden showed up on the scene in Dallas, it must have brought it all back to him. The

259

police in L.A. say she died from a drug overdose more than a year ago."

Jaden's head snapped up and her eyes were wide with disbelief. Sloane saw how white she was and took her hand. "We don't know if it was her or not," she said softly.

"What is it?" Detective Tillis asked.

Sloane looked at Jaden for permission to tell the story. She was trembling and she was clearly agitated. She jumped from her chair and paced quickly away and back again, her hands to her face. "Jaden, we have to tell him what happened." She paced again and came back to the chair, but didn't sit down. She looked at Sloane steadily but knew what she had to do. She nodded once.

Sloane turned back to the detective again. "Jaden told me the night she left California she went to a drug house to get Kendall. There was another woman there. She had OD'd and was already dead. Jaden tried to help her but the dealer came after her and she had to run. She called the police about it as soon as she got away. That was the last she heard about it. They never contacted her about giving a statement or following up on it or anything."

He contemplated them for a long moment before nodding. "Okay. I'll send an inquiry out there and see what they have on it." He looked at Jaden until she sat down again. "How long ago was this?" She wrote on his notepad after a thoughtful moment and turned it back to him. She shrugged as if to say it was the best guess she could give him. He nodded again. "Okay. Like I said, I'll see if they have anything on it but it may not even be her. There are a lot of drug deaths and this could just be a coincidence. Thanks for coming in to sign your statement. I'll be in touch."

Chapter 23

Sloane opened her eyes slowly, not wanting to release sleep just yet. The bed next to her was empty. She put a hand on the adjacent pillow and found it cold. Time to get up then because who knew what Jaden might be up to all by herself. She sat up and reached for her robe.

She found her in the kitchen drinking coffee and reading the paper. She was wearing flannel boxers and a torn tee shirt and she looked marvelous. A smile touched Sloane's lips at the first sight of her. Jaden looked up as she entered the room and smiled. Sloane stopped behind her chair and bent to kiss her on the neck.

"Good morning, beautiful," she whispered in her ear.

Jaden leaned her head back and her smile got bigger. "Morning," she whispered back.

"Shush," Sloane admonished her. "I promised your doctor I'd keep you from talking for another day." She moved to the counter and poured herself a cup of coffee. She sat across from Jaden at the table and raised the cup for a sip before saying, "The next time I hear a sound from you I want it to be a scream...as you're coming in my mouth."

Jaden's mouth dropped open and her heart stuttered in her chest. When she could restart her brain, she grabbed the notepad and scribbled.

Sloane laughed when she read it. *When*, it said. "That's up to you," she told her. "When you're able to scream let me know."

She gave Sloane a look that melted her heart. She took the notepad back and wrote for a minute. Sloane put a hand to her eyes when she read it. It said she was not going to Denver to play. She was going to get a job in Dallas and stay here. Sloane sniffed and shook her head. "No, Jaden, no. You need to play ball. I know that now. I was an idiot." She wiped her eyes. "I should have trusted you."

Jaden shook her head and scribbled again. *I can't leave you*, it said. She grabbed it back and wrote, *not for you—for me*. She looked at Sloane hopefully.

Sloane had to wipe her eyes again. "Oh, baby, I can't let you do that. We'll work something out. Okay?"

Jaden nodded vigorously. *I love you*, she mouthed silently. She reached for her hand and entwined their fingers, her eyes never leaving Sloane's.

"Shit, Jaden, you're making me cry again."

Chapter 24

Jaden hung on the fence near the bullpen and observed the pitchers and catchers. She hadn't been able to hook up with a new team yet and Georgia asked if she could keep an eye on the pitchers whenever she had some free time. She had been excited at the prospect of helping out; anything to keep her involved in the game. She stepped away from the fence and approached Erin Coe.

"Erin, you're not finishing your delivery," she said quietly.

Erin caught the return throw from Gillian and looked at her with a question in her eyes. "Yeah?"

"Yeah," she nodded. She stood next to her and mimicked her wind up and delivery in slow motion. At the last second, she adjusted her stance a little as if getting ready for the ball to be in play. She'd been hit by a line drive before and Jaden knew the fear of it happening again was in her sub-conscious. "At the very end, just before you release, you move your foot. See?"

Erin nodded. "I'm doing that?"

"Yes."

"Huh. I didn't realize."

Jaden smiled. "It's no big deal and it's easy to correct." They went through Erin's motion for a few minutes until she was back on track and then Jaden faded back against the fence again. She had worried about giving instructions to the players she had been teammates with just a short time ago. She had no idea they would do anything she said in regards to their play.

It wasn't long before Georgia called across the field and motioned for them to take batting practice and they all trooped down to home plate.

"How are they looking?" Georgia asked.

"Pretty good," Jaden nodded. "Nothing to worry about."

"I need a favor."

Jaden swiveled her head to look at her. Something in her tone caught her attention. "Anything."

"I have an appointment tomorrow afternoon," she said. "She looked away for a second. "It can't wait."

"We...the team have an afternoon game tomorrow."

"I know. That's the favor. Will you take the team in my absence?"

Jaden stared, her mind a swirl. "You want me to coach the team?"

"Yeah," Georgia nodded and then grinned at her. "You're available, right?"

"Yeah," she grinned. "My schedule is pretty empty these days."

"Good. We can go over the batting order and the pitching strategy after practice today."

Jaden was still grinning. "Okay. Great."

*

"Tell Ms Tate to come in now." Donald Sutton, owner of the DSG Group and therefore, the Dallas Metros, released the intercom button on his phone and rose to greet Georgia.

"Coach Tate." He held out his hand and Georgia shook it before taking a seat in front of his desk. He sat and regarded her silently for a moment. "Can I safely assume this has something to do with Jaden Hawke?"

Georgia relaxed in the chair and crossed her legs. "Yes," she nodded.

"Can I ask why you didn't talk to Steve Cutter first?"

"We all know Steve doesn't do anything without your approval," she stated. "I don't have time to waste on corporate games." She maintained her relaxed posture even though she wanted to reach across the desk and shake some sense into him. "I think there are two options here."

"And those would be what?"

Georgia knew he needed to think he still had a choice in the matter even though he didn't, so she said, "Either give her a new contract or hire her as the assistant coach." She stopped there. She didn't want to shove it in his face yet about what a mess he'd made of the whole situation so far.

He appeared to ponder what she'd said for a long moment. It wouldn't do to let her think she'd won too quickly. He tapped his fingers against his chin as if in thought. "I don't know if that's possible," he said, keeping his eyes on her.

Georgia sighed and shook her head. What a stupid fucking asshole! She uncrossed her legs and stood up. "Well, in that case, I'll see…"

"Now, wait a minute," he interrupted quickly. "Don't get all crazy on me."

"Don, I don't have time for this crap! I've already told you that. Either give her a new contract, or get your ass down to the field and coach the team yourself!" She stood with her arms crossed, her stance wide and uncompromising.

"Now, Georgia, you can't be serious." He put a smile on his face and made a placating gesture toward her. "Sit down. Let's talk this over."

Georgia was tired of the whole situation. "You hired a psychotic killer for my assistant. You rescinded the contract of an innocent player. A player, I might add, who would have taken us all the way this year. Now, what in the hell could you possibly want to discuss?"

"I can't just put her back on the team," he protested.

"Can you coach? Can you hire a coach today? Do you even know what to look for in a coach? Do you care?"

"You won't quit," he said with false assurance.

In answer, she started for the door. "I'll expect a good recommendation when my next team calls."

"Okay," he barked before she could leave. She stood with her hand on the doorknob. "Okay," he said again.

She turned back into the room. "I expect her agent to call me by tomorrow night with a signed contract. And I expect her to be happy with it, even if it hurts your checkbook. And I expect her to be in uniform for the next game." She calmly opened the door and walked out.

Made in the USA
San Bernardino, CA
10 December 2012